Church Girl

Also by Naima Simone

The Single Dad Project
Her Best Kept Secret
An Off-Limits Merger

Visit the Author Profile page at Harlequin.com for more titles.

NAIMA SIMONE

Recycling programs for this product may not exist in your area.

ISBN-13: 978-1-335-57487-9

Church Girl

For questions and comments about the quality of this book, please contact us at CustomerService@Harlequin.com.

Harlequin Enterprises ULC
22 Adelaide St. West, 41st Floor
Toronto, Ontario M5H 4E3, Canada
www.Harlequin.com

Printed in U.S.A.

To Gary. 143.

To Connie Marie Butts.

I'll miss you forever and love you longer than that.

To A.C. Arthur.

Thank you for inviting me to the cookout.

One

"Technically, I'm not a runaway bride since I powerwalked to the waiting Uber. No running involved."

Aaliyah

"This isn't what it looks like."

Crossing her tattooed arms over her ample chest, my cousin Tamara steps out of her hotel room and onto the breezeway, scanning me from the top of my cathedral-length veil to the pearl-encrusted hem of my bridal ball gown.

"Really?" She jerks her chin up, her knotless butterfly braids swinging against her cheek. "Because it looks like you bailed on your own wedding and left that preacher boy at the altar."

I wince.

"Okay, so maybe it is what it looks like." I glance over my shoulder like SWAT has its rifle scope centered on my back.

I'm not saying my father is having me followed…but I'm not *not* saying it, either. "Can I come in? Please?"

Yes, I'm begging, but at this point, desperation has settled inside me, and pride has left the building.

Tamara squints at me for several long moments where the itchy feeling of being exposed crawls over my nape like a line of marching ants set out to destroy a picnic. Just when I'm about to plead with her again, she blows out a loud, aggrieved breath and steps aside, granting me entrance.

The room isn't anything to write home about, given this is one of those chain motels that sits right off I-20. The nondescript room with its plain dresser, TV, round table with one chair and two full-size beds proclaims its middle-of-the-road status. Right now, though? It feels like something better than a luxurious hotel. It feels like sanctuary.

And for the first time since running out of my father's church and hopping into the back of an Uber, I exhale a long, relieved breath. Not an easy feat in this tightly laced corset.

"Well." Tamara plops down on the bed closest to the door. "I guess it's a good thing I wasn't invited to the wedding. It would've been a waste of a trip," she drawls.

I wince again, hiding the nervous clenching of my fingers in my full skirt. "Yes, I'm sorry about that," I apologize.

Tamara is my first cousin, my aunt Trulie's youngest daughter. And according to my father, the wildest and most unrepentant of my cousins. A huge sin in his book. Hence Tamara not being invited to the wedding. And I stress *the* wedding, not *my* wedding. Because the only decision I made regarding it was saying yes to Gregory's proposal. And I still can't believe I did that.

Who am I kidding? Yes, I can; I know why.

Because as Bishop Timothy James Montgomery's daughter, I was expected to. And like the obedient preacher's kid I am, I fell in line. Just like always.

Until about thirty minutes ago, when I fled Greater Faith Christian Ministries a mere twenty minutes before I was set to walk down the aisle and marry Apostle Gregory L. Riley, executive pastor and my father's right hand.

I guess that makes me a sinner in Dad's eyes. Probably, a worse one than Tamara because my disappearing act will no doubt humiliate him. Though Dad preaches the importance and power of forgiveness, I don't foresee that coming my way anytime soon. And yes, just the thought of disappointing Dad has fear crouching at the base of my throat like a cottonmouth right before it strikes.

Yet…here I am, a literal runaway bride hiding out in my cousin's hotel room.

I sink down to the other bed—or I try to. Between the corset and the voluminous skirt, this dress isn't conducive to lounging.

Forget it. I'm too anxious to sit anyway.

Pacing the short length of the room, I smooth my hands over my hair and bump the small tiara holding my veil in place. With a tiny growl, I snatch the thing off my head and toss it aside.

"Aaliyah. Here." Tamara thrusts something at me, and on reflex, I grab the squat bottle labeled Patrón. "Drink this.

Then we'll talk. And either find a way to remove all that shit from under your gown and sitcho ass down or stop walking. I'm still half drunk from last night, and you're making me queasy."

She doesn't return to the bed, but instead pops her hands on her gorgeous full hips and gives me a hard stare. Deciding it's wise to obey—and because a drink doesn't sound *terrible* right now—I twist off the cap and down a healthy swig. Immediately, fire races down my throat, incinerating my esophagus. No, seriously, it's cauterized.

I start coughing, my eyes watering. Tamara's lips lift in a small smirk. "Go on. Take another sip. This one will be smoother, I promise."

Wincing, I follow her instructions, and either the lining of my throat has been seared away or she's right about the second round going down easier. Because I don't feel anything except the warm burst of heat in my chest and belly.

So, I take another sip because, why not?

"All right now," Tamara drawls, nabbing the bottle and setting it on the dresser behind her. "Slow down because if you fall out on the floor, I'm just gonna roll your little ass up in all that tulle and step over you on my way out."

"That's fair," I rasp.

I move to the bed, and hiking up my voluminous skirt and the hoop petticoat under it, I drop to the mattress with a grunt. I lean my back against the plain headboard and make grabby hands at the tequila bottle. Rolling her eyes, my cousin picks it up and walks the short distance to give it to me. She's not smiling, but I swear there's humor in her dark eyes.

"I feel like I'm going to regret this," she mutters, passing me the alcohol. Shaking her head, she plops down on the other bed, crossing her legs. "Uncle Tim already thinks I'm going to hell. If he could see me enabling your corruption, he might call ahead and reserve my staycation there."

I gulp down more tequila then hold up a finger. I start to shake my head, too, but *whoa.* The room feels wavy…or maybe that's me.

"Believe me, you are the least of his worries. Right now, he's probably too busy interceding on my behalf to blame you for anything."

"Please." She flicks her hand, and I can't help but notice her long, pink nails with tiny diamonds. "If any of them—your father, mother, my father—found out you're here with me, I would get blamed for…" She waves her fingers up and down my form. "Whatever this is. You ready to talk now? And—no offense—but why are you here?"

I cradle the bottle to my chest as if it will jump out of my arms and flee. It's difficult to meet her direct gaze because the truth is, we're not close. Though Tamara's only a year older than me, once we hit high school, my parents "discouraged" me from hanging around her. Claimed she was a bad influence. Back then—and shoot, up until about an hour ago—I followed their edicts.

But desperation and panic are strange bedfellows. Add fear, and you have a ménage that's downright messy.

I could give Tamara some made-up story right now. Attempt to hold on to the scraps of my pride. But I mean… I'm in a wedding gown clutching a bottle like it's my best friend.

So I go for honesty.

"I don't have anyone else to go to."

Something flickers in Tamara's light brown eyes, but it's there and gone, too quick for me to decipher it. But then her lips twist into a sardonic…well, I can't call it a smile. She arches a dark eyebrow.

"And you thought of me. I don't know whether to be offended or, shit, offended." Heaving another sigh, she tucks thick, long legs bared by a pair of pink boy shorts under her. "What happened?"

"I left my fiancé at the altar."

"Well, I already got that," she scoffs. "Why? What happened to have you pulling a jailbreak?"

"I wouldn't call it a—" Tamara cocks her head to the side, and okay, fine. It's too late for me to play semantics. "You're right," I murmur. "There's no point in lying about it now. *In vino veritas*, and all that."

"You're drinking tequila, but whatever." She waves a hand. "Go ahead."

Closing my eyes, I press my head back against the headboard. "Tamara, there I was, standing in the children's church room, staring at myself in the mirror, waiting for Daddy to come get me so he could escort me down the aisle. One moment, I was fine. And in the next…" I swallow, my mouth suddenly as dry as it'd gone in that room with finger paintings of Noah's ark decorating the walls. "In the next, I started to suffocate. Honest to God suffocate. It was like I was having an allergic reaction to strawberries, except I hadn't eaten any of them. But my throat started closing shut. I couldn't breathe. My eyes started to water. I thought I was dying."

"You were having a panic attack."

"Yes, I get that now. But then..." I shiver. "Then, I was terrified Daddy would walk in and find my body sprawled on the Jesus-feeding-the-hundreds play mats." Worried about how annoyed he would be over the inconvenience of my untimely passing. "But even more, I was terrified I would be fine and have to enter the church sanctuary, walk down that aisle and vow 'til death do us part to Gregory."

"Breathe, babe," Tamara murmurs.

I give a jerky nod and lift the Patrón for another sip. This story is best told drunk, where the consequences of my reckless actions don't seem so...what's the word I'm looking for? Oh right.

Apocalyptic.

"So, I grabbed my phone and purse, opened that door, made sure no one was in the hallway and ran. I didn't stop until the church was no longer in sight, and only then did I call an Uber. And well, here I am."

"Suddenly, I'm thinking you've bumped me out of first place for the most petitions at intercessory prayer."

I grimace. She's not wrong. Daddy is always praying for her soul in that godless place she works—his words, not mine. I personally don't think there's anything wrong with Tamara being a stripper. I mean, if she's anything like Mercedes on *P-Valley*—and my cousin definitely has a body that rivals hers—then more power to her.

But now, I bet Daddy would rather have me tatted up and swinging around a pole than abandoning Gregory at the altar and humiliating him. Both of them.

"You might be right."

The knot binding my chest pulls even tighter. I rub my knuckles over the spot, but it doesn't loosen. So I tip the tequila bottle and down another sip.

Tamara scoffs. "I know I'm right. So what now? You can't hide out in this room forever. One—" she pops up a finger "—Parsons is way too small. Matter of fact, if the front desk clerk saw you hauling ass out that Uber, your father is probably on his way over here right now."

Oh God. I didn't think of that.

"And two, this isn't some extended-stay motel. So what's your plan? Because I just came through town for my homegirl's bachelorette party, and as fun as this family reunion has been, I'm headed back to Chicago tonight. You can sleep here if you want since the room is paid through tomorrow—"

"Take me with you."

The words—the plea—burst from me before I have a chance to reconsider.

Even now, I'm still doubting this decision. But that's part and parcel of being…me. Of being Bishop Montgomery's daughter. I question and dissect every choice of my own that doesn't line up with his. His deep, melodic voice echoes in my head, criticizing, picking this decision apart—picking *me* apart.

How're you going to survive? Just what do you plan on doing for money? You've never lived outside your parents' home—what do you know about paying your own bills, supporting yourself?

The questions slam against my skull. Yes, the answers are murky, as is my immediate future, but I don't rescind my plea. Something deep inside me shimmers bright—and no, it's not the Patrón.

It's this sense of being in the right place at the right time.

"Take me with you, Tamara," I say again.

She stares at me, not blinking. Finally, she exhales a breath that ends on a chuckle as dry as the air pushing through the antiquated air conditioner.

"Okay, that's enough alcohol for you." She swings her legs over the edge of the bed and stands, her hand outstretched toward me.

I cradle the Patrón against my chest.

"I'm not drunk," I protest. Feeling *reeaally* relaxed maybe, but not drunk. "And this isn't me being impulsive. Well, not completely." Tamara props her fists on her hips, eyeing me with a healthy dose of suspicion, and I can't blame her. I mean, I did just ask her if I could tag along with her cross-country while hugging a bottle of tequila. Still… "No, I didn't plan on running away from my wedding. And no, I didn't come here with the intention of asking you to take me with you. But I *have* thought of leaving Parsons. I even…"

I pause, my throat closing around the secret I'd been keeping for over three months now. It's a conditioned response, limiting what I share with anyone, especially my parents. With my father, because eight times out of ten he's going to criticize it. And with my mother, because a hundred times out of a hundred she will tell my father everything. So to avoid judgment and the inevitable fallout, I carefully dole out information.

To be fair, my father taught me that not all secrets are bad, especially if they're to cover your own behind.

And this…this particular secret would've caused World War Z. And I would've been patient zero and the first person to be eaten alive.

"You even what?" Tamara softly asks.

I lick my suddenly dry lips, swallow past a too tight throat.

"I…I even applied to college."

Her eyebrows wing high, and surprise flickers through her honey-colored eyes. "Seriously?" Then, with disbelief dripping from her voice, "You?"

I shouldn't be offended at the incredulity or the question. I get it. I've never shown any inclination to be anything other than a dutiful and obedient pastor's daughter, perfectly content with serving in the women's and youth ministries, teaching in children's church and one day becoming first lady of my husband's church. I've never rocked the boat or colored outside the lines. At least, not where others could see.

So no, I shouldn't feel this flash of irritation with Tamara.

But I do.

I'm more. I want more.

Yet, how do I expect her to believe that when I have trouble convincing myself?

"Yes, me," I say. "And I've been accepted, too. In three weeks, I start at the University of Chicago to earn my bachelor's in visual arts."

"And Uncle Tim doesn't know anything about it?"

"No." I shake my head, ignoring the nerves and, okay, a smidge of fear in my stomach. "I didn't tell him or Mom."

Frankly, I'm *still* shocked that neither of them discovered the truth. My father has never claimed to be God in flesh, but sometimes he seems to have divine omniscience. Nothing gets past him. Well, almost nothing.

And I want to get out of Dodge—or Parsons, Alabama—before he finds out.

"That's…wow. That's amazing, Aaliyah. Congratulations. But—" she shakes her head, sinking back down on the edge of the mattress "—have you thought this out? Getting accepted is one thing. Actually having the money to attend school and live in Chicago is another. And I don't mean to discourage you, but Chicago might as well be a whole 'notha world from here. Hell, different galaxy."

"I know. Of course I know that." I set the bottle on the other side of me and lean toward her. "But am I supposed to let not having traveled farther than Huntsville stop me from leaving? Keep me trapped here to live the life mapped out for me, the life I had no input in?" *That I went along with.* "Shouldn't I at least try?"

The thought of trying and failing hunts me like a stalking beast. I can already taste the faint, metallic flavor of it in the back of my throat. But I can't allow that to stop me, either. Shoot, whether it's here or Chicago, I'll be alone. I might as well be alone doing something *I* want.

For once.

Sympathy flashes in Tamara's eyes, and that burns through my veins like acid. I don't want her pity. I need her help.

"Aaliyah..." she murmurs, and I catch the regret in her voice.

Desperation surges inside of me, and my body charges into fight-or-flight mode.

"No," I sharply say, cutting off her gentle letdown. "You got out, Tamara. You know firsthand what it is to feel like you're slowly suffocating under the heavy weight of expectation, of standards so high that trying to reach them is just a setup for failure. You know what freedom tastes like. Please," I rasp, my anger and passion ebbing, replaced by a quiet sadness. "Help me to leave here. Help me to finally *live*."

Humiliation sears me as my desperation echoes in the room and inside my head. I can't run from it, can't hide. It's all there, out in the open, and I feel so damn exposed. It's uncomfortable, and I cringe away from it. Vulnerability isn't an asset or an admirable quality. At best, it's an emotionally out-of-control state. At worst...well, at worst, it's a weapon willingly handed over to be abused.

Physically and emotionally.

I don't know if Tamara will tell me to get a grip and compose myself, or view my confession as an opportunity to hold something over my head.

Yet, she's the only person I've felt close to for a long time. And that includes my almost husband.

God, I sound so pathetic. Not that I'm going to let that stop me. It's dramatic to claim this is a matter of life or death. But that's how I feel. This emptiness and fear are so consuming that I'm seconds from being swallowed up by it. And then I will be nothing.

"I've been saving up money for three years," I softly confess. "Even before I consciously made the decision to leave, I started saving for it. This is my chance, Tamara. I don't think I'll have another one. And I'm not talking about my father, I'm talking about me. I don't know if I'll have the courage to do this again."

Tamara stares at me for a long while. So long my heart sinks toward my belly and disappointment embeds itself in my chest.

"Fine." Tamara sighs, pinching the bridge of her nose.

"What?" Shock propels the air from my lungs so the question emerges on a wheeze.

Sighing, my cousin lifts her head, and those light brown eyes narrow on me. "I know I'm bound to regret this but fine. You can come with me."

Still not sure I've heard her correctly, I lean forward—as far as my corset and skirt will allow. "Are you serious? You're..."

"Yeah, Aaliyah, I'm serious." She shakes her head, and when she looks at me, her indecision and irritation are abundantly clear. Standing from the bed, she waves a hand. "Now get up. We need to get you out of this dress. And then we need to get on the road before they come knocking at my door."

Shoving off the bed, I get to my feet and turn around, giving her my back. Immediately, her fingers go to the long row of delicate buttons that march down my spine.

"Tamara," I whisper.

"Yeah?"

"Thank you."

"Whatever. I'm not certain I'm doing the right thing, and I'm sure both of us are going to regret this." Several beats of silence pass between us. "You're welcome."

I smile at the far wall, and moments later, when the wedding gown falls to the floor in a billowing heap, it's as if I've shed dead skin. As if I'm standing in a brand-new, soft, untried body.

Words I've heard my father say a million times take on new meaning.

I'm born again.

Two

"I'on trust nobody that makes Mary Poppins look like Lizzy Borden."

Von

"Fuck. You have *got* to be shittin' me."

I read over the paper in my hand two more times, and I still can't believe what I'm looking at.

No, correction. I *can* completely believe this. It's Sheree, after all. And my ex-wife has nothing but bitterness and time on her hands to pull this bullshit.

Tossing the petition for modification of our divorce on my desk, I snatch up my cell and dial a number I know by heart now. Shit, it's listed in my Favorites because I've used it so often over the last year.

Ten minutes later, I end the call, and some of my anger and, yes, panic, has subsided.

According to Ronald Waller, my divorce attorney, Sheree

filing the modification petition doesn't mean shit if she can't prove there have been significant changes in my circumstances from those repeatedly hashed out in the original decree. And last I checked, those "circumstances" remain the same. I owned my tattoo shop before we even met one another. But for some reason, she believes the five years we were married, plus the two weeks she helped me out by working the front desk when my employee up and quit, affords her fifty percent of my shit. Hell, I even paid her for those two weeks.

Leaning back in my battered leather chair, I link my fingers behind my head, blowing out a long breath. It's only twelve thirty, and I'm tired as hell. That's the usual result of anything having to do with Sheree. She's fucking exhausting.

A knock on the door echoes in the office, and seconds later, my employee and best friend, Michelle Carter, pokes her head inside.

"Aye, I didn't say come in." I lower my arms, scowling at her. "What if I'd been in here fucking?"

She walks in, closing the door behind her. Crossing the room, she drops into the armchair in front of my desk. "This is you we're talking about. While I or Jah might get some dick and pussy up in here, that ain't you." She arches a pierced eyebrow. "Besides, are you forgetting I know what it sounds like when you fuck? Shit was too quiet in here for that."

Yeah, Chelle and I have a past. But that was years ago. When I brought her into the shop as an artist, we'd cooled on that. I don't shit where I eat. Ever. Not only is it bad business, but it's messy as hell. And contrary to how tattoo shops are portrayed on reality TV, King Tattoos is drama free.

"What do you want?"

That's the great thing about best friends. They don't get their feelings hurt when you're rude. It's practically a prerequisite for friendship with me.

"Nothing." She shrugs, stretching her lightly muscled, heavily inked arms above her head. More tattoos peek above the round neckline of her white tank top. "My one o'clock canceled, so I'm free until three. And I already have that piece drawn up. So I came in here to see what you got going on."

Instead of answering, I pick up the petition and toss it toward the edge of the desk. Chelle picks it up and scans it. A sneer curls the corner of her mouth, and when she lifts her head, disgust gleams in her dark brown eyes.

"She just doesn't stop, does she?" Chelle drops the paper back on the desk, sucking her teeth. "She already gets spousal support. But she's not going to be satisfied until she can take everything from you." She claps her hands together in the prayer position and rolls her eyes toward the ceiling. "Lord, if I'm ever a bitter bitch, please just strike me down and put me out of my misery." In spite of the anger still seething in my gut, I chuckle. "Seriously, though. You know Sheree only wants to get her hands on this shop because she knows how much you love it. Especially since you were awarded primary physical custody of Gia. She doesn't have anything but space and opportunity to fuck with you."

"Yeah, I know." I drag a hand over my stitch braids then

down my face. My beard scratches my skin, and I'm reminded that it's past time for a line up. "But this isn't going to work. I'll still have to go through the pain-in-the-ass hearing, wasting time I could be getting money, but she'll have to try again."

"And she will," Chelle mutters.

She's not wrong. What's the saying? The person you divorce isn't the one you married. I'm living proof of that. The woman I met and fell in love with ten years ago is not the same Sheree who dragged me through hell and back in our divorce. I don't know that person. And don't want to.

"Forget her. Sheree gon' keep Sheree-ing. Ain't shit we can do about it right now." Chelle reaches into her pocket and removes her ever-present pack of spearmint gum. Unwrapping it, she eyes me. "When's your next tattoo?"

"Three. But I have an interview before then at..." I pick up my cell and touch the screen. "Well, damn. In about ten minutes."

She frowns, popping in the piece of gum. "Interview for what? A new artist? You didn't mention bringing someone in."

"Nah, it's for a nanny position. I haven't found a reliable one since Ms. Anne left. I can't keep going through all these babysitters. Gia needs stability."

Frustration trips through me, and I clench my jaw against it. Not like I begrudge our longtime nanny the opportunity to be with her grandchildren in Florida. Ms. Anne had been with us since Gia was two—for five years—and she'd become family. So even though we miss her, Gia especially, Ms.

Anne deserves to be with her daughter, son-in-law and their children. Still, it's been almost a month, and I haven't found anyone to replace her long-term. I'm damn near desperate.

"Well, make sure whoever you hire knows how to cook. No one bakes banana nut bread like Ms. A, but we need someone who comes close."

"I'm glad your priorities are straight when it comes to my daughter's childcare."

"Now, you know lil' G's my heart."

Chelle might've been teasing about the banana nut bread—well, not really—but she does love my little girl, considers Gia one of her five nieces. Which was another problem with Sheree. She hadn't wanted "one of my hoes" around our daughter—her words, definitely not mine. My ex-wife couldn't seem to grasp the fact that there was nothing but friendship between me and Chelle. I loved Sheree, but I wasn't getting rid of a relationship that had been around longer than her, or letting go of a dope-ass artist for her petty jealousy. Particularly since I'd never given her a reason to be jealous.

Yeah, the joke was on me.

I pick up my phone again, looking for the email that has the information regarding the person I'm interviewing. She's late. Technically, she still has seven minutes until one thirty. But I'm of the school of thought, if you're on time, you're ten minutes late.

Glancing up at Chelle, I snort. "And yet, I don't see you volunteering to babysit."

Chelle raises her hand, studies her short, red-painted nails.

"If you want me to cancel appointments so I can hang with my niece, then I'm all for it. But I don't do that for free."

"There's something wrong with you," I mutter.

She cackles, and a knock sounds at my office door. Unlike Chelle, the person on the other side waits until I invite them to enter.

"Yeah," I call out.

A moment later, Malcolm, the front desk employee, opens the door. "Hey, you have a woman out here who says she has a nanny interview with you."

"Aight. Here I come."

Four minutes to spare.

Shoving back my chair, I stand and round the desk. Chelle rises, too, and follows me out of the room. I toss her a look over my shoulder, but she smiles. Shaking my head, I don't tell her to mind the business that pays her. Not like she's going to listen anyway.

We pass the open area with six large cubicles, where the murmur of voices and the whir of tattoo machines punctuate the air. I employ five tattoo artists, and each of them are damn good at what they do. Every one of them has a style they specialize in—Chelle is a beast at black-and-gray portraits, and not many can get with Zion when it comes to new school—and I'm thankful to have them in my shop. They're the reason the schedule stays booked months out, and clients come from all over the country to King Tattoos to get ink.

I head down the hallway, reaching the open entrance that leads to the lobby. As soon as I pass through, my gaze falls on the woman standing at the front desk. She turns to look at me, and I frown. There has to be some mistake.

I'm supposed to be meeting Aaliyah Montgomery for the nanny position, not fucking Pollyanna. I let my gaze run over the short woman who looks like an escapee from a Disney movie. My scowl deepens. Okay, maybe she possesses long, thick, dark hair, thicker curves and a beautiful pecan complexion instead of blond pigtails, freckles and pale skin…

Aw, fuck. Correct that.

On closer inspection, actual freckles scatter across the bridge of her nose and upper cheekbones like cinnamon sprinkled across buttered toast.

Nope.

Innocence radiates from her. She wears it like the tattoos that cover my body—inked in and permanent. And it disturbs the hell out of me. All I know is it—she—has no business here. Not in my shop. Shit, not in Chicago. For her safety, she needs to return to whatever small town with singing birds and domestic-prone mice she came from.

"Hi." A hesitant smile curves her mouth, and I pretend not to notice that those full, dick-tease lips don't fit her angelic appearance. Those lips are all sin and destruction. "I'm Aaliyah Montgomery. Are you Von Howard?"

She extends her hand toward me, and I drop my gaze to it, staring. After a moment, she lowers her arm back to her side, and that smile trembles, but she holds on to it. Uncertainty flickers in her eyes. Eyes that remind me of the sweet and delicious toffee Gia and I get every time we visit Navy Pier.

Yeah, I'm being rude as fuck, but I need her gone. It's a

damn near primal urge to usher her out the front door and lock it behind her—an urge I can't explain.

"Yeah, I'm Von." I dip my chin, sliding my hands into my front pockets. "You're here to interview for the nanny job?"

I already know the answer—I've read her email and résumé several times, and both include her name. Still, a tiny glimmer of hope rises that this is a mistake. That she's supposed to be at the deli next door, interviewing there. Not a place that's too rough, too coarse, too…much for her. And no, she wouldn't be watching Gia here, but this is my world, one that I rule. And I reiterate, she doesn't belong here.

"Yes," she says, her smile brightening. Aaand she has dimples. *Fuck.* "I'm pleased to meet you, Mr. Howard. And thank you for the interview."

"Von. And I wouldn't thank me just yet."

I turn, heading back the way I came, leaving her to follow. Hoping she doesn't.

"Hi. Oh wow. Your tattoos are gorgeous," Aaliyah says behind me, and for a second, I think she's talking to me.

My chest tightens at the delight in her voice. Again, inexplicable. As is the pleasure that trickles through me before I shut that shit down. Delight, my ass. She seems more like the type to cross the street to avoid someone covered in ink than the kind to admire it.

I glance over my shoulder, the sharp retort ready. But then I notice her gaze fixed on Chelle, not me. And that's not fucking disappointment prickling my skin. It's not, goddammit.

It's another mark against Aaliyah Montgomery.

"Thanks." Chelle beams. *Beams.* My best friend is one of those people who needs to know you for six months before she even has a whole conversation with you. The only exception was Gia. But not many people can meet a Disney princess and *not* melt. Except me. I want no part of this. Of her. "Aaliyah, right? I'm Michelle. Most people call me Chelle."

And by "most people" she means the five or six people she actually likes.

I stare at my friend. Who *is* this person right now?

"Yes, Aaliyah. It's awesome to meet you, Chelle."

Awesome. What're we at fucking band camp? I don't look over my shoulder again, but I can hear the smile in Aaliyah's voice. Can mentally see those dimples in her cheeks.

"Same. Are you from around here?" Chelle asks.

Not with that warm, honeyed accent.

"No, I—"

"Last time I checked, this was my interview. Ms. Montgomery, this way."

I walk away, and the clack of her modest heels echoes in the hallway behind me. Reaching my office, I open the door and allow her to step through first. When I enter and close the door, it's in Chelle's grinning face.

I don't know what's up with her, but she can have it on the other side of the door.

Crossing the room to my desk, I glance at Aaliyah, who stands in the middle of the room, her hands clasped in front of her. Does she even realize how her fingers twist, exposing her nerves? Probably not. And asshole that I am, I stare down at them, making her aware. Following the direction of my gaze, she dips her head, and her slim shoulders stiffen as her arms drop to her sides.

"Have a seat." I wave toward one of the two armchairs and sink in my own seat.

"Thank you," she murmurs. "And please, call me Aaliyah."

I frown, recalling that I did formally address her. But we don't need to be on a first-name basis; she won't be around long enough. The only reason I insisted she call me Von is because…

Shit, I don't know why I told her to do it.

That seems to be my mantra in the less than ten minutes I've been in her company. *I don't know why.*

Another mark against her.

Yeah, it's unfair of me to be so biased against her, but I can't find it within myself to give a fuck. She *bothers* me. And I don't—*dammit.*

I refuse to think or say it again.

Aaliyah fidgets in the chair before she stills. Tugging her shoulders back, she visibly controls her body, and my frown deepens. Not at the rigidity in her frame—well, not only that. It's the composed, damn near blank expression that covers her face, darkens her eyes to a deep brown. The difference between now and a minute ago is like a heavy door being slammed shut on a bright, clear day.

Someone only closes down completely like that with practice.

I should know.

The question of why Pollyanna would need to adopt that

particular form of self-defense drops into the grab bag with all the other ones I have about Aaliyah Montgomery. And not one of them have to do with whether she would be a good fit for Gia.

Leaning back in my chair, I move the mouse, and my laptop screen blinks to life. Quickly typing in my password, I navigate to my inbox and pull up the email with her info and résumé.

"Where're you from? It's not here." Not my intended first question, but it'll do.

She shakes her head, her wavy hair moving with the motion. And damn if my gaze doesn't follow the sway and swing of the thick strands.

Sheree would hate her on sight. Aaliyah's too fresh-faced, too pretty. My ex-wife couldn't stand not being the best-looking woman in the room, being the center of attention. Knowing how Sheree would feel is almost enough to make me change my mind about hiring Aaliyah. Good thing I care more about my baby girl's well-being than aggravating my ex.

"No, I'm from Alabama. I just moved to Chicago a couple of weeks ago."

"For family?"

"For school. I started taking classes at the University of Chicago."

I frown. "How old are you?"

Again, rude as hell. If my mother was here, she would've popped me in the back of the head for asking a woman her age. But shit, I want to know. With the freckles, wide eyes that turn down at the corners and slightly rounded cheeks, she could be anywhere from nineteen to twenty-five.

"Twenty-four."

Not jailbait young, but she's ten years my junior.

I'm guessing there's a story behind her just starting college at her age when most have graduated, but it's not my concern. Especially since I won't be seeing her in about ten minutes—the amount of time it'll take me to finish this interview and show her the door.

"So you're about to be a full-time college student, and you'll still have time to be a full-time nanny?" I don't try to hide my skepticism.

"Yes." She leans forward, and her face warms slightly, losing some of that guarded stoicism. "The agency said your daughter is seven years old, so I'm assuming she's in school. Most of my classes are during the morning and early afternoon. And the one that isn't is an online class, and I can handle that course load after I get off work. Or after your daughter goes to bed since your job description included a couple of late nights during the week."

"And you don't think that will be too much?"

Again, she shakes her head, and this time I swear a delicate, fruity scent permeates the air. Her shampoo? Or maybe my imagination, fucking with me.

"Not at all. I'm used to juggling several different schedules and agendas." That too-lush-for-her-own-good mouth tightens. Have no business noticing that, but I do. "Going to school and working for you won't be a conflict."

"Uh-huh." I stroke a hand down my beard, studying her.

Have I said she bothers me? It's like an itch in a place I can't quite reach. "I'm a little surprised Angel Care hired you," I say, mentioning the name of the nanny service I contracted. "Your résumé is pretty light on work history. Babysitting, Sunday school and children's church ain't exactly the experience for a position like this."

"I understand that on paper it may look like my experience is slim—"

"More than looks like, ma. It is."

Her eyes narrow, and flame licks my skin. Maybe she's not so Pollyanna, after all.

Nope. Again, not my business. I deliberately snuff out that flash of heat until there's nothing left but smoke.

"That doesn't mean I haven't spent the last ten years around children. As you can see under the responsibilities section, I didn't just watch over them but taught and tutored them as well. And those were multiple children at one time."

"Yeah, I peeped that. My argument still stands. Teaching some kid about Noah's ark doesn't instill much confidence that you can care for my daughter, though."

Hell, Gia can be a handful. She's sweet, but she's also a daddy's girl, and I freely admit to spoiling her a little. Aaliyah Montgomery doesn't look like she could wrangle a fly much less an active seven-year-old.

"That's understandable." She pauses, inhales an audible breath. Her head tilts to the side, and the full weight of that unwavering stare settles on me. And for the first time, she appears older than her years. "Can I ask you a question?" I spread my hands wide, gesturing for her to ask it. "You made up your mind about not giving me the job before this interview, didn't you?"

"Yeah." Why lie?

"Will you tell me why?"

I roll my chair forward, propping my forearms on the desk. "Because you don't belong here," I say, not sugarcoating shit. "I want to roll you up in Bubble Wrap and ship you back to wherever you came from. You don't look like you can withstand a Chicago winter, much less life outside of whatever small town you left. I can't trust that kind of inexperience. Damn sure can't trust my kid with it."

Not gon' lie. I half expect her to bust out in tears. Another thing that's a strike against her—and they keep adding up. My mouth is reckless as fuck, and anyone around me with thin skin is asking for their feelings to be hurt. I've never been savage—well, not with someone who didn't deserve it—but blunt to a fault? Yeah. And I don't plan on changing.

"It's your decision to not offer me this job, and I have no problem with that. What I do have an issue with is you judging me before even officially meeting me."

She inhales, and when she releases it seconds later, it's not tears glistening in her eyes. It's anger. The sight rocks through me like a punch to the chest. Like a stroke to my cock. Fury shouldn't sit right on her angelic features, but for some reason it fits. As if a missing puzzle piece has been found and fixed into place. And fuck if I don't find it fascinating.

"You don't know anything about me, and you haven't tried to find out. So whether you believe I belong here or not doesn't matter. It's what I believe that does. And I know you're not the first or only person who's tried to discount me or put me into a box that's comfortable for them. I also know that proving you and them wrong has become my favorite pastime."

An unwanted flicker of admiration sparks in my chest, as does curiosity. Who were these other people that supposedly discounted her? Did her move here having anything to do with proving them wrong?

Again—not. My. Fucking. Business.

She rises, smoothing her skirt over her full hips and thick thighs. And my gaze lingers on those curves, how the material hugs them, before I give myself a mental shake and lift my regard to her face. She might've come in here dressed like a nun, but that body… Shit, it's all sinner.

"Thank you for your time," she says with a nod then spins on her ugly heels, walking toward the door. Dismissing me.

And as I silently study her—the strands of her hair brushing the middle of her shoulder blades, the slim back, flared hips and goddamn beautiful ass—it's like someone dragged back a curtain, and the thing that has been nagging me becomes crystal clear.

Now I get why she bothers me.

Part of me sneers at this kind of innocence. And the other half? The other half wants to sully it. Corrupt it. Dirty it so she's unrecognizable.

Stain that smooth brown skin until she can't wash me away.

Aaliyah opens the door and walks out, not glancing behind her. Only then do I scrub a hand down my face, tugging on my beard. And now that my office is no longer infused with the delicate scent of peaches and vanilla, I can admit the truth to myself.

It isn't only her inexperience that would've made her a bad fit for the nanny position. There's also the fact that I might've ended up fucking the help.

Yup. It's for the best that she walked out.

Now if I can just convince my dick of that.

Three

"Y'all gonna get up off Mary Poppins…"

Aaliyah

I march into Tamara's apartment, barely managing not to slam the door closed behind me. I've been in Chicago and out from under my parents' thumbs for two weeks, yet years of conditioning don't disappear in days. Outward displays of emotion—unless in church—weren't welcome. Even in church, go on too long and you'd get ushered out the sanctuary. Apparently, even the Holy Ghost got a time limit.

No, in my world—former world—emotional displays were derided, disdained. So for the second time in hours, I check the need to "display" all over the place.

Now, I quietly shut the door.

Earlier, I restrained myself from telling Von Howard to go to hell.

Still, not acting on my fury doesn't mean it isn't burning a hole in my chest.

"What the fuck is wrong with you?" Tamara emerges from the kitchen with a bowl in one hand and a spoon in the other. "And where are you coming from?"

I move farther into the apartment, cutting a left into the living room and plopping down on her couch. Bending down, I slip my shoes off, setting them neatly to the side. Heel to heel. Toe to toe. Cleanliness wasn't just next to godliness, order was, too.

I stare at them too long while a closed fist of anger, frustration and sadness squeezes my throat. I'm not home anymore. I'm on my own. I don't need to abide by anyone's rules but my own. And yet…

Yet I don't move the shoes.

Sighing, I fall back against the couch, staring at the recessed ceiling.

"Girl, I know you hear me talking to you." The cushion next to me sinks as Tamara drops down. "Where're you coming from? Classes don't start until a couple weeks from now, as you've been telling me. Often."

Okay, so I'm a wee bit excited about starting college and may have been talking about it. A lot.

Shifting my body to face hers, I lift my legs up and curl them under me. Propping an elbow on the back of the couch, I lean my head against my hand. "I had a job interview. I put it on the calendar on the refrigerator," I say.

She waves her spoon before digging it into the bowl. "I told you I wasn't paying attention to that," she says around a bite. "Damn, Aaliyah." She moans. "You put your whole foot in this banana pudding. I'ma have to spend a few more hours in the gym, but it'll be worth it."

"Thanks. I'm glad you like it."

I smile, my delight probably disproportionate to her compliment. Tamara wouldn't let me help pay rent out of the money I brought with me, ordering me to save it along with the first few paychecks I'll eventually earn. I very much appreciate her generosity. I hadn't planned on staying with her, but she'd insisted, claiming I would end up on the back of a milk carton with my green ass—her words, not mine. The least I can do to earn my way here is cook and keep her gorgeous condo neat.

And by cook, I mean secretly DoorDash meals and transfer the food to plates.

Because my mother tried, but the cooking gene? It skipped a generation. Aside from banana pudding, I got burgers and boiled eggs covered. Other than that?

Peace be with you.

But Tamara doesn't need to know that. She would just be upset over me spending my money to get us food. So why get her blood pressure up?

Why yes, I am justifying me lying and being sneaky.

"So where was this interview at and with who?"

I sigh, thoughts of the past few hours snuffing out any positive feels. "You remember that I signed on with that nanny service?"

Tamara nods. "And the temp agency. And you've been submitting applications to every grocery store between here and the Gold Coast. Yeah." She squints at me, jabbing the spoon in my direction. "I've told you repeatedly you don't have to worry about getting a job right away. I'm not trying to kick you out. There's more than enough room here for both of us, and shit, half the time, I don't even know you're here."

"Here" being her beautiful apartment in the South Loop neighborhood of Chicago. For all her talk in that motel room back home, Tamara wouldn't hear of me posting up in an extended-stay motel. Speaking of motels…

I don't know what I expected, but given the, uh, *modest* motel I found her at in Alabama, I figured her apartment would be nothing exceptional. But I couldn't have been more wrong.

The spacious three-bedroom, two-bath condo sits on the sixteenth floor of a towering high-rise. Wide, high-ceilinged rooms that seamlessly flow into each other, hardwood floors, free-standing fireplaces, and a whole wall of glass that faces east and offers a breathtaking, panoramic view of Lake Michigan, Museum Campus and Soldier Field. Out of all the rooms, ironically, her kitchen is my favorite. It's not as big as the one in my childhood home, but the amenities make up for the lack of space. Glossy wood cabinets, quartz countertops on the breakfast bar and counters, a marble backsplash and top-of-the-line appliances that need a master's in engineering to operate. It's beautiful.

My cousin is living her best life as "Jade" down at Inferno, the strip club where she works. She pays her bills, owns her condo and the newest Audi A8, and always looks like she just rolled up out of a salon. I can't lie: I'm trying to be like Tamara. Well, not the stripping part. Aside from the fact that I don't have the guts to strut out on stage mostly naked, I can't dance to save my life. I blow that stereotype about all Black people having rhythm out the water.

But she's gorgeous, confident, self-reliant and doesn't give a damn what people think or say about her.

That's admirable.

That's powerful.

I shrug, lifting my hand and studying my cuticles. The acrylics I'd gotten on my wedding day were long gone, leaving my nails short, unadorned. "I know, but I want to contribute. It's important that I do."

She doesn't ask why; she and I come from the same place, the same family. She understands why.

Tamara shrugs, scooping up more banana pudding. "Whatever. So, back to your job hunting. Where'd you go? And I hope you Uber-ed. God knows you're not familiar enough with Chicago to take public transportation."

"No." I shake my head. "I took a rideshare. I had an interview for a nanny position, but I had to meet the father at his job. It was a tattoo shop over in Irving Park."

Tamara slowly straightens. Setting the bowl and spoon on the coffee table in front of the couch, she studies me for several long moments.

"One, why didn't you tell me you needed a ride? I would've driven you. Irving Park is damn near a half hour away from here. Too far to Uber. I thought you wanted to save your money," she points out.

"In my defense, I didn't know it was so far."

"Uh-huh. You didn't seem to have a problem asking me to bring you with me to Chicago, but now you have an issue with asking me for help. If something happens to you, that's gonna be my ass. So for my ass's sake since it's literally my moneymaker, stop being too proud." She cocks her head, squinting at me. "Now, second. You interviewed at a tattoo shop? Which one?"

"King Tattoos, I think?"

"King Tattoos?" Tamara's eyes widen as she leans forward. "Von Howard's shop?"

"Yes, that's who I met with. Do you know him?"

"Know him? Hell, girl, who doesn't know him? He's only one of the best tattoo artists in the city. Shit, the country. People from all over come to get work done by him. Including athletes and celebrities."

"Oh." I had no clue. But since I've never had the occasion to get a tattoo, why would I? "Well, he's looking for a nanny, but I sincerely doubt that nanny will be me." I suck my teeth. "He was an ass."

Tamara blinks, then releases a crack of laughter. "Well damn, Aaliyah. If you're cursing, he must've really rubbed you the wrong way." Her lips twist into a smirk. "What did he do?"

"He didn't give me a chance. At all. His mind was already made up before we spoke."

She balls up her face. "Did you wear that to the interview?"

I glance down at my white silk blouse with the big bow

at the neck and the dark blue pencil skirt. It's one of my favorite outfits, not to mention it's professional-looking. "Yes." I lift my hands, giving myself another once-over. "What's wrong with what I'm wearing?"

"Nothing...if you're going to share the good news of Jesus Christ."

"Seriously, Tamara?"

"I'm just sayin'. He took one look at you and probably thought you were Mary Poppins's sister from another mister."

Laughter rolls out of me, and Tamara grins, shaking her head.

"You're ridiculous. I mean, I was applying to be a nanny. You'd think he'd appreciate the Mary Poppins look. But instead, he just called me into his office and told me how I didn't belong anywhere near his daughter. Didn't belong in Chicago. He was so cold. And mean."

"And fine." Tamara reaches for her bowl again. Twirling her spoon, she arches an eyebrow. "Tell me I'm lying."

"He's aight," I mutter.

I'm lying. And from Tamara's smirk, she knows it.

Okay, so the man was gorgeous. And even that seems too lackluster a description for the giant, wide-shouldered man with the chestnut skin, heavy dark brows, deep-set gray eyes and thick black beard. His dark hair, weaved into long stitch braids, revealed a face of stark, almost severe angles. A sleeveless black shirt and jeans didn't hide the tight muscles in his big body or the miles of tattoos that covered his arms, hands and neck. The piercing at the corner of his full bottom lip drew attention to the carnal cruelty that was his mouth.

Von Howard was brutal beauty.

And an asshole.

But that didn't seem to matter to my body as I sat across from him. Even now, my belly pulls and knots at the thought of that harshly pretty face and intimidating body. My coochie spasms, and I curl my legs closer as if that can extinguish the ache. An ache I never once felt with my fiancé—ex-fiancé. I'm chalking it up to fascination; they didn't grow 'em like Von in Parsons.

"He's aight, huh?" Tamara mocks me, snickering. "So he really said you didn't belong in Chicago?"

"Yes," I grumble, bending my head and picking a piece of nonexistent lint off my skirt. I don't want her to see the hurt that still resonates in my chest. Silly to have my feelings all sore by a man who doesn't know me from Adam. "And I told him his thoughts on the matter were irrelevant."

"You didn't."

I chuckle at Tamara's surprise. "I did. What? Don't let the church girl fool you."

"Yeah, okay." She laughs again, scraping the last of the banana pudding from the bowl then setting it aside. "I tell you what. Make some more of that—" she points at the empty bowl "—and I'll take you clothes shopping. Because lil' cuz, you can't go out on any more interviews looking like a disciple."

"You're gonna get off my outfit," I snap, but then ruin it by grinning. "I'll have you know, I wore this on my first date with Gregory, and it bagged me a man and a proposal."

Tamara snorts, rising from the couch. "And we see where

that got you, right?" Not waiting for my response—not that I had one because, y'know, she's right—she strolls toward the kitchen. "Go and get changed. We're leaving out in twenty."

Grabbing my shoes and standing, I follow her, stopping at the mouth of the hallway leading to the bedrooms.

"Hey, can I ask you a question? It's been on my mind for a minute, but I don't want it to seem like I'm in your business..."

"Just ask it, Aaliyah."

"When you came to visit home, you stayed in the Barrington Arms. Not saying it's a dump, but clearly—" I turn, waving a hand at the living and dining rooms and kitchen "—you can afford better. Why go there?"

"The same reason I've never invited your family here to visit me—to keep them out of my pockets. Because the people who talk shit about me and what I do are the same people who would expect ten percent of it when that offering plate goes by. Nope. If what I do isn't good enough for them, then neither is my money."

My cousin wears a hard demeanor, and with reason. I've heard with my own ears how Dad runs her down to Mom's sister, my aunt Trulie. And while Tamara's mother doesn't take that with a closed mouth, most of our family follows Dad's lead. It's no wonder my cousin opts to stay in a hotel rather than with her own relatives when visiting. While she and Aunt Trulie get along, her father is another story. So yes, her defensive manner is warranted. Yet...

Yet, I still catch the note of hurt in her voice. Family is supposed to love and accept you, even if they don't necessarily agree with all your decisions. With mine, their love and acceptance are conditional on obedience. On submission.

How well someone takes to the gilded cage comprised of expectation and Scripture.

I should know. All my life, Dad has tried to keep me behind the same bars my mother so willingly accepted.

"I get that," I murmur. "I'll be ready in twenty." Nodding at my cousin, I continue down the hall to the guest room.

It's funny.

I've left Parsons. Physically escaped my father's house and my mother's suffocating silence.

But then there are moments like this one where it just feels like geography.

I'm as trapped now as I've ever been.

Four

"Crow tastes like ass."

Von

"Gotdammit."

I jab the screen of my cell, glaring like it just told me to fuck myself. Tossing it on the breakfast bar, I scrub my palm down my face, tugging on my beard.

"Ain't this some shit?" I mutter, flattening my palms on the marble top and leaning all my weight on my arms.

"Ooh, Daddy. You said a bad word. That's five dollars in the swear jar."

I sigh, lifting my head and meeting Gia's gleeful smile. Little mercenary. The swear jar was my way of deterring her from parroting me and forcing myself to clean up my language. Let's just say, I keep singles on me at all times.

Wincing, I cross to the bedazzled glass container that's damn near full of bills. Removing five ones from my wallet,

I stuff them through the slit in the top. We've emptied the thing four, soon to be five, times. My mouth isn't getting any cleaner, and she's earning her college tuition.

"Aren't you supposed to be getting dressed?" I eye her Barbie pajamas. "I laid your clothes on the back of your chair."

She climbs up the step stool in front of the bar and settles on the high-backed chair. "I know. But I have to eat first then get dressed. Mommy said you do things ass-backward."

"G," I growl, and she shrugs her shoulders, eyes wide.

"That's what Mommy said," she whines.

"Okay, but you know that's a bad word. You ain't slick, and I'm taking one of my dollars back."

"Aw, Daddy." She pouts, her bottom lip poking out.

"Fix your face, G. You know better."

"Yes, sir," she mutters, a frown drawing her eyebrows down over the bridge of her nose.

Her mother knew better, too. Or she should. Anger simmers inside me at a slow boil. I make it a point not to say anything negative about Sheree in front of Gia. Apparently, my ex-wife doesn't give me the same courtesy. There's no telling what other shit Sheree says or does—I don't put a fucking thing past her.

This isn't the first time she's done some petty-ass things just to disrupt my house. Last month, it was changing Gia's bedtime from eight o'clock to nine thirty, so when Gia returned home, she expected to stay up later as she'd done at her mother's place. The month before that, it'd been getting our daughter's ears pierced even though, previously, we'd both agreed on waiting until she was ten. I'd been so pissed, Chelle had to talk me out of driving over to my ex's apartment.

The fucked-up part is Sheree isn't hurting me with her antics. It's Gia who's paying the price. Sheree is shifting her around like a chess piece, and it's confusing the hell out of our daughter. But my ex is too caught up in her own petty bullshit to see the consequences of her actions.

"Here." I set the bowl of her favorite cereal with only a quarter cup of milk—just the way she prefers it—in front of Gia. Rounding the breakfast bar, I bend down and press a kiss to the top of her braids. "I love you, G."

"Love you, too, Daddy." Her pout gone, Gia beams up at me.

That's just one of the many things I adore about her. That sunny personality won't allow her to remain in a funk long. With her pretty hazel eyes and rounded cheeks, she's the best thing I've ever done in this life. Gia's a daddy's girl, so yeah, she's a bit spoiled. But even with the big changes our divorce has brought into her everyday world, she still remains sweet, kind and funny. After everything I've been through with her mother, you'd think Gia being the spitting image of Sheree would have pain knocking at me every time I looked at Gia. But my daughter *isn't* her mother. I've worked hard to make sure that stays true.

Still, Gia adores Sheree, and I'm not naïve enough to believe that the breaking of our family hasn't affected her. I've made a promise to myself to be there for her in any way possible, no matter the time. This divorce isn't her fault, so she shouldn't be the one paying the cost.

Speaking of cost…

Crossing into the living room, I palm my cell, go to the call log and hit Redial on the top number. I lift the phone to my ear and listen to it ring again. And again. When a cheery voice invites me to leave a message, I swallow the curse burning my tongue. I've already put enough money in that jar. I end the call and tip my head back.

My nanny should've been here a half hour ago, and she isn't answering her phone. I have to be at the shop in a couple of hours to do a big back piece for a client. The nanny has only been working for me five days, and she's been late three out of those five. Now, she's not even answering her phone or showing up. This is the second nanny Angel Care has sent. The first one didn't even last a whole day. Once she grabbed my dick after putting Gia down for bed, I had to put her ass out.

So far, this nanny service was zero for two.

Well, three if you count the one with Aaliyah Montgomery.

Point is, I don't have time to set up an appointment for a replacement.

Shit.

I quickly scroll to my Favorites and press the top name. After a couple of rings, my mother's voice gives a scratchy but happy hello.

"Hey, Ma. Sorry to be calling so early and waking you up."

"No problem, sweet pea," she says, and I shake my head

at the nickname she's called me since I was a kid. I'm thirty-four years old, and she still hasn't let it go. "What's wrong?"

I sigh, rubbing a hand over my braids. "The nanny is an hour late, and she's not answering her phone. Gia's school has an e-learning day, and I have no one to watch her. I have a client coming in, and since he's from out of town, I can't reschedule." I blow out another breath, even more aggravated now that I'm saying it aloud. "I hate to impose, Ma, but do you think you could watch Gia today? This piece is going to go until the afternoon, but I'll call the nanny agency as soon as I get to work."

"Sweet pea, you know I'm always ready to jump at the chance to spend more time with my grandbaby. But I'm on call at the hospital. I agreed to take on an extra shift. I'm sorry."

Ma has worked at Chicago's Mass General for over a decade. When my sister and I were kids, Ma worked at the hospital in reception for the regular hours since Dad's truck-driving job only had him home three or four days out of the week. But when I was fifteen and Leslie thirteen, and Ma deemed us old enough to not need as much supervision, she returned to school to pursue a nursing degree, the dream she'd put to the side years ago. She's now an RN, and I might be biased, but one of the best Mass General ever hired. The hospital and her patients are lucky to have her.

But damn, as selfish as it is, I really wish they could do without her today.

"No need to apologize. This is my problem, not yours."

"Now you know, in this family, that's not true. If one of

us has an issue, we all do. What about Sheree? She can't take her for the day?"

I snort. "Yeah, right. She's not answering, either. Probably because she sees it's me."

"That girl." Ma tsks. "I just don't get her. At all. I promise you, she better be glad I'm saved. But she don't know, I'm from the south side of the kingdom. She can still get these hands if she don't stop fucking with you." She sucks her teeth. "The way she's acting you'd think you hoe'd up one side of the East Coast and down the other. Given the dirt she's done, no one would blame you if you did."

Ma is the sweetest person until you mess with her kids. Just 'cause she's a deaconess don't mean she won't kick some ass.

"Nah, Ma. You would blame me."

"True." She sighs. "Damn me for raising you with principles."

I laugh, even though a hard knot tightens in my chest. I'm looking forward to the day when any mention of the shit show that was my marriage won't leave me teetering between a panic attack and rage.

"Yeah, me not slinging dick on some get-back is your fault. I hope it weighs on you."

Most mothers would be completely scandalized with my language. But not Jerusha Monae Howard. This is our relationship. Mother and son and best friends.

"Sweet pea, I really try not to think about your dick in any capacity. I'll shoulder this guilt, though." After her snickering dies down, she says, "Let me know what you work out for Gia. I'm going to worry until I hear from you."

"All right, Ma, I will. Love you."

"Love you the most," she says, ending our call the way we have for as long as I can remember.

Sighing, I try Sheree again. After the fifth ring, I hang up. If this was anyone else, I would give them the benefit of the doubt; the ringer might be off. But I can't extend my ex that courtesy. As long as I've known her, that phone ringer has never been turned down—not even in a movie theater or church. And she's always been a light sleeper—hell, the flip of a bathroom switch could bring her out of REM. Sheree is ignoring me, and her childishness is just another thing to piss me off.

Dammit. What am I going to...

"Hold up," I murmur to myself.

It's a long shot, and if this works out, I'll be eating a fuck-load of crow, but I have to try. I don't have any other choice. Switching over to my email app, I quickly locate the message that contains the information I'm looking for. Once I have the phone number, I dial it before I change my mind.

I literally can't afford to change my mind.

She's my last hope.

One ring. Two. Three. My lips roll in, and I'm about to end the call when the soft yet husky voice that has been following me into sleep echoes in my ear.

"Hello?"

I unclench my teeth to reply. "Aye, is this Aaliyah Montgomery?"

A long pause. "Yes."

Throwing a glance over my shoulder toward Gia, who's

still bent over her cereal bowl, I move farther into the living room.

"Aaliyah, this is Von Howard. You came to King Tattoos a week ago to interview for a nanny position."

"I remember who you are," she says. And the tone, while not *what the fuck do you want?* isn't exactly friendly, either.

Not that I blame her given our last interaction.

Yeah, this is going to be tougher than I imagined. But I'm desperate.

"Listen," I forge ahead, squeezing the back of my neck, "I don't know if Angel Care has found you another job. If they haven't, I'd like to offer you the one with me."

Another long pause. I'm waiting for her to tell me to take a short trip to hell, and I hold my breath. Yeah, I really do.

"What happened? Did the other option fall through? Because I'm assuming I'm still as naïve and inexperienced today as I was when we met."

Releasing that pent-up breath, I pinch the bridge of my nose, debating whether to be honest or lie to get her here. I pull the phone away from my ear and peep the time. I now have an hour and a half before my client pulls up.

I need her. But it's not in me to lie. And besides, green as she may be, something tells me she would smell my bullshit a Chicago mile away.

"I won't lie to you—"

"I appreciate that," she says, tone dry.

I should be annoyed at the interruption. And a part of me is, but that doesn't stop amusement from trickling through me. "No, my mind hasn't changed about your job experience, and yeah, the other nanny fell through as in I fired her because she's gone from being late most days to not showing up at all. I can't have that kind of inconsistency when it comes to my daughter. And right now, I don't have any options. Except you. I need to be at work in a little over an hour, and there's no one to watch my baby girl."

More quiet over the line, and my gut dips, filling with apprehension.

"Listen," I continue, "while I don't apologize for putting my daughter and her welfare as my first priority, I am sorry for my delivery. I'ma be honest, I'm still not one hundred percent certain you are the right person for this job. But I have a strong feeling you wouldn't leave my girl high and dry or be unprofessional—" i.e., grabbing my shit. Hell, Aaliyah looked like she might be a little scared of dick. "I'm willing to give you the opportunity if you're willing to take it."

Another beat of silence, and God—I might've called her out of desperation, but in this moment, I *want* Aaliyah Montgomery to say yes. Don't know when that changed—don't even know why there's urgency humming under my skin, but it's there. And I'm damn near close to begging her.

"Aaliyah."

"I'm thinking," she says. A pause, and then a sigh. "Fine. Only because I haven't found a job yet, and I really need one. Let's be clear, though. I won't put up with how you spoke to me before." A tremble works through her words, and I wonder if she's aware of it. Even so, her voice remains low and strong. "The first time you do that, I'm out. I also won't allow my feelings toward the father affect how I treat the daughter."

In other words, she don't fuck with me. Cool. I prefer it that way. As long as her focus is Gia. That's what's important. That and how fast she can get here. "I get that and accept it. We don't have to be best friends. Just be there and be good for my kid."

"Okay then."

Relief washes through me, and my eyes close on a long exhale. "Thanks, Aaliyah. I hate to rush you, but will you be able to start today? Like in an hour?"

The sound of rustling comes through the line, and I can easily imagine her throwing back the covers, revealing that curvy, stacked body.

Shit. No, I can't. I can*not* imagine that. I *won't* imagine that.

"An hour? Probably not since I still have to shower, get dressed and get over to wherever you are. Speaking of, where are you?"

Shit. Rubbing a knuckle over my eyebrow, I frown. "I'm in Edison Park. Your résumé has your current address in the South Loop, right?" At her hum of affirmation, I shake my head even though she can't see the gesture. "That's about a half hour from me. Damn." Striding back over to Gia, I glance over her shoulder to see if she's finished. And she is, thank God. "Hold up a sec," I tell Aaliyah. "G, go get dressed. And don't start playing with that sticker kit. We need to get out of here."

"Okay, Daddy." She climbs down off the stool and takes

off down the hall. I don't bother reminding her about the running-in-the-house rule. The faster she gets to her bedroom and ready, the better.

"Hey, sorry 'bout that," I say, returning my attention to the phone. "Okay, if I bring my daughter to my shop, could you meet us there?"

"Uh, yeah, I can do that. I can be there in about an hour and a half. Is that okay?"

It would have to be.

"Yeah, that's fine. Just get there as soon as you can. I don't mind having Gia at King Tattoos for a little while, but not all day."

I'm good with my employees, and most of our clients are cool people. But a tattoo shop with strangers coming in and out, and language that isn't always clean isn't the best environment for a seven-year-old.

"Okay, I understand. I'll be there as soon as possible. And, Mr. Howard?"

"Von," I correct, a note of impatience creeping into my voice. All the other details we can hash out at the shop. I need to get Gia and be out.

"Von," she murmurs, and that soft yet husky lilt wrapped around my name slides right through me, strokes over my skin. Fists my dick. *Gotdammit.* "I just wanted to say thank you for the opportunity. I look forward to proving you wrong."

A smile curves my lips before I can contain it. But as soon as it tips the corners of my mouth, I deliberately straighten it. "I hope you do, Aaliyah. See you in a little bit."

Without waiting for her to say goodbye, I end the call. And stare down at the phone screen. Giving my head one last hard shake, I turn to find G. It's a little too quiet, and something tells me there's more playing with stickers going on in there than dressing.

It's never a dull moment around here.

"Hey, Von. Aaliyah Montgomery is here."

I glance up from adding ink to the caps lined up on the red tool chest and give Malcolm a nod. "Cool. Thanks. I'll be right out. Gia still up front with you?"

"Yeah. Heads up. She's rearranged the piercing case by prettiest to ugliest."

I cock my head. "Malcolm, seriously? I left her up there with a week's full of coloring books. And you let her fuck with the jewelry?"

He shrugs, completely unrepentant. "Listen, man. I don't know how it happened. One second, I was saying no, stick with the crayons, and in the next, she hit me with the lip tremble. I'on care what you say. Drag me. But yeah, I gave in and let her do whatever she wanted. Your daughter's a savage, bruh."

"Weak ass," I mutter. I can't really blame him, though. Gia uses her cuteness like a weapon of mass destruction. "Here I come."

"Bet." He claps the doorjamb and disappears.

"Terrel, can you give me a minute? This won't take long at all," I say to my client, peeling off my black gloves.

"Yeah, no problem. Handle your business."

He gives me a chin jerk over his shoulder. I already transposed the design for his back tattoo onto his skin. The blue outline of a grim reaper grasping a scythe and a pocket watch dangling from his long, bony fingers looks bad as fuck, and I haven't even started tattooing it yet. Terrel is a longtime customer, and one of my firsts. He's allowed only me to do his ink for the past fifteen years. The first five when I worked in my uncle's shop and the last ten here at King Tattoos. Even though he no longer lives in the Chicago area, having moved to Charlotte, North Carolina, a couple of years ago, he still comes to see me and get new work done when he's here visiting his family. Which is why I couldn't miss this appointment. Not only could he not reschedule since he leaves for Charlotte in the morning, but he's a friend and loyal client who I didn't want to cancel on.

I head out of my room, closing the door behind me. It's a perk of being the owner. My artists have wide, spacious booths, but I work in my own room. Plus, if I have celebrity clients like athletes or artists, it affords them privacy.

Reaching the opening that leads into the lobby, I frown at the sight of Gia's head poked into the jewelry display case. The fuck? Now we're going to have to sterilize everything in that damn thing. Still, watching her jerk and shift to the latest Gunna hit playing through the shop's speakers in what, I guess, is her idea of dancing almost draws a smile from my face. Then I remember she's fucking with my shit *and* rapping along to a song she has no business knowing the words to.

"Gia," I growl.

She stills, and slowly—because her little ass knows she's wrong—emerges from the jewelry case.

"Hi, Daddy." She beams, and while that smile might pinch my heart, I fold my arms across my chest and don't lose the frown. Seeing this, she even has the nerve to give me a little finger wave. Again, I have to force myself not to smile. "I was helping Malcolm! Do you like it?"

"Gia, what did we talk about on our way here?" Her eyes lower and shift to the side, her mouth twisting into a small pout. Yeah, she knows she's wrong as hell. "G? What did I say?"

"To sit my little ass down and color and don't touch nuthin'," she mumbles.

"That's right. And when you get your allowance Friday, you gon' give me a dollar for the swear jar."

"But, Daddy," she whines, her face balling up. "That's what you said!"

"Aye, lower your voice when talking to me. You know I don't do that. And yeah, I said it. But *you* know not to repeat that word. You think you being slick. For trying to play me, I should make you give me two dollars."

Wisely, she doesn't say anything back. Even though she's seven, my baby values those five dollars she earns at the end of every week. She probably has more money in that dragon-shaped bank than I have in my bank account.

"I'm sorry, Daddy," she says, tilting her head back and looking me in the eye. "I won't touch nuthin' else."

"That's my girl. And thank you for the apology. You showing me what a big girl you are."

At my praise, a grin breaks across her face again. Thank God she has no idea how much I adore her or that I would burn this fucking world to the ground for her. She would be a goddamn terror if she did.

A soft cough reminds me that we have an audience, and damn. For a moment, I forgot about Aaliyah being here. I switch my attention from Gia to the petite woman standing on the other side of the front desk.

"Hey, Aali—" I scowl, cocking my head and staring at her. "What the fuck happened to you?"

The smile softening her face evaporates, and she matches my frown. In spite of the glare she's shooting my way, amusement wells up within me. It's almost like watching a panda mug me. Too cute to be taken seriously.

Yeah, I need to shut that shit down.

There's nothing cute about my new nanny. Not that I can notice anyway. One, I need her, since my last two were absolute shit shows. Two, all that innocence makes my ass itch.

And three, no matter how beautiful this woman is, she has trouble written all over her, like the time Gia took a blue crayon to her wall when she was three. Bright as fuck and impossible to get rid of.

Last time I didn't heed that shit, I ended up with a wife who turned into my bitter and bitchy ex. As George Bush once said, "Fool me once, shame on you. Fool me—you can't get fooled again." Ol' boy fucked that saying up, but he ain't wrong.

"What's wrong with me?" Aaliyah asks. There's an edge to her tone, but a hint of red stains her rounded cheekbones.

"Last time you walked up in here looking like you were headed to a Sunday prayer service and now..." I wave a hand up and down her small, ridiculously hot frame. Shit, even if that soft, honeyed drawl hadn't announced she came from the South, that corn bread–fed body would. Baby girl's curves are sick. And damn, I wish she was back in that nun's habit.

"And now, what?" She pops her fists on the wide, dick-hardening flare of her hips.

I shrug. "Now you look like you're ready for hot girl summer."

She glances down at herself, and shit, so do I.

So I exaggerated. But given what she wore in here last time, the short-sleeved green shirt conforming to her small, perfect breasts and gently rounded belly, and the tight, high-waisted jeans shrink-wrapped to those thick thighs might as well be some shorts and shirt with her ass and tits hanging out. Those cinnamon-colored freckles splashed across her nose and cheeks don't even diminish her sexiness.

She stares at me, seemingly speechless. For a moment, uncertainty flickers across her face, but in the next second, it's gone. So fast that maybe I imagined it because her face blanks just as it'd done over a week ago when she'd been in my office. And like then, a curiosity I don't want gnaws at me. Who taught her that defense mechanism? More, why? Deliberately hurting this woman would be like kicking a puppy.

"Let's start over," she says, her voice as even as her expression is bland. "I'm here in the hour and a half I promised when you called. Now, can I meet your daughter?"

Oh okay. The kitten has claws. Tiny, baby claws, but there, nonetheless. I'm analyzing why this pleases me, but damn if it doesn't. She might sound tougher if her voice didn't hold a slight quiver, but I'm feeling grateful today, so I won't point it out. If she really wants to scare somebody, lil' mama better work on that. Other people out here will take that as a sign of weakness and eat her up.

And not in the way that will have her thighs shaking around someone's head as she screams their name.

Fuck. My gaze drops to said thighs because, shit, I'm human.

But I'm also her new employer, for fuck's sake. That reminder snatches a knot in my ass real quick, and I shift my focus back where it should be—Gia.

"G." She looks at me, and surprise that she's remained quiet all this time flashes through me. I reach my hand out to her, and she wraps her small fingers around mine. I walk her over to Aaliyah. "This is your new nanny, Miss Aaliyah. Aaliyah, my daughter, Gia Howard."

"Hi," Gia whispers, crowding closer to my leg. While she's talkative as hell, that's only after she warms up to a person. The fact that she doesn't even ask why Aaliyah's here instead of her old nanny says a whole sermon.

"Hi, Gia. That's such a pretty name. But then again, you're a pretty girl." Smiling, Aaliyah hunkers down in front of us. So this is what she'd look like if she knelt for my—*gotdammit, no.* I shut that thought down with so much force, I feel a twinge at my temples. Aaliyah offers Gia her hand. "You can call me

Aaliyah. No need for Miss, okay? Can I call you Gia or do you prefer Miss Gia?"

I swallow a snort as my daughter's giggle vibrates against my leg. "I'm not a Miss."

"Really? Are you sure?" Aaliyah scrunches her face up. "You look like a Miss. What're you? Twelve? Fourteen?"

"I'm seven!" Gia announces, moving away from me.

Aaliyah gives a shocked gasp, covering her mouth with her hand. "Wow. Seven. You had me fooled." She grins, and hand still hovering between them, she waits for Gia to take it, which she does. Aaliyah pumps her hand up and down then releases Gia. Rising to her feet, she says, "Since you're a big ol' seven, and I'm new here, you want to show me the ropes? My cousin told me about this place we can try out. You heard of Sloomoo?"

Gia steps closer to Aaliyah. Her wide eyes and smile betray her excitement. As does the bounce she gives on her toes. "Yes!" All it took was the promise to play in some slime, and Gia's moving to Aaliyah's side, taking her hand once more. "It's so much fun! Bye, Daddy!"

"Bye, Daddy? Wow, it's like that?" I arch an eyebrow. I'm pleased their first meeting went well. Still, it stings a little that she's willing to ditch me for her new friend and slime. I look at Aaliyah. "How you two getting over there? You drive?"

"I do drive, but I don't have a car. I was just going to Uber over there then back to your house after some lunch."

I nod. "Aight. But you can't take a rideshare everywhere. That'll work for today but not when you need to pick her up for school and go other places. All that will eventually add up."

"I understand, but unfortunately, I don't have a car for the time being, so Uber it is."

"That's not gon' work. I don't want my little girl getting in cars with strangers. People on some foul shit out here. Hold up."

I turn around and stride back toward my office before she opens that mouth and contradicts me again. She doesn't know yet, but I don't run no damn democracy. I have the final say. Especially when it comes to Gia.

A minute later, I return and hold out the keys to my Ford F-150 XLT. After a brief hesitation, she accepts the keys, staring down at them like they're foreign objects.

"I thought you said you could drive," I say.

She snaps her gaze up to me. "I can but… I don't know about being responsible for someone else's car."

"You're good. It's safer than climbing in and out of different people's cars. And it has GPS, so you don't have to worry about getting lost. Chicago no doubt has more traffic than you're used to in—wherever you come from."

"Parsons," she says, that spicy edge back in her voice. "Parsons, Alabama."

"Uh-huh, lil' mama. I don't care what way you say it, that shit still sounds country as fuck." Her eyes narrow, and I'm pretty sure she's calling me about six different kinds of dicks in her head. I don't care about that, either. "I'll get a ride home after I'm through here for the day, and then we can figure out the rest."

"Fine."

"I got your number, and you should have mine now. Save it and text me when you get to Sloomoo. Know what? Just hit me up when you move to different places so I know where you at."

"Yes, sir."

I pause, studying her face, taking in the irritation shadowing those toffee-colored eyes, the sprinkle of freckles, the heavy bottom lip and the delicate but stubborn chin. The dimples are nowhere in sight. Good. Those shits are overkill in a face that belongs on somebody's fresco wall, and not in a Chicago tattoo shop.

What also doesn't belong?

The heat licking up my spine and the underside of my dick. I'm not into BDSM, but I'm a fucking man. And hearing her utter those two words while staring at me with that damn innocence bleeding from her pores like an expensive perfume? Yeah, my dick's bricking up and ain't a damn thing I can do about it.

"You might want to kill that shit, ma," I murmur low enough for only her to hear. "That and the little attitude you call yourself having gon' get you in trouble you don't want."

Her eyes flare wide, and her lips part as red rushes into her face, staining that flawless brown skin. My gaze drops to those still-parted lips, and a better man than me could keep away the image of tapping his dick on that lush bottom one before pushing deep inside.

I'm not that man.

Clearing her throat, she steps back, and I have to check the urge to disappear that space she placed between us.

Employee.

Gia's nanny.

Both reasons are enough to cool the lust whistling through me like one of those tornadoes that whip through her home state. I can't afford to antagonize her because I don't have another nanny option right now. And Gia needs her. So do I.

Besides, as hot as Aaliyah is, that Disney-princess shit she got going on is a turnoff. I already spent more years than I should've with a woman who acted like she didn't know how to operate in this world without me providing for her, buying for her, telling her what to do. Dependence isn't sexy on a full-grown woman.

Yeah, Aaliyah has this job and she mentioned attending school, but that doesn't mask the fact that she's a lamb in a lion's den. I give her two months, tops. She's going to be headed back to Parsons, Alabama.

"I'll text you when we get to Sloomoo," she murmurs. Switching her attention to Gia, she smiles, and nope, I don't miss the relief in her tone. "You ready, Gia?"

"Yep." She heads toward the exit, tugging a laughing Aaliyah behind her. "See you later, Daddy!"

"Bye, G. Behave yourself."

"I will." She waves to me, not even bothering to look over her shoulder. That girl has slime on her mind.

Just as Aaliyah pushes the entrance door open, it swings back, and Chelle steps in, nearly bumping into my new nanny. "Oh, my bad. Hey, G." Grinning, Chelle bends down and holds her hand up for a high five. After Gia slaps her palm, Chelle pulls her in for a quick hug. "And hello again. Aaliyah, isn't it?"

Aaliyah nods. "Yes, and it's nice to see you again."

"Same—"

"Auntie Chelle, Aaliyah's taking me to Sloomoo!" Gia interrupts, back to bouncing on her toes in her excitement and impatience. "We have to go."

"Okay, okay, dang. I won't hold you up." Chelle laughs then says, "Aaliyah, I guess we'll be seeing more of each other since you're taking care of lil' G. I'ma get your number from Von, and maybe we can get some drinks later."

Even with the distance of the lobby between us, the wide smile that lights up Aaliyah's face has me blinking.

Damn.

She's so fucking beautiful. And she doesn't even know it.

"I'd love that." Gia tugs on Aaliyah's hand again, and she chuckles. "We need to get out of here, but I'll see you later."

"Bet."

Aaliyah turns back to the door, pushing it open for Gia. Because I'm a glutton for punishment with an eye problem, my gaze drops, skimming over that work-of-art ass that's just sitting up there.

Fuck.

My fingers and palms itch with the urge to shape my hands to those firm, lush curves.

"Let me find out you into young, fresh-off-the-Greyhound chicks."

I jerk my head toward a grinning Chelle. She cocks her

head, staring after Aaliyah and Gia as they pass by the shop's storefront window. Then she returns her gaze to me. "That ass is pretty, ain't it?" She smirks.

"Leave her ass alone, Chelle," I growl. "Literally."

My best friend's attracted to who she's attracted to. Gender doesn't factor into it. He, she, they… As long as they're sexy to her, she'll pursue them.

"Is that an order from my friend or…"

"It's an order from your employer, who would be mad as hell if the nanny quits because my tattoo artist breaks her heart."

That's another thing about Chelle. Monogamy is just a word after *money* and before *monopoly* in the dictionary. As long as I've known her, she's never been in a situationship that lasted longer than three months. She has her reasons, and some of them are valid, I'll give her that. But mostly, she don't trust not one muthafucka if it ain't me or her brother.

She shrugs, but that little smile still rides her mouth. "If you wanna save Dolly for yourself, just say that."

"Dolly?" I mug her. "Who the fuck is Dolly?"

"Her." She tips her head toward the door. "With that accent, hair and smile, tell me you don't think of Dolly Parton. I mean, she doesn't have the tits but…" She shrugs.

"Nah. She definitely doesn't bring Dolly Parton to mind."

Now Lauren London with that tiny waist, fat ass, thick thighs, big brown eyes and dimples? Yeah, her I can see.

"Whatever." Chelle waves off my words and goes back to grinning. "I notice you didn't say anything about not wanting her."

"He gave her the keys to the F-150, too, Chelle," Malcolm chimes in.

I glare at him. "Aye, bruh. Don't you have some business to take care of?"

"Nope." He snickers.

"Say what?" Chelle leans back, dragging her gaze up and down my body. "Hold up, hold up." She pops up her hand. "You let Dolly drive your precious F-150? You don't even let me sit my ass in the driver's seat. And you've known her, what? All of five minutes?"

"Yep," Malcolm throws in.

"The fuck happened to Von Howard and when is he phoning home? 'Cause some muthafucking body snatchers had to beam down here and grab his ass."

Flipping her off, I stalk back toward the desk. "I don't have time for this. I got a client I need to get back to."

"This ain't over," Chelle calls after me.

The fuck it ain't. I don't have anything else to say.

I also don't have an explanation. Nothing either of them would accept. And the one I gave Aaliyah is true but even in my head falls flat when they're absolutely right. No one drives my baby but me. I can't make it make sense.

So I don't bother.

As I pass the display case, I slow my steps. And peer through the glass to where Gia had been hard at work. A smile spreads across my face and I chuckle. She really had started organizing the pieces from prettiest to ugliest, in her opinion. The butterfly, flower, and diamond-crusted studs and loops lined up along the front while the plain bells, bars and skulls are shoved to the back.

"Malcolm, since you don't have no work and so much free time on your hands, sterilize this jewelry and get it all put back."

"Damn. I walked right into that one, didn't I?"

I don't answer but keep moving until I'm outside the room where I left Terrel. Pausing a few seconds, I briefly close my eyes and will my body to calm down.

It wouldn't do to enter back in there with a hard dick.

Shit. Aaliyah is already fucking with me, and she's only been working for me twenty minutes.

Trouble.

That woman is trouble, just like I said.

Five

"I can't kill my boss. I can't kill my boss. But God didn't say anything about maiming in the Ten Commandments..."

Aaliyah

"Gia, you have ten more minutes in the bath, okay?" I call to Von's adorable little girl from the other side of her bathroom door.

"Okay!" Then the humming starts back up.

Is that "Bongos," though? What she know about Cardi B? Shoot, *I* barely know anything about Cardi B.

Shaking my head, I move across Gia's bedroom, locate her pajamas in the top drawer of her dresser and lay them out on her Bratz-themed bedspread. Then I go about straightening up the room, putting away the games we played after returning home from Sloomoo and finishing her schoolwork from her e-learning day. Who would've thought there was a whole place devoted to making slime? There were interactive displays as well, but the main draw was definitely the slime. I smile. Gia had loved it. And truthfully, so had I.

She's lovely. Funny. Sweet. Talkative and a little bit demanding but not so much she's rotten. Must take after her mother in personality as well as looks.

In spite of her father's, uh, rough disposition, I can tell Gia's well-loved and maybe a wee bit spoiled. Still, I've enjoyed my first day. Hopefully, the rest of my time with her goes this smoothly because I need this job. I can't live off Tamara forever, no matter what she says. I came to Chicago to be independent, to finally discover what it is to stand on my own two feet. I can't do that leaning on her for something as basic as where I lay my head.

My phone vibrates against my butt, and I pull it from my back pocket. Speak of the devil. This is probably Tamara checking in on me, even though she should be heading to the club by now. When I called her earlier to let her know I wouldn't be home until after nine, since Von texted earlier to see if I could stay because his last appointment was running late, she hadn't been happy about me taking a rideshare late at night.

I glance down at the phone's screen, and my stomach bottoms out. Dread rushes in like the Coosa River during rainy season. I suck in air like my head just broke over those rushing waters, making me lightheaded. I stumble over to Gia's bed and sink down onto it.

My mother.

It isn't the first time she or my father or Gregory has called. Oh no. In the first week after I disappeared from the church, they'd called nonstop. Almost as if they could bully me into answering. But they obviously underestimated my fear of talking to them. I'm afraid that if I did, I'd cave and let them convince me into returning home. I'm not foolish enough to believe that just because I've been out from under my father's thumb for a couple of weeks, I've suddenly developed a backbone when it comes to him.

No, I'm still weak. Still that daughter desperate to please him. To win his approval.

Maybe deep inside, I'll always be her.

But I'm determined to give myself a chance to find out if that's true. And I can't do that by speaking to Bishop Timothy James Montgomery. The commanding, imposing Bishop of Greater Faith Christian Ministries. And as one of his flock, he would expect me to obey.

I sit there, staring at the phone long enough for it to stop ringing. Just as I exhale a relieved breath, it begins ringing again.

This is silly. I can't not speak to them forever.

If I came to Chicago for change, to stand on my own, then running and avoiding calls isn't the way to start off. Here I am at my new job, a week away from college starting. I did these things by myself, no help or input—or demands—from anyone. I can talk to my parents. Mom anyway. She'll be an easier place to start than Dad.

Closing my eyes and offering up a small prayer for strength, I press Answer. "Hey, Mom."

A beat of silence passes then, *"Aaliyah Renee Montgomery, where have you been?"*

I pinch the bridge of my nose. Not only is she using my full government name, but her voice is raised. I can count on one hand the number of times I've heard Georgia Marie Montgomery use her outside voice. And one of them was when a bat flew into the house and the other when...well, there was that other time.

Skirting away from that thought, I clear my throat. "I've missed your calls, Mom. I'm sorry about that."

"Missed my calls," she repeats, her volume down about half a notch. "That would imply you mistakenly turned your ringer off, misplaced your phone or didn't see all the missed calls. No, Aaliyah Renee, you've been avoiding me and your father."

Since she's right, I don't say anything.

Her heavy sigh echoes in my ear, and the disappointment weighing down the sound settles on top of my chest like a soaked blanket. Forget Catholic guilt. My mother has sackcloth and ashes down to a perfect science.

"I don't understand any of this," she says, and I can imagine her shaking her head, a confused frown wrinkling her forehead. "What can you possibly be thinking to just up and disappear like this? And without a word—"

"I texted you and Daddy to let you know I was safe," I interject.

"Two days after you left," she snaps, and a moment later, I catch her quiet but audible indrawn breath. "Do you know what those two days were like for me? For your father? Torture. Not knowing what happened to you. If you were safe or dead on the side of a road somewhere."

"I'm sorry, Mom," I murmur. "That was selfish of me not to contact you sooner. I didn't think."

"No, you didn't," she says. Another pause and another soft inhale. "Okay, baby. What's done is done. Where are you now?"

On a reflex that's inbred in me, I part my lips to tell her my location. An elder asks you a question, you answer. That's how I was raised, and you better be quick about it. But at the last second, I snap my mouth shut and swallow the information. No. That was the old Aaliyah. This one is in self-preservation mode. And it's only the fear that she'll show up here, my father and Gregory right with her, that keeps me quiet.

Fear. I tell you, it's a motivation stronger than love.

One of my father's favorite Scriptures to quote is 2 Timothy, chapter 1, verse 7. *"For God has not given us a spirit of fear, but of power, and of love, and a sound mind."*

Well, in this moment, I don't have any of those virtues. Fear is definitely driving this bus.

"Aaliyah, you don't hear me talking to you?"

"I heard you, Mom."

"Then answer me. Where are you?"

I swallow, staring at the closed door of Gia's bathroom, her innocent humming—now Beyonce's "Cuff It"—a discordant soundtrack to this conversation.

"I can't…tell you that, Mom."

Silence buzzes in my ear. I close my eyes, waiting on the explosion. I don't have to wait long.

"Excuse me?" she asks, her tone low, angry. Even a little confused.

Join the club. I'm confused about where I found the courage to disobey her.

Obedience. To the Lord. To my father. To my future husband. To my mother. That's the hierarchy that's been drummed into me from the time I could grasp the meaning. Obedience above all, and to not submit is an offense not just against my parents and now Gregory, but also against God.

The nearly instinctive urge to give in, to surrender, rises within me so strong, if I wasn't sitting, I might sway on my feet. But I look around this little girl's room, and it's pink-and-purple color scheme symbolizes the new beginning I'm trying to carve out for myself. That gives me an iota of strength, just enough to hold out and not buckle under the weight of expectations that have sat on my shoulders and chest for…well, forever.

"I'm sorry, but I can't tell you where I am."

"You mean you *won't* tell me."

I shrug although she can't see it. "That, too." Before she can speak again, I say, "I don't mean to hurt or embarrass you and Daddy, but this is a decision I made, and I'm sticking to it. I'm sorry for the way I handled it—"

"Handled it like a thief sneaking out in the middle of the night."

I blow out a breath. She's right. That's exactly what I did. And though I did what I had to, I am a little ashamed of how I went about it. I was in survival mode. But Mom wouldn't understand that if I tried to explain my reasons. She's perfectly content as first lady of my father's church. As his wife. With her voice being an exact reflection of his. And I'm not looking down on her for her choices. But they're not mine. Not any longer. Maybe not ever.

"I did, and I apologized for that. If you need for me to do it again, then I'm sorry."

"I don't want your apology, Aaliyah Renee. I want you to use the money I just sent you to buy a plane ticket and come home. Everything else we can talk about when you get here—with your family. Gregory has been at his wit's end, but he's willing to forgive and reschedule the wedding. Although because of the wasted time and money, it will be decidedly smaller—"

I commit the cardinal sin of interrupting her and say, "That's not going to happen, Mom. After leaving Gregory at the altar, there's no way he's forgiving me, and he most definitely isn't forgetting." I have zero doubts he'd go through with the wedding anyway. But it would be less about being madly in love with me and more about being related to the great Bishop Montgomery. But I'll keep that to myself. "And I don't want to marry him. Which is why I left in the first place."

Part of the reason, but a major one.

"You don't know what you want." She sucks her teeth, and in my head, I can easily picture Mom rubbing her forehead. "You never said anything—"

"I did, Mom. In so many ways. You just weren't listening. But I definitely said it when I left the church."

And yet here she was, on my phone, ordering me to return home and consign myself to a stifling life that would suffocate me, silence me. No, she still wasn't listening. I'd literally *run away*, and she still didn't see.

"You are not four, young lady, you're twenty-four. Much too old to be throwing temper tantrums and acting rashly. Our God is not one of confusion, Aaliyah. He keeps His word, and doesn't go back on it. We are supposed to model our own lives and actions after Him, and this is not godly. It's not righteous. We've raised you better than this." She tsks. "Your actions don't just affect you, Aaliyah. Your father, the church, Gregory, his family... Do you have any idea how it makes them—us—look? You've humiliated us by this behavior—especially your father in the eyes of the church. How do you expect people to believe he can lead his flock when his own daughter doesn't follow him? No, ma'am, now isn't the time for childish excuses. You have to be an adult and make it right. So buy that ticket and use it. I don't want to hear anything else unless you're telling it to my face. I will see you in two days when we pick you up at the airport."

She hangs up on me, and for a long moment, I hold the cell to my ear, listening to the silence that echoes with her cutting words. Her disappointment in me is a physical thing, and I lift my other hand to my throat, rubbing it. As if the gesture can open my lungs and expel the grime that's impossible to wash away. It's embedded in my skin, my heart... my soul.

"Aaliyah!" Gia's voice penetrates the cloud wrapped around me in the wake of that phone call. "I'm finished!"

Slowly exhaling, I stand and move toward the bathroom. The heaviness doesn't evaporate from my chest, but I can't dwell on that or the two-day ultimatum Mom issued. I have a job to do.

"I'm coming, Gia." Knocking on the door, I wait a couple of seconds before entering.

Forty-five minutes and three bedtime stories later, I close the door on Gia's room, her nightlight spilling a soft glow that pushes back the dark. Smiling, I head down the hall, detouring to the kitchen. I've had the stove fan blowing since my, uh, attempt at cooking Gia dinner. I flip the switch, shutting off the noise. I sniff the air several times. Nope. I think the lingering odor of burned ground beef has finally dissipated. Note to self: if I'm going to be here late and have to make dinner again, DoorDash it. It's not only more edible but also not a fire hazard.

Sighing, I make my way to the living room and sink down to the couch, grabbing my bag. Removing my sketch pad and pencils, I settle down, losing myself in the drawing of Gia I'd started while she went wild with slime. Not a long time later, the front door opens and Von walks into the foyer.

Or stalks.

This man doesn't do anything as simple as "walk." With power and sexuality that wraps around him, he charges ahead like the perfect male animal he is, expecting everyone to get out of his way.

Perfect on the outside anyway.

That inside could use a little work, though.

Just thinking back on how he talked to me at the tattoo

shop earlier makes my whole head itch. I can honestly say I've never met anyone like Von before in my life. Someone who doesn't seem to care what flies out of his mouth or if it'll offend. Who commands a room just by walking into it and expects everyone to bend to his will.

He reminds me of Dad in that, but while Dad uses Scripture and a paternal affect, Von uses the handiest four-letter word and that intimidating growl.

And then there's the way he has of making everything sound so…erotic. Dirty.

I shiver as I recall his threat from earlier.

You might want to kill that shit, ma. That and the little attitude you call yourself having gon' get you in trouble you don't want.

I might be inexperienced, but I'm not naïve. I know the "trouble" he referred to. I've seen *365 Days* and have read my fair share of urban fiction. All on the down-low since I didn't feel like being shamed by my parents, but still…

Knowing what he's talking about and experiencing it? Two totally different things. And while my mind is all, *Girl, please. You pass out after one flutter of that rose against your clit,* my body—okay, my vagina, my whole vagina—is yelling, *Assume the position and get your back broke!*

It's very disconcerting.

Maybe a tiny, secret-even-from-myself part of me didn't accept the…vanilla kind of relationship I would have had with Gregory. But I would've walked down that aisle even if I wasn't fully content. Satisfied.

And that's the problem, isn't it?

Just one look into Von's beautiful gray eyes has my poor

kitty cat throbbing in a way that makes me acutely aware of what I've been lacking.

As he moves into the living room, that silver gaze centered on me, it takes every bit of control not to lower my eyes to avoid the intensity that seems to be part and parcel of him.

"Hey." He stops next to the couch, taking in my curled up legs and the pad in my lap before returning his scrutiny to my face. Quickly, I shove the sketch pad and pencils back in my bag. "Gia in bed?"

Grudgingly, I give him cool points for asking about his daughter first. I can't say he doesn't love Gia and put her welfare first. Too bad he's an ass about it.

See? He's already a bad influence. Got me cursing. Even to myself.

"Yes, she's been out like a light for the last ten minutes or so."

He nods. "You fuck my truck up?"

I squint at him. "No."

"You didn't reply to my text after you got back here."

"Sorry about that. I figured the text before that telling you we made it home would suffice."

"I don't pay you to 'figure' anything. Especially not when it comes to Gia. Until both of us are comfortable with this new arrangement, I'm staying on your ass about my daughter. I don't play about that one."

Had I said he was beautiful? That attitude makes him look like an orc.

"I understand," I say, proud of the unbothered note in my voice.

"How did the day go? You make out okay?"

"It went well. We made slime, had lunch, came back, completed her schoolwork, played some games and then got prison tats to commemorate the day's success."

Oh God. Did I say that out loud?

"Yeah, ma, you did," he says, and though his tone remains even, his eyes narrow on me.

I wince and try to make up for my loose lips. "I'm sorry. Not a good time for humor—"

"No, it isn't. Not when it comes to my daughter."

"I'm sorry," I apologize again and rise from the couch. Now seems as good a time as any to get out of here. While I still have a job. "Well, if that's all, I'll get going. What time should I be here in the morning?" I ask, grabbing my purse and my phone. I tap on the rideshare app. By the time I put on my coat and make it outside, my Uber should be here. And I can leave before I talk myself out of a job.

"What're you doing?" he asks.

"Just requesting an Uber." I frown. Well shoot. The nearest one is ten minutes away. There's no telling what might fly out of my mouth given that amount of time. Anything from "Your daughter must get her sunny disposition from her mother" to "You must work out a lot, huh? Tattooing don't give you thighs like that."

"Nah, cancel that. You're not going to need it."

I glance up from my phone. "I'm not?" Then it dawns on me what he's saying, and I'm shaking my head so hard, the end of my high ponytail smacks the corner of my eye. "No, I appreciate the thought, but you don't have to give me a ride.

I'm fine. And besides, you shouldn't wake Gia after she's already in bed. I have pepper spray on my key chain that my cousin bought me the first day I got here..."

My babbling trails off when I realize that, *A*, I'm babbling, and *B*, he's silently staring at me like I've lost my mind. Or I could be projecting.

"You finished?" he finally asks.

"Yes."

"Good. As I was saying, cancel the Uber and come with me."

He doesn't wait for my reply, just turns and walks out of the living room. I frown at his retreating back. He could've at least asked instead of ordering me. I mean, is that so hard? To be polite? Sheesh...

"Aye, you can talk shit and walk. Let's go."

Heaving a sigh, I slide my crossbody purse over my head and follow him. I move into the foyer, where he stands beside the front door, big hand grasping the knob.

"And to answer your question, that was me being polite. I can show you mean as fuck if you want..." he offers, eyebrow arched.

"No, thanks, I'll pass."

He stares at me another long moment, one where I fight not to squirm. I even hike my chin up for good measure.

Ain't nobody scared of him.

Mostly.

"Anyone ever tell you getting mouthy with your employer is a good way to get your lil' ass fired?"

No. Mainly because this is my first real job. Babysitting

and children's church didn't count. One never gave me a W-2, and the other didn't pay. But this probably isn't the best time to point that out. I should also wait to point out that addressing me in any manner that includes my ass doesn't seem appropriate. Since he's pulling the door open and moving outside, he most likely doesn't expect an answer anyway.

As soon as I step out onto the porch, Von trots down the front steps and strides over to his driveway. I follow behind him at a slower pace, confusion swirling in my head.

On the top step, I glance behind me at the door he left wide open. If he is taking me home, shouldn't he be going back for Gia? Anyone could walk into the house. Even in Parsons, we lock our doors, and we haven't had a murder in our town since '04.

"Aaliyah." The impatience he pours into my name is etched into his frown. "I've been standing here for fucking eighty-four years. Could you bring your ass?"

I can't quit. I need this job. And I can't cut him. If leaving Gregory at the altar embarrassed my father, going to jail for assault with a deadly weapon will send him to the upper room. I remind myself of all the consequences as I—cough—bring my ass down the stairs and over to him.

"Here." He dangles a key chain in front of me.

"What's this?" I return his frown. "I don't need a key to your truck. I appreciate it, but I don't feel comfortable driving it home. I'm not even on your insurance—"

He snorts. "Yeah, like hell that's happening again. Today was a one-off. Here," he repeats, but this time, he grabs my hand and drops the keys into my open palm. "These are for that."

He nods to the jeep behind his truck, and nope, I'm still not getting it. Partly because my brain short-circuited when he touched me. It was the first time we had contact of any kind, and that hard, calloused hand cupping mine sent a bolt of lightning through me. Residual currents still crackle, and I force air through my lungs. As if he'd stroked that big hand over my breasts, my nipples and between my thighs?

I've never gone instantly wet. Even with my clit vibrator, it takes a few minutes to get to that point. But with one platonic touch, he's done it. High and deep, I throb, ache.

Oh God. This isn't good. Not good at all.

I step back, knocking his hand from mine, the uneven edges of the key denting my palm. If Von is wondering about my odd reaction, he doesn't show it. He opens the driver's-side door, reaches inside and pulls out a couple of papers.

"Here." He extends them toward me, and when I don't immediately take them, he shifts closer. "Take them, Aaliyah."

Without my permission, my fingers grab the papers. I don't know. Maybe it's years of being obedient that has me unconsciously reacting to his demand. I glance down at the sheets, and three words across the top snare my attention.

Bill of Sale.

"What is this?" I'm staring at the form, but the meaning of it… "Why are you handing me a bill of sale for this—" I drop my gaze to the sheet again "—2021 Jeep Grand Cherokee Laredo X?"

"Because it's yours, Aaliyah," he enunciates as if he's speaking to a kindergartner who's learning syllables. "And you're going to need to keep that paperwork in the car while I get your permanent tag and the final title."

"What?" I gasp. "Nope. Nopenopenope. You can't try to make me sound like I'm crazy because I'm questioning *why you've bought me a car.*"

I promise, I didn't mean to yell at him. On my mama, I didn't. And when his chin jerks back, I pinch the bridge of my nose, silently praying for the patience of Job *and* Jesus.

"Who you yelling at, lil' mama?" He mugs me. "I know you gon' take that bass out your voice."

I exhale, long and low. Dropping my arm, I meet his glare.

"Excuse me for being a little shocked when someone—a someone I've known a matter of hours—gifts me with a car."

"That's the most fucked-up way I've heard someone say thank you." He crosses his arms over his wide chest. "Look, Aaliyah, I haven't forgotten that you start school soon. What if you get out of class late and my daughter has to wait around while you get a ride? Nah, at the end of the day, this ain't got shit to do with you and everything to do with my daughter. This isn't Bumfuck, Alabama. I told you before, bad shit can and does happen."

"And I can't let you just give me a car."

When his brow arches higher, I turn down the volume of my voice. "Sorry, but even in *Parsons, Alabama,* we don't just gift people with vehicles." I blow out another hard breath. "Look, Von, I appreciate the gesture but— Hey! We're not finished talking!"

"I am. And I'm also tired and hungry," Von throws over his shoulder as he walks toward his house, not even glancing back at me. "Get your *Parsons, Alabama*, ass in that car and go home. And be back here no later than 7:15. School starts at 7:45, and my baby hates being late."

"But we're not finished—"

"'Night, Aaliyah." He climbs the front steps, and seconds later, the front door slams shut.

I stand there in the cool night air, hearing only the faint sound of traffic from several streets over and the cheerful chirping of insects. I wait a couple of minutes, certain he's going to come back outside so we can discuss this like rational adults. But not only doesn't he return, he shuts the porch light off, casting me in shadows.

This mutha—nope. I shut the thought down. He will not take me there. But whew, was I close.

Opening my hand, I stare down at the keys then shift my gaze to the bill of sale. Then over to the Jeep Cherokee. Then back to the paper again.

"Holy..."

My eyes bug out of my head. No. No way. He paid *eighteen thousand dollars* for this car! I shift through the other papers, praying I see something about financing and him putting down like two or three—and even that is way too much!—for a deposit. But no, he paid out all that money, and I own the car, free and clear.

Who does that? No, seriously, who. Does. That?

Drug dealers.

Oh, so he got to be a drug dealer 'cause he Black and has available cash.

No, because who you know got that much cash just sitting around?

This successful Black man who owns and runs his own business. Stop counting his money!

While the voices in my head go back and forth, I stare at the new-to-me car that's still there. Not going anywhere.

My phone buzzes in my pocket, and I pull it free and glance down at the screen.

Bad Boss: If I have 2 come back out there & put u in that truck u not gon like it. I will but u wont

Dammit.

Completely inappropriate excitement filters through my veins at that not-so-subtle warning. My belly bottoms out, and not from hunger. What is wrong with me? I should be angry, offended that he just threatened to manhandle me, not, not…*turned on.*

Forget him.

I'm his nanny, not his property. I'm my own person. I have free will, and he can't steal that from me. He's the boss of my job not my life.

"And I'm taking this damn car because I want to, not because he told me to," I mutter, marching over to the Jeep and climbing in.

Great. Now he's had me curse two times in as many minutes.

That man is a menace.

"And no, the new-car smell *isn't* amazing." I let loose a squeal seeing its keyless ignition, but quickly cut it off. "No, that's not cool. Heated seats? Get. Out," I whisper, cringing at the awe in my voice.

The 2015 Camry my parents bought for me to use, but did not put in my name, didn't have all these amenities. I feel like I'm sitting in a luxury car.

I mean, it's aight.

Shifting the car into Reverse, I carefully back out of Von's driveway. The car has a navigation system, but for now, I'll use the GPS on my phone to get back to Tamara's.

Speaking of Tamara…

I pull up to the stop sign at the end of Von's street, head to my Favorites list and tap my cousin's name. The phone barely rings once before her voice pours through the cell's speaker.

"Girl, you need to be glad you called me when you did. I was about to tell these people fuck that pole and come find you. Where you been, Liyah?" she demands.

Though her irritation pours out of each word, so does her concern. And it's that last emotion that has my lips curling into a smile. Her worry is so different from my mother's during our earlier conversation. Mom's had been smothering, guilt-inducing and controlling. But Tamara's is genuine and not selfish.

"I'm sorry, Tamara. I intended to call you back. I'm just leaving work now."

"Now? It's almost nine thirty. I don't like you having to take a rideshare so late. Not when you're still new here. Is this going to be a normal thing?"

I shrug and slowly roll out into the intersection. The GPS instructs me to keep straight for another quarter mile.

"I don't think so, although he did warn me there would be a few late nights a month. It's fine, though. The little girl is sweet." Unlike her daddy. "And once we had dinner—"

"Aw, hell no. Please tell me you didn't cook for that baby." She sounds truly appalled and about six seconds away from calling CPS.

"Really, Tamara? Really?"

I huff out a breath. Tamara must've been Sherlock in another life because that DoorDash cover story didn't work for long. The spirit of deduction is strong in that one.

"Listen, you can do a bomb-ass banana pudding. But I don't know what the fuck you called yourself trying to fry the other night."

"Chicken." I frown. "It was chicken."

"Mmkay. I'ma let you make it. Make that delusional shit you talking, that is. But not chicken. You can't ever make no more of that. Had to take my damn curtains to the cleaners," she mutters.

"It wasn't that—" I cut my own self off from uttering that lie.

"Ma'am? It wasn't what?" Tamara snorts. "Uh-huh. For the life of me, I don't get it, though. I've had Auntie Georgia's cooking. She can throw down in the kitchen. How that gene just skip a generation?" She chuckles. "How you Black, Southern as hell and can't cook? That's like breaking some law, ain't it?"

"Don't you need to get to work?" I grind out.

"Yeah, I do. And can do it in peace now that I know you're good. How close are you to home? Do I need to stay on the phone until you make it there?"

"No, that won't be necessary. I'm, um..." I hedge, flicking my signal light on to turn right toward the interstate exit. "I'm not in an Uber."

Tamara's quiet for a beat. "Why didn't you tell me you were in that man's car?" she hisses.

"Von isn't giving me a ride home."

"Yeah, I give in. I'm lost."

"Tamara." I slow down at another four-way stop and scan the dashboard, console and passenger seat like it's the first time I've seen them. "Why this man buy me a car?"

Another beat of silence. This one so long I catch the faint sound of music and the loud chatter of women in the background.

"Say what now?" The noise in the background dulls, and I'm guessing she must've moved to another room. "Now, repeat that. He did what?"

"He bought me a car." I huff out a laugh and guide my new Jeep toward the on-ramp. "I don't care how many times I say it, I still can't believe it. And I'm sitting in the thing!"

"Bitch! Girl, not you. Mind your business." I'm assuming she didn't direct that last part toward me. "Sorry 'bout that. One thing I can't stand about working around a bunch of women is they always in your business with their petty asses," she mutters. "But anyway... Bitch! You're driving home in a new car? Right now?"

"Yes! With seat warmers!" I shake my head, hearing myself sounding like a country bumpkin, but I can't help it. Dad's Rolls Royce Ghost has heated seats, but I've never driven it. Shoot, he barely lets me sit in it. And this is supposedly *mine.* "And he paid eighteen thousand dollars for it."

I don't know why I'm back to whispering that when it's just me in the car and her on the line. It just feels like that amount of money needs to be uttered with some kind of reverence.

"Now, cous..." She clears her throat. "I'm not judging, I promise. But you taking care of more than his daughter?"

"What?" I gape at the car in front of me on the interstate. "You don't mean... Hell no!"

"My bad, damn. I've made you curse." Tamara cracks up, and my frown deepens at her laughter. "I had to ask. These men in here have handed me thousands in cash, vacations, Chanel purses, red-bottom shoes and even the key to a time-share. But never gifted a car. Shiiiit, I wanted to ask for pointers." She cracks up again, and after a moment, I snicker. "But for real, though. What did he say? I mean, I knew Von Howard was paid but *damn.*"

"He brought me outside and just handed me the keys and a bill of sale, saying it wasn't safe for his daughter to be riding back and forth in Ubers. And then he threatened me into taking it. God, how can a man be generous and so rude at the same time?"

Tamara laughs again, and I'm glad one of us finds this amusing. I guess she didn't hear the part where I said he threatened me.

"Aaliyah, you're so damn dramatic."

Dramatic? Me? I mean, yes, I did run away from the altar like I was about to be sacrificed on it, but that was the most *dramatic* thing I've done in my life.

"Listen, real talk," she says, "this is like the third time you've mentioned him being rude or mean. Babe, you're no doormat. That may be hard for you to remember given you're on the run..." I snort, and she chuckles. "Where the lie? Like your ass in witness protection the way you got me lying to the family about if I've heard from you. But I mean what I said. You have issues standing up to your parents, especially Uncle Tim, but you've never had that issue with anyone else."

I stay quiet because, right now, contrary to what she's said, I can feel the footprints marching up and down my back.

"Yeah, you're on the quiet side, but you always checked anyone who mistook that for weakness. I remember that time Mother Johnson came at you and asked when you were going to lose weight, that men didn't want big women. You looked her straight in the eye and told her that if God had a ram in the bush for her then, surely, He would find one for you, too." She cracks up. "The shade! Your ass even smiled like you were complimenting that old biddy."

"She kept trying me," I mutter. "Thinking just 'cause she older she got a pass to say whatever she wants. Age should give you wisdom not a license to be hurtful. I said what I said, and I'm still not taking it back." Chuckling, I switch lanes, obeying the GPS's directions. "She didn't say anything else to me, though."

"That's what I'm talking about, Liyah. When you get out

of your head and feelings, you don't take shit from anyone. You're a helluva lot nicer than me and use less profanity, but you have a mouth and a backbone. I overheard what you told Von this morning when he called asking for your help. That he couldn't speak to you any ol' way. Stand on that, babe. He seems like the kind of man who will roll right over you if you allow it. You need to start that job how you mean to continue. You a bad bitch, but if you don't believe it, how you expect anyone else to?"

She's right. I know she's right. About Von and definitely about setting the stage for where our employer-employee relationship will go from here.

"You're right," I murmur.

"I know I'm right."

I smile then huff out a breath. "Can I be honest?"

"Of course."

"He scares me," I softly admit.

"Hol' the fuck up," Tamara snarls, and her anger streams through the line, damn near burning my cheek. "I laughed off that threatening shit, but were you serious? Has he done something? Did he touch you? Nope, nope, he got me all the way fucked-up—"

"No, Tamara, no." I laugh. "Please don't leave that club and pull up on his shop." I laugh harder as she continues to hurl insults at Von's head. And dick. Okay, no, not going down that road. "Other than what I told you, he hasn't been abusive or anything. And by *threatening*, I meant he told me to get in the truck or he would put me in there."

An involuntary shiver trips down my spine.

"Oh. Girl, you should've led with that because I was about to say fuck this job and go find him. Big muthafucka or not, he was about to see me," she mumbles.

Since I'm alone, I do nothing to contain my grin. My cousin plays tough, but she possesses the hugest heart.

"So, what're you talking about that he scares you?" she asks.

I sigh, and a part of me wishes I hadn't said anything. Not because I don't trust Tamara. But because I feel kind of silly now.

"Aaliyah?" she presses.

"Maybe *scare* is the wrong word. He makes me nervous. Like, tonight I started babbling a couple of times. I feel like I don't even know myself, but at the same time I feel more myself than I've been in a long time." I shake my head. "I know I'm not making much sense."

"Oh, babe." Tamara sighs and falls silent. The muted cacophony of women's voices and the thump of heavy music pulses in my ear. "Don't fall for him."

"What?" I practically screech. Coughing, I clear my throat and repeat, "What?"

"You heard me. Don't fall for him."

"I wouldn't—that's not even… Of course not," I protest.

"That's what you're saying. Liyah, I see the appeal. He's gorgeous, tatted up, has BDE and is successful. And no matter how much you talk about how rude he is, I bet a part of you even likes that. Or, at least, your pussy does. But I'm warning you," she says over my sputtering at the casual mention of my…vagina, "don't do it. He might be fine, but he's also a shitload of heartache and pain. Promise me you'll keep it professional and won't get involved with him."

"I promise," I quickly say, and when I'm greeted with a very loaded silence on her end, I repeat, "I promise, Tamara. Even though you have it all wrong. It's not like that."

Of course, I've noticed how hot he is, and okay, my body perks up like a groundhog seeing its shadow when he's within breathing distance. But *fall for him*?

No. Excuse my language, but hell, no.

I just escaped—a terrible relationship. God knows, the last thing I need is another one. And nothing about Von Howard screams commitment. Call me a prude or an uptight preacher's kid, but I'm not built for one-night stands, or no strings attached...situationships.

But if I were to lose every God-given sense I own and have sex with Von... What would happen when all that ended? And let's be clear—it would eventually end. I wouldn't be able to separate sex from emotion. Then I would be out of a job.

Bottom line. I need this job. It's making a way for me to stay in Chicago, to go to school, to be self-sufficient.

To be free.

I don't care how big Von's dick is or how good he can sling it. It's not worth my freedom.

And dang it, I have to stop thinking about that man's penis!

"Uh-huh." Skepticism drips from her tone. "All right, Liyah, I have to go. If that girl pokes her head in here one more time to see what I'm doing, she gon' see another side of me. Since I don't want to lose my job, let me get out there. You good?"

"Yes, I'm not far from your place now."

"Good. Still text me when you get there."

"I will. Bye and have a great night."

I end the call and set the phone in the middle console.

Her concern sends warmth spreading through me like a sip of hot coffee. I'll make it back to her apartment nice and safe, and I'll stay that way with Von. I know she's uncertain, but I can show her better than I can tell her.

I'm here to go to college and stand on my own two feet. Nothing and no one will get in the way of that. I won't let it.

Six

"My kingdom. My kingdom for a baby mama that got some damn act right."

Von

"Aw fuck."

"Incoming."

That's all the warning I get from Chelle and Malcolm as I glance up from my plate of oxtails and see my ex-wife crossing the small dine-in section of my favorite soul food restaurant. Usually, coming here for lunch is one of the highlights of my workweek. Mama Zee's food comes in second only to my ma's cooking. And quiet as kept, they're neck and neck. I'd just never admit that to Jerusha Monae Howard. Not if I want to keep my head on my shoulders. So I keep my mouth shut and enjoy Mama Zee's at least three times a week.

Or I *was* enjoying my food.

But Sheree has that effect. Sucking the joy out of every damn thing.

"Hey, Von." She sidles up to our table, ignoring Chelle and Malcolm.

"Sheree. What're you doing here?"

"Damn." She tries to reach for offended, but that smirk riding her mouth ruins it. "I can't just come and speak?"

"Don't see a point in it." I shrug. "What're you doing here?" I repeat. "And don't try that in-the-neighborhood shit. You don't live over this way, and you don't even like the food here. So say what you gotta say and move around."

"Who do you think you're talking to?" she snaps.

"Here we go," Chelle mutters around a forkful of mac 'n' cheese.

"Nobody's talking to you." Her head whips around, and she glares at Chelle, who arches her brow and slips more food in her mouth. "You need to mind your business."

"Well, boo, I would but you not giving me or anybody much of a choice." Chelle turns in her chair, to the left and then to the right, in an exaggerated sweep of the restaurant. "If you gon' hold me hostage to the bullshit, I'ma speak on it."

"See, that's the problem right there." Sheree jerks her attention back to me because she don't want no smoke with Chelle, for real. My ex-wife likes to run her mouth, but when it comes to backing it up, baby girl has no hands. Chelle, though? She'll drag anyone's ass, no discrimination. "Your *friends* are always in our business."

And there it is.

From the beginning of our relationship, Sheree never accepted that me and Chelle are just friends and colleagues. Sheree even tried to make me choose between her and Chelle. And this was *before* I married her. That should've been my first red flag.

That's where thinking with my dick landed me.

Divorced and permanently attached to her through our daughter.

Looking at her, I can objectively see why I fell for her. My ex-wife is beautiful. Pretty face with hazel eyes and lips that could suck the skin off my dick. Dark hair in a sleek, shoulder-length bob, nice-size titties, a fat ass and thick thighs. She got that body women will pay Dr. Miami to give them on a surgical table. Only hers is natural. Yeah, Sheree is gorgeous, as the tight, green Fenty sweatpants and cropped sweatshirt attest to. Too bad that beauty goes away whenever she opens her mouth.

Like now.

"*We* don't have business anymore, Sheree," I remind her, shoveling more rice and gravy onto my fork even though my appetite is shot. "We're divorced, remember? Which means whatever this—" I slide the food in my mouth and then wave the fork back and forth between us "—is about, I don't have to entertain it. For the sake of our daughter, I'ma be generous. Say what you want then let me eat so I can get back to my shop."

That smirk returns to her mouth. "Don't you mean *our* shop?" Her voice raises a little, just enough to draw attention our way.

This was her intention all along. To find me and that bullshit lawsuit. To embarrass me. 'Cause she could've brought her greedy ass on to the shop if she didn't want an audience. You'd think she knew me by now. Nearly ten years together and she still thinks she can play with me.

Leaning back in my chair, I set my fork down on my plate and meet her hazel gaze. "You sure you want to do this here?" I calmly offer her one last chance to get the fuck on. I may sound unbothered, but inside, anger seethes in my gut.

Uncertainty flickers in her eyes, but in the next second, her smirk widens, and she crosses her arms over her chest. "Why not? You don't answer the phone when I call, and my attorney says you've been ignoring his messages and emails. I know the thought of losing half that damn shop probably has you feeling some kind of way, but you can't ignore a court document, Von. And since we're going to be co-owners soon..." She shrugs like the shit has been ruled on and it's a done deal.

"This bitch..." Chelle laughs, falling back in her chair, and Malcolm shakes his head, disgust for Sheree etched on his face.

There's no love lost between her and any of my employees. She had a chance to get to know them, to get their respect, but that's hard to do when every time she rolls up in my place of business it's with some drama. I've lost clients behind her ass. And me losing clients means my tattoo artists did, too. So yeah, they don't fuck with her.

"Who you calling a bitch?" Sheree shouts at Chelle, and when she laughs harder, I want to warn my ex-wife. Past experience taught me, the harder Chelle smiles, the closer she is to swinging. But in typical Sheree fashion, she's writing a check her ass can't cash. "You just gon' sit there and let her call me out my name?" she directs back to me.

"Aye, who you yelling at? You need to talk to me like you got some sense," I say, voice still even, but my leg starts to jump under the table. "And you're not my woman anymore. Take that shit up with her."

"I'm your daughter's mother," she snaps.

As if I can forget. I shrug again. "And that means I gotta co-parent with you. Everything else is a wrap."

Fire damn near shoots out of her eyes and she leans forward. Then at the last second, as if she catches herself, she straightens. "I'ma need this energy right here when I come and take half your shop—"

"You ain't taking shit, Sheree." I cock my head, studying her. "I don't know what you thought you were going to accomplish by this, but it's not gonna end how you want it to. Now, you walked up in here, calling yourself checking me. Baby girl, if you want me to hurt your feelings in front of all these people by airing your files, I will. Because if I start talking about our divorce, I ain't stopping with this recent bullshit. I'm going to end with why we divorced in the first place. Is that what you want? You let me know."

Real fear flashes in her eyes, and I know her decision before she opens her mouth. "You're such an asshole, Von," she hisses.

"I'll take that as a no." Yeah, she doesn't want me telling her business. She doesn't want me to tell the whole truth. "If you're done spoiling my lunch, you can go. And you better hope I don't send the video from one of these muthafuckas recording us to my attorney. Maybe I'll get paid for harassment along with his fees."

She glances around. Several people have their phones up and aimed toward us. Probably got this whole shit on a live right now.

"Fuck you," she snarls then stomps off.

"I don't get it, Von." Malcolm squints after Sheree, waiting until she shoves through the door. "I don't even fuck with the cops like that, but even I might get a restraining order on her." He shakes his head, lifting cabbage to his mouth. "She loose."

"Get a restraining order because my ex-wife is bitter and trifling?" I snort, shoving my plate away. "Yeah, I don't think it works like that. Hell, even Hallmark ain't got a card for that."

Chelle rubs a hand over the shaved side of her head then props her inked forearms on the table. "I told you she had issues when you first started dating her. A woman knows when another one doesn't have some damn sense. And Sheree never did. But no." She draws out "no" until it's about five syllables long. "She got a fat ass and good pussy."

"Chelle," I warn on a low growl.

"Okay, okay." She holds up her hands. "But for real, I got a question. What did you mean by telling the reason you got divorced? There's something else besides catching her cheating and stealing your money?"

It's cliché and laughable how I discovered Sheree was

fucking around on me. The one time she didn't take her phone into the bathroom with her, and "Kia" called her. I answered it, and it was Malik, one of my boys. Finding that out on top of my accountant informing me money had gone missing from my business account? I was done. Past done.

Like those two offenses weren't enough.

But no. There's more.

And that fucking more damn near broke me.

A very familiar fury throbs in my head, beating in sync with my pulse. Even if I could get past the cheating or the stealing, I'll never forgive her for the *more.*

"Von?" Chelle presses when I go silent.

"Yeah?" I scratch my beard-covered jaw. "It doesn't—hold up."

My cell vibrates against the table. I frown. Why is Gia's school calling me? My gaze flicks to the time at the top of the screen, and I note that it's only 12:34 p.m. My heart gives a hard thump. Silly. They could be calling for any reason, but that's my baby. Picking up the phone, I press Answer and lift it to my ear.

"Hello?"

"Mr. Howard?" the voice on the other end asks.

I tamp down my impatience and say, "Yeah, this is him. How can I help you?"

"Hello, Mr. Howard, this is Principal Laurence Hutchinson at Gia's school."

"Is everything okay with G?"

Chelle's and Malcolm's gazes fly to me at the mention of Gia.

"Your daughter is fine, but..." My jaw locks, barely trapping the "Speak the fuck up" behind my teeth. "Sir, we have a problem with her caretaker and need you to come up to the school."

Her care... "Aaliyah?"

"Yes, sir. Ms. Aaliyah Howard. You have her listed in Gia's file as a person permitted to drop off and pick up Gia from school as well as a contact in case of emergency. Which is why, when we had a situation here, we called her when we couldn't get in touch with you."

"What kind of situation?" I bark, anxiety spiking inside me. "What time did you call me earlier?"

"It was about 11:15," he says. And after a brief hesitation, he adds, "I'd rather discuss the other part of this in person as it pertains to another child in Gia's class, sir. Can I expect you at the school soon?"

I drag a hand down my face. At eleven, I was in the middle of a tattoo, but because of Gia, I never turn my phone off or silence it. I don't know how I missed the call. Yeah, I added Aaliyah to her file as an emergency contact—and in the three weeks Aaliyah has been with G, they've been super tight—but Gia's *my* daughter. And my stomach curdles. She's my first priority, and it doesn't sit well with me that I failed to be there for her today.

"I'm on my way." Not bothering to wait for his response, I end the call and shove back my chair, standing.

"What's going on, Von?" Chelle fires at me, rising from her chair, too. "What's wrong with G?"

"I don't know. The principal said she's fine, but something's going on if they want me up at the school."

"Call me as soon as you find out." She follows me out the restaurant door and onto the sidewalk. "I mean it, Von. Don't make me have to blow up your phone."

"I got you. Have Malcolm call my afternoon clients and reschedule them for me."

"Yeah, I will. Give her a kiss from her auntie."

I wave to her as I climb into my truck, focused on getting to the school in record time. Soon I'm striding through the quiet elementary school entrance, my mind flooded with all kinds of scenarios about what could be happening with Gia.

As soon as I reach the front office, I pull the door open and move directly to the administrative assistant's desk. The older woman looks up, and recognition flashes in her blue eyes. Gia has never been a problem child, but I'm no deadbeat parent, either. They know me up here because I haven't missed a parent-teacher conference, a bake sale, a book sale or anything in between. And though Sheree gets on my fucking nerves, she's the same. Or at least she was before the divorce. She's been slipping a little since then. Still, she might be a bum-ass wife, but for the most part, I can't shit on her as a mother.

Clenching my teeth, I shove thoughts of my ex-wife aside. I've had enough of her today. Still mad she spoiled my goddamn oxtails.

"Good afternoon, Mr. Howard," Mrs. Terrance says with a small smile. "Principal Hutchinson is expecting you. Go right on in."

"Thanks."

I walk toward the door on the other side of the room. Giving it the barest of knocks, I twist the knob and enter.

My gaze immediately zeroes in on Gia, sitting at the child-size table and chair set in the corner of the large office. I study her, settling on her frown before scanning her little body. Once satisfied she's indeed fine—looking pissed off but fine—I shift my attention to the woman next to her.

Instead of taking one of the *adult-size* armchairs in front of the desk, Aaliyah is damn near spilling over the other chair, her body turned to the side since her knees ain't fitting under that table. I'd laugh at how ridiculous she looks if it weren't for the fact that we are up at my daughter's school. Aaliyah wears a composed, cool expression, as if she's chilling at my place on the couch, definitely not like she's in the fucking *principal's office.* But then she lifts her eyes to mine and…

Yeah, maybe not so composed.

There's worry in those pretty brown eyes, but anger, too.

Aaliyah is hot, and since I haven't done anything to her little ass, it must be directed toward Principal Hutchinson.

Swinging my gaze his way, I narrow my eyes on him. Both my daughter and Aaliyah ain't fucking with him so that already makes the other man suspect in my book. Gia, because of the obvious. And Aaliyah… Well, shorty don't mess with anybody. She's still too nice, too naïve, in my opinion, although I don't have one complaint on how she takes care of my daughter. But, making her mad is like enraging a fucking Disney princess. It ain't natural.

I've only seen her mad one time, and that's when I had

to strong-arm her into accepting a car from me. A car she clearly needed so she wasn't riding around Chicago with strangers, at the mercy of some rideshare app.

She got over that mad, though. Not that she had a choice.

"Mr. Howard." The principal rises from behind his desk and stretches his hand out to me. I stare down at it for several seconds before briefly shaking it. He's been principal here since Gia started kindergarten. She's now in second grade, and I've never had to be called to his office. "Please have a seat."

He waves toward the visitor chairs, and I catch the quick, impatient glance he shoots in Aaliyah's direction.

Sinking to one, I don't waste any time. "What's this about? And why they over there looking like you sat both of them in timeout?" I dip my head toward Gia and Aaliyah.

His mouth flattens, but he smooths his hand over his tie and the front of his shirt, lowering back to his chair. Clearing his throat, he says, "Yes, well, I asked Ms. Montgomery if she wouldn't be more comfortable over here—" he nods at the vacant chair next to me "—but she opted to sit with Gia."

Despite the circumstances, amusement bubbles in my chest. Yeah, I've encountered that stubborn streak. In the three weeks she's worked for me, it's raised its head. And flipped me off. She's soft-spoken and sweet 'n' all, but I can practically see her cussing me out in her head at times. Sometimes, I wish she'd just let the shit fly. A nice, gentle Aaliyah is damn hard to ignore. But the Aaliyah that would tell me to go fuck myself with the same sentiment in her eyes?

Yeah, maybe it's a good thing she keeps her cool. Otherwise, I'd be too tempted to give her something else to do with that mouth instead of go off on me. Shit, who am I kidding? I'm tempted to do that regardless.

Fucking focus.

"Aaliyah, come here, please?"

I don't glance over my shoulder, but after a beat of several seconds, the sound of her chair legs scraping over the floor fills the office, and a moment later, she appears at my side. The annoyed, grim set of her mouth telegraphs her displeasure with me calling her over here. If she knew how fast and hard I brick up at her obedience, she'd run back over to that table. Maybe crawl up under it.

Principal Hutchinson's gaze skates down Aaliyah's curves as she settles in the visitor chair, lingering on her firm, high breasts and those wide, sexy-as-fuck hips. He must think I don't catch that shit. Even though I can hardly blame him, given how thick and gorgeous her body is—yeah, fuck that. I can blame him.

"Aye, up here," I growl, not caring one gotdamn bit if I embarrass him.

I'm not here for him to eye-fuck Aaliyah. Matter of fact, he should just keep his eyes off her altogether before I move some furniture up in here. And no, I'm not analyzing why that shit bothers me to my soul. It just does.

He clears his throat again. "I'm sorry to have to call you up here during the workday, Mr. Howard, but there was an incident here at the school earlier that we need to address." I stare at him, and he dips his chin. Next to me, Aaliyah shifts in her chair. "Gia had an altercation with another student in her class this morning. Things turned physical, and we have a zero tolerance policy for violence—"

"Tell him why she resorted to putting her hands on the other…girl," Aaliyah interjects, leaning forward in the chair. That little pause… If I didn't know better, I'd think Pollyanna was about to call a child a bitch. "It wasn't unprovoked."

"That's a matter of she said, she said, Ms. Montgomery."

"No, it is not. It's a matter of the truth. There are no two sides to it."

"Gia is saying one thing while the other student tells a different story—"

"And she's lying, but you don't want to acknowledge that. You'd rather cover your own a—" She bit off the sentence before she cursed, and I blink at her near uttering of profanity. She sucks in a deep breath and slowly releases it before continuing. "You'd rather cover your own behind," she amends, "rather than admit you didn't listen and protect Gia when she asked for help. You'd rather give the message to a child that even when she goes through all the right avenues, even when she follows the rules, she'll be punished by the adults who failed her in the first place."

Holy. Shit.

Who is this and what happened to my nanny?

She's reading the fuck outta him, and all the principal can do is sit there, taking it.

Shaking my head, I tear my gaze from this…so *un-Disney* version of Aaliyah and focus back on Principal Hutchinson. "What is she talking about you failed to protect Gia? From what?" I growl.

What the hell does my daughter need protection from, and why is this the first I'm hearing of it? Whew. Anger flashes inside me like a lighter flaring to life. Somebody better have some answers. I don't, and will never, play about Gia.

"Ms. Montgomery claims that Gia has been bullied," he says, an edge to his voice.

"Claims?" Aaliyah barks out a sharp laugh, her fingers curling around the arms of the chair. "Why don't you just come on out and call both of us liars? But here's the thing, sir, I don't need to lie. Not when I have proof."

She removes a phone from the purse slung across her body, taps on the screen and passes it to me.

At first, I'm not sure what the fuck I'm looking at. But then I realize it's a piece of blue paper and a rough drawing of a girl with squiggly lines for hair and a pig's face. Above it is scrawled Piggy Gia.

Pure fury roars inside my head. I swear to God, I'm sweating, and my pulse drowns out everything. Deliberately, I pass the phone back to Aaliyah when I feel like throwing it across the room to smash against the wall.

The. Fuck.

I glance behind me at Gia, and she stares down at her clasped hands. Battling the urge to flip a desk—and the man sitting behind it—I softly call her name. And truthfully, it ain't all that soft. But it's the best I can do with this rage riding me.

"You okay, G?"

She nods her head.

"Look at me, baby girl," I gently order. And when she lifts her head and meets my gaze, I ask again, "You okay?"

"Yes, Daddy," she whispers. And my heart aches.

Pain radiates behind my ribs. I want to pick her up, hug her close and run out of this office, this school. Want to shield her from the shitty people in the world. Somehow, I forgot that kids can be just as horrible as adults. And I hate that I couldn't protect my baby from that ugliness, from that hurt. Hate that it even touched her.

"Okay, do me a favor? Go outside and sit with Mrs. Terrance."

"Okay."

As soon as she leaves and the door closes behind her, I return my focus to the principal. He flinches before he straightens his shoulders and tries to appear like he's the one in control. He can kill that. I got something for him.

"Did you see that?" I jab a finger toward Aaliyah's phone.

"Yes, I did," he says. "And like I told Ms. Montgomery, that's not necessarily proof. Anyone could've drawn that, not the other stud—"

"Are you fucking kidding me?" I seethe. "As a principal, a fucking man, you're really gon' sit here and defend that shit?"

"Mr. Howard, I understand you're upset, but I won't condone that language."

"Oh, so you have standards." I lean forward, propping my elbows on my knees and clasping my fingers between my spread thighs. It's either that or wrap them around his neck. "A little girl being harassed doesn't offend you, but my language does?" I chuckle, shaking my head. "Get the fuck outta here with that, bruh."

"Now, wait just a—"

Throwing up a hand toward him, I turn to Aaliyah. "What happened? Since I'm obviously not going to get the full truth out of him."

"Last week, Gia came home upset. I finally got it out of her that she was being bullied by a girl in her class, and she showed me that…drawing. The other girl had given it to her during recess and started calling her names. Apparently, this isn't the first time. It's been going on since the beginning of the year." She shoots a dirty look at the principal and under different circumstances, it would be comical. "Anyway—" she returns her attention to me "—I told her to tell her teacher. And if things didn't change, tell her teacher again. She did that the next two days, and her teacher did nothing." Aaliyah's voice thickens, and her eyes glisten though they remain hot with hurt and anger for my little girl.

Shit, I don't think I've ever found her more beautiful.

"When she let me know, I told her to tell a different teacher, and she did that as well. She let another second-grade teacher know what was going on, and still, nothing. Then I got a call from *him* today." She hikes her chin in the principal's direction. "Gia got in a fight. And apparently because that little heffa got a lot of mouth she can't back up with her hands, Gia is the one in trouble and about to be suspended."

"Gia could've come to me at any time if she was experiencing difficulties in class."

Before I can turn and tell him in detail how to go fuck

himself, Aaliyah beats me to it. Her head whips in his direction, her long waves falling over her shoulder. "Oh really? She should've gone to you? Because the teachers she trusted did nothing to intervene? As the head of this school, their neglect falls on you. Do I condone violence? No, not ordinarily. But she followed the rules, reached out to the authority figure, three times, and she was failed. At. Every. Turn. So when the bully came at her again, she defended herself. Or maybe you think she should've sucked it up and persevered for the rest of the year? Maybe you believe being tormented would've built character? God gave John a thorn in the flesh to endure, but I'm proud of Gia for plucking hers out."

I frown, confused. Thorn in the flesh? Must be all that Sunday school she taught.

"I sympathize with Gia. I really do. I'm not so heartless that I don't understand the why behind what occurred. But be that as it may, we have a zero tolerance policy, and I can't let her be the exception."

I cock my head, running a hand down my beard. "And what about the zero tolerance policy about bullying? I haven't heard you say shit about that yet."

Back to clearing his throat. "We know Gia hit another student, while we can't prove the bullying by—"

I hold up my hand again. "Let me stop you right there. Are you trying to tell me that my daughter will be punished, but the other student won't face any consequences?"

Principal Hutchinson sighs like he's tired of this conversation. And he needs to head to Bible study tonight and give thanks we're in his office. Because if we were out on the street…

"I'll take that as a yes." I nod. "Bet."

His shoulders sink, and relief flashes across his face. Cupping his fingers together, he leans forward on his desk. "I'm glad you can understand why—"

"I don't understand shit," I correct him, and Hutchinson's jaw clenches. He's probably been interrupted more in these fifteen minutes than he has in his career. "I just wanted to make sure this is where you stand. So when I go down to the board of education and file a complaint, I have my facts straight. Also, when I hit up my social media with the over one million followers, that I have it right. Now, usually, I'm no keyboard warrior. But for you? I'll make an exception. By the time I'm done, everyone will know that bullies are tolerated at this school. I'll make sure to include that lil' drawing. You don't consider it proof, but I'm 'bout a hundred percent certain other people will view it differently."

"And that doesn't even begin to cover what I'll do." Aaliyah scoots forward to the edge of her seat. "My father is a pastor. A renowned pastor with a large following and many connections. By the time he rallies his fellow clergymen and their congregations, we will have a prayer rally in downtown Chicago about the trauma of bullying and the systemic failures in the administration that refuses to address the problems." She tsks, her mouth turning down at the corners. "I can just see the rally cry now. They took God out the schools and now look at what happens. Jesus, please protect our children." She tilts her head back, palms up, crying out to the ceiling before smiling at the dumbfounded principal. "It should really bring the city together in solidarity."

I bring a fist to my mouth, covering the smile threatening to spread across my damn face.

This girl.

Just an hour ago, I'd been wondering what an angered Aaliyah would look like. Now I didn't have to speculate anymore. A fucking goddess. That's what she looks like. And she did more with a Bible reference than I could with a bag of *fuck-yous*, *bitches* and *muthafuckas*.

I was right about one thing, though. She was hot as fuck.

"Are you threatening me?" the principal snaps.

"Nah, bruh." I lean back in the chair. "I don't need to threaten when a promise works better."

He stares at both of us, that jaw still working. He's doing right. Principal or not, if he comes out his mouth foul at Aaliyah, I'll drag him across that desk.

"What are you suggesting, Mr. Howard? Gia must face consequences."

"And I'm not suggesting she doesn't. Do I feel she was justified? Yeah. But I do teach my daughter that violence is the last option. Since she told two of your teachers and received no help, maybe she *did* feel she had no other choice." I pause and let that sink in. And he best believe, I would be scheduling a meeting with him and her teacher *real soon*. "So she'll take those suspension days, but so will the other student. She needs to learn a lesson about bullying. Now either you do it, or I find her parents, and I have a one-on-one talk with her father."

Hutchinson's eyebrows arrow down, and he flicks a glance at Aaliyah. "Like I told Ms. Montgomery, that kind of talk on school premises can't be allowed."

For the moment, I'm choosing to ignore him trying to check me. Because another thing he said catches my attention. "What do you mean, like you told Ms. Montgomery?"

"Well, that's not important," Aaliyah rushes in, waving her hands as if she can brush away my question. "But I got it, Principal Hutchinson."

I stare at her for several long seconds, but she doesn't glance over at me, keeping her gaze trained on the principal. All right, I'ma let her make it—both of them. For now. But she's gonna give me some answers.

"If that's it—" I shove to my feet "—I'm taking my daughter out of here. How many days are you giving her?"

"She can return in three days. I already had her teachers gather her schoolwork, and it should be waiting for you at the front desk."

"Thanks," I say dryly. "And the other student?"

His lips flatten as if he's about to refuse to give me that information. But as I stand there, not moving and peering down at him, his gaze drops away from mine, and he smooths his hand down the front of his shirt again.

"She's already left school for the day with her family. I will call to deliver my decision to them as well."

"Yeah, okay." After giving him one last hard stare, I look at Aaliyah. "Ready?"

"Yes. Have a good day, Mr. Hutchinson," she says politely, almost sweetly.

And if I hadn't just witnessed her snatch the man a new asshole, I might've believed she meant that shit. But I had witnessed it, and I wouldn't be forgetting it.

Neither would my dick, unfortunately.

I toss him a head jerk and purposefully wait for Aaliyah to walk out of the office first so I can follow her. If that muthafucka thinks he's going to stare at her ass as she walks out, he better think again.

Settling a hand on the small of her back, I guide her out and into the front office. Mrs. Terrance glances up, her fingers halting mid-type as we emerge. Her face softens as she glances at Gia, who sits across from her on one of the chairs, her little feet swinging an inch or so above the ground.

"She's been sweet as always," the older woman says. "No problem at all."

"Thanks," I say, approaching Gia.

My daughter tips her head back, and her fear and hurt are obvious in the subtle tremble of her chin. "I'm sorry, Daddy," she whispers.

I shake my head, and tears glisten in her eyes. Hunkering down in front of her, I cup her shoulder. "Hey, baby girl. Stop that, okay. You know I don't like you fighting, but am I mad at you? No. Daddy's not mad at all. The adults are more to blame here than you are. So get rid of those tears, okay? I love you, G."

"I love you, too, Daddy." She swipes the backs of her hands over her cheeks and rubs her fists into her eyes, momentarily making her seem much younger than her seven years.

"Aight, c'mon." Standing, I hold out my hand, and she takes it, jumping down off the chair.

"See you when you're back, Gia," Mrs. Terrance calls out, and though it's small, G smiles and waves at the administrative assistant.

I go to leave the office, but Gia pulls up short, turning to Aaliyah and holding out her hand. "Come on, Aaliyah."

Aaliyah doesn't hesitate to accept Gia's hand, which speaks volumes—this woman will never reject my daughter. Hell, Aaliyah had gone to bat for her like she'd pushed Gia out her own pussy. Still, the quick look she shoots me, full of indecision, has my chest pulling tight.

I abruptly nod, and relief flashes across her face.

Together, with Gia between us, we leave the school.

"Let me ask you a question."

I twist the eye under the spaghetti down to a simmer and turn around to face Aaliyah, who sits at the breakfast bar. Out of habit, I look over her shoulder toward the living room, checking for Gia. But she's sitting in front of the television, engrossed in *She-Ra and the Princesses of Power.* She loves that cartoon and can watch it for hours. It's aight for a remake. Still ain't the original.

"You think she's really okay?" I ask.

Aaliyah twists on the stool and peers over at Gia, too. When she faces me again, a small, soft smile curves her pretty mouth.

Yeah, I have no business noticing how pretty—and fuckable—that mouth is.

"Honestly," she says, thankfully dragging my attention away from thoughts that are inappropriate and dangerous, "I think the fact that we believed and stood by Gia is why she can shake it off and be at ease now. There's a comfort and...security in knowing your parent unconditionally loves and believes you."

At the wistful note in her voice that I'm not even sure she's aware of, I narrow my gaze on her. Frowning, I study her, my curiosity sharp, greedy. Hard to believe when I first met her, my initial assumption was naïve, innocent...simple. I stand on naïve, and she still carries that air of innocence that's so tempting to a man like me—a man likes to get his hands dirty. But simple? Nah. She's far more complicated; there's a lot more underneath that good-girl exterior.

And against my better judgment, I want to dig deep, uncover all that is Aaliyah Montgomery. Just from some of her revelations in that office today, I have questions.

First among them is the one that's been scratching at me since before we left the principal's office. "She'll always have my support. Even if she does shit I can't get behind, that doesn't mean I won't love her and help her in any way I can. If somebody comes for her, they come for me." Something glints in her eyes, and I don't miss how she swallows hard. "But I got another question."

I cross my arms, and her gaze dips, lingering on my chest, as if she can't help but follow my body's movement. Lust bullies its way into my veins, flooding them. It solidifies inside me like a separate, new organ. My dick hardens, and if she glances down toward my black joggers, she's probably going to get an eyeful. Crossing the kitchen, I don't stop until the high counter hides my erection.

"What is it?" she asks.

"What did Hutchinson mean by telling you about 'that kind of talk' up at the school? Something happen I should know about? And before you say you don't know what I'm talking about, ma, the way you cut him off was sus as hell. Don't think I didn't catch that."

She balls up her face, but a moment later, sighs, her shoulders sinking like a deflated balloon. "When I first got to the school, the other girl's mother was there, and she was loud, yelling at the principal. But when she tried to scream at Gia, I..." She scratches the side of her nose then lifts her gaze to mine. "I might've threatened her."

"You...might have threatened her," I repeat slowly. "What did you say, Liyah? Exactly?"

Her body gives a tiny jolt, and I'm not sure if it's from my low tone that vibrates with anger at that bitch for daring to address my daughter or my shortening her name. The nickname seemed too familiar, too...intimate.

I mentally cringe at my slip.

Another sigh. "I told her, 'Don't let the cross around my neck fool you. I will beat the hell out of you now then hold it while I pray for you later.'"

I stare at her. Blink. "You said what?"

"Don't let the cross—"

"Yeah, I heard you." I slice a hand through the air between us. And I had. But my brain is having the damnedest time catching up to my ears. I squint at her. "You told that woman you would beat the… Do you even know how to fight?"

Her head jerks back as if I offended her. But then she shrugs, a sheepish smile twisting her lips. "Actually, no. But she didn't know that."

I bark out a loud crack of laughter. Studying her and the discomfort on her face, I laugh harder, longer. So long that tears sting my eyes and my chest twinges from not being able to catch my breath.

"I'm glad you find it funny. Principal Hutchinson warned me I could be banned from the school's campus for threatening violence," she grumbles.

That cut my hilarity off like a switch. "He got me fucked-up," I snap. "Why didn't you say anything? Bet. I'll be back up there tom—"

"No need to do that. Like I said, he *warned* me. I'm good to still pick Gia up and drop her off. But I can't make any promises if I see that witch in the line. What grown woman screams at a kid?"

"Thank you," I murmur, and my tone is low, gritty. Unless it has to do with my daughter, Sheree cauterized most of the softness out of me. And the fact that this warmth is mixed with a grinding, dirty need… Yeah, not much has been familiar since Aaliyah showed up in my tattoo shop. "I appreciate what you did for Gia today. And for staying this evening. With me here, you didn't have to come back to the house, but Gia appreciates it."

So do I.

When Gia pleaded with Aaliyah to come home with us,

indecision had wavered over Aaliyah's face, darkened her eyes. I got why she was hesitant. Her returning home with us… It felt personal. I didn't need her here in a nanny capacity; she was strictly here because she cared about my girl.

And fuck if that didn't make her even more gorgeous. I didn't know that was possible, but here we are.

Shoving away from the bar, I turn, heading back to the stove to place much needed distance between us. So I can take a breath that isn't infused with her fresh, fruity scent. That has to be more than her shampoo. I bet it's embedded in her skin. Saturates her pussy…

Shit.

"How's school going?" I ask, desperate to latch onto any subject to distract my thoughts from the swollen, drenched flesh between those thick thighs. "You're going to the University of Chicago, right?"

"Yes, that's right."

I slowly stir the sauce, lifting the spoon to my mouth for a quick taste. Frowning, I open the cabinet above the stove and grab the garlic and onion powder as well as the oregano.

"And?" I glance over my shoulder at her, eyebrow arched, before shaking the seasonings in the sauce. "You're liking it?"

The beat of silence has me looking at her again, and she tucks thick strands of hair behind her ear. I frown harder at the gesture that smacks of embarrassment.

"Yes, I love it actually," she says. "My classes are interesting, even the prerequisites. Well, maybe not calculus." She scrunches her face up, and the expression is adorable and startlingly…young. Damn. That mix of guilelessness and sensuality is so damn fascinating. "But the other classes? I enjoy going to them. My professors are great. I enjoy the discussion, even the homework." She chuckles, shaking her head. "I'm sounding like a nerd."

"Ain't nothing wrong with that. Whoever says brains isn't sexy as fuck has obviously never had a crush on Velma."

She tilts her head, eyebrows wrinkling. "Scooby-Doo's Velma?"

"Hell yeah. I get most people thought Daphne was hot, but it was Velma for me. Those glasses, bangs, that skirt and sweater that no doubt covered real thickness underneath. And then, of course, her figuring out every mystery. Nah, man. I need my girl to add to me, not just be pretty window dressing like Daphne. Velma was sexy and a beast."

I check the pot of water, and seeing that it's finally bubbling, I grab the spaghetti and drop the pasta in. When I turn around to grab the salt from the counter, I catch her staring at me, her full lips slightly parted.

"What?" I shake a little salt into my palm and toss it into the water.

"That was...awesome," she breathes. "And also a little disturbing considering you broke all this down when you were younger."

I snort. "My ass was fast when I was a kid. Come here." I jerk my head for emphasis, beckoning her over to me.

Her gaze remains on me as she slides from the bar stool, rounds the corner and approaches me. I'm a tattoo artist; I'm used to being in close proximity to people. But the closer she gets, the more my skin is on fire. It even crackles in the soles of my feet like the herald of a nut. Fuck. That's impossible. I can't come from just looking at her, from inhaling her scent.

I should give my dick a heads up on that impossibility since my balls are tightening and blood pounds there, thickening my shit.

"Here, taste this." I lift the spoon to her mouth, hovering just in front of that pouty bottom lip. "What do you think?"

She stares at me, and for a moment, the big kitchen seems small. Tight. And she fills every inch of the limited space. I watch her mouth, focused on the moment when those luscious lips will part and I'll get my first peek at her tongue. Imagine it tasting me instead of the red sauce.

Like time has slowed, she leans forward, closing her mouth around the spoon. Her tongue slicks over her lips, as if ensuring she captures every bit. Her eyes close, and when she releases a moan, an answering one claws its way up my throat. Only by sheer will, held together by tape and prayer, do I contain the hungry sound.

And it's an act of God that I don't grab my dick and give it a good, hard pump.

"Delicious." She hums, her thick lashes lifting and granting me up-close-and-personal access to those beautiful brown eyes.

"Good." I clear my throat, trying to hide the gravel coating my throat.

It takes everything in me not to close my mouth over the same spot hers just occupied. Clenching my jaw, I deliberately lower the utensil to the platter next to the stove.

"I gotta ask, so don't get your lil' sensitive ass all uptight. There are a lot of good schools in Alabama or Georgia, even

Florida. Why come all the way to Chicago, where you don't know anyone and you only have a, what? Cousin, right? Wouldn't staying closer to home have provided a safety net and bigger support system?"

Silence greets my question, and I look over to her. Seeing her expression, I once again wonder how she became so proficient at shutting down. *Who* made her so proficient.

"You good, ma?"

She nods, but shifts so I can only see her profile, and I stuff my hands in the pockets of my jeans or risk putting them on her so I can study that face. Try to pick apart that blank expression for clues to her thoughts.

"Yes, I'm fine." She opens a cabinet door and removes plates. Does she really believe I can't see through this evasion tactic? Yeah, the fact that she won't even look at me says she's not *fine*. "And you're right, there are plenty of great colleges and universities in Alabama. But they weren't for me, and their programs didn't offer what I was looking for. The University of Chicago does."

"Aye." I wait until she sets the last plate on the counter and cants her head to look at me. "Thank you. 'Cause if you're going to lie to me, at least look me in the eye. Or better yet, just tell me you don't want to talk about it or it's none of my business. I prefer that to you lying to me."

"That's fair." She dips her head before meeting my gaze again. "I don't want to talk about it."

I nod.

"What're you going to school for again? I don't think you mentioned it."

"Visual arts with a concentration in illustration."

Surprise ripples through me, and I go still, the colander for the pasta hanging next to my thigh. This woman is like one of those Russian dolls my nana used to collect. Open one and there's another on the inside. And another. And another. I'm constantly discovering something new about Aaliyah. Discovering another side to the unassuming woman who walked into my tattoo shop weeks ago.

Unassuming. Shit.

It's not easy admitting I misjudged someone, but I did.

Yes, she's who she first appeared to be. But also so much more.

Like a dependable, capable employee.

A fierce defender.

And an artist.

I hate that I'm fascinated. That a nagging curiosity to know more scratches at me.

"Illustration, huh?" I finally say, and she nods, still not looking at me. "What do you plan on doing with your degree?"

She shrugs, and I grunt out an irritated sound. "What did I say about lying to me?"

This time, her head tilts toward me. "You're my boss, but I don't owe you a conversation. Or my thoughts. As a matter of fact—" she backs away from the counter "—my workday is over, and I'm not on the clock."

"So you're a runner." I flick off the heat underneath the spaghetti. "I'm learning so many things about you today, Liyah."

"*Aa*liyah," she corrects, voice low.

Tension practically vibrates from her, drawing her so stiff one Chicago autumn breeze would crack her in half. Interesting that of all the things I've let fly from my savage mouth, *this*—a question about her college major—gets such a dramatic reaction.

She might not have wanted to let me see that I got under her skin. I don't know how to back off, how to let go. It's a good trait when you're opening a new business in a crowded field, but, as I've also been told, it's an annoying one as well. I can easily guess which camp Aaliyah falls in.

"*Aa*liyah," I murmur, giving her that. For now. "Do you feel better getting that off your chest? Good." I nod, not giving her a chance to answer. I already know what her little stubborn ass will say anyway. "Now go put those plates on the table so we can get ready to eat."

Her lips flatten—or try to. Good luck with that. The Bears have a better chance of winning another Super Bowl than that damn dick tease of a mouth has of disappearing.

"You have selective hearing," she growls.

I arch an eyebrow. "When it comes to bullshit, yeah. And we both know you leaving right now and disappointing G is bullshit. So I tuned that all the way out. Now—" I jut my chin toward the small breakfast nook "—go. I'm hungry."

She doesn't move, though. And my brow rises higher, irritated and…riveted by the play of emotions flickering over her face like a movie reel. Some of them I recognize—anger, frustration, surprise. Arousal.

My dick jerks in my joggers, and it takes everything in me

not to reach inside my boxers to readjust the flesh that's been at some semi-state of hard in her presence these past weeks.

The other emotions that whisper across her face, though? They're tougher to evaluate, dissect or label. Maybe grief? Anxiety…defeat?

That last one has a need to protect roaring loud in my head, clenching my gut. Only Gia has ever stirred an urge—an instinctive need—so strong in me. Not even Sheree did. And that's sad as fuck. But it's also what it is.

"Liyah." Frowning, I move toward her. The loud, jarring ringtone from her cell halts me mid-step.

Her petite body flinches. Sucking in a low but audible breath, she reaches in the back pocket of her jeans and removes her phone. She glances down at the screen then answers it, pressing it to her ear. She does all this without glancing my way.

But she does return to the counter and pick up the plates.

"Hey, Tamara." She moves to the table and sets out the dishes. "Yeah, I'm going to be here a little later, but I should be home before you leave for work."

Listening to Tamara, she crosses back over into the kitchen and opens the drawers with the silverware. Another thing she changed. Before she got here, I could've bought stock in plastic forks and knives.

"Yes, ma'am." That honeyed accent sounds even more pronounced wrapped around those two words. She laughs and the light note directly contradicts the mood she wore like a soaked blanket only moments ago. "At some point, you're going to stop worrying about me—" She breaks off, a scowl darkening her features as she snatches the cutlery from the drawer. "Her stomach's just fine, thank you. Heffa."

Both my eyebrows jack upward as a loud but muffled bark of laughter emanates from the other end of the phone.

"Bye, girl." She pulls the phone away from her ear and presses her thumb to the screen, still glaring down at it.

"Your cousin?" I ask. "The one here in Chicago?"

"Yes, Tamara. She's letting me stay with her since I only have a partial scholarship," she mutters, nudging the drawer closed and returning to the table, silverware in hand. "She worries about me more than my mama."

Her disgruntlement tugs at the corner of my mouth.

"Is she older?"

"Only by a year."

"Must be pretty close then. Especially if she's letting you live with her. I love my sister, but ain't no way in hell she's staying with me. We're not a death penalty state, but I'm not built for life in jail, either."

"You're not close?" she asks, the first personal question about me since she's started this job.

"With a father who's a truck driver and more out the house than in and a working mother, we didn't have a choice but to be close. She's my best friend other than Chelle."

I could've just said "yes," but something I refuse to scrutinize compelled me to give her more. Usually, if it didn't have anything to do with tattoos or the money paid to get one, then it wasn't anyone's business.

"I don't know if we're close or not," she says after carefully setting the forks and knives beside the plates—just a fork next to G's. "Growing up, no. Actually, not until very recently would I say that we're *closer* than we've ever been. She's been nicer than I deserve," she quietly adds, but not so low I don't catch it.

"Than you deserve?" I snort, moving the colander to the sink then pouring the pasta in. "I can't see you purposefully hurting or offending anyone, ma."

"Just because it's not on purpose doesn't make the hurt any less."

I still, the empty pot hovering over the sink. Her words sinking so deep, they grow claws and cling tight.

How fucking true.

"What'd you do to hurt her?" I ask, deliberately keeping my voice even. Free of judgment.

Another pause, and for a few seconds, I don't think she's going to answer. Then, "Didn't think for myself. Being a coward."

My involuntary response is to contradict her, tell her the woman who stood up to a principal, threatened a parent and defended a small girl like a lioness isn't a coward. And that same woman, who left the safety and familiarity of her hometown to travel to another state so different it might as well be a new country, definitely owns her own mind.

But I don't say it.

Because, though it's true, that feels like lip service. And something—call it instinct, call it a knowledge gained by dealing with a lot of people's shit—tells me that not many people in her life have listened to her. Truly *listened.*

Crossing the distance separating us, I stop next to her, cup her shoulder and gently but firmly turn her around to face me. Like earlier at the school, an electrical current sizzles from my palm, up my arm, arcs across my chest and works its way down to my dick.

Damn. The way even the littlest thing causes me to brick up around her, I might need to start wearing a fucking jockstrap. Clenching my jaw against that jolt, I grip her other shoulder.

"So what if you were a follower? Or a coward? So the fuck what? Weren't we all something else other than who and what we are today? Everything in our lives shapes us into who's standing here now. Not just the good shit but the bad, too. The shit we're proud of and the things we don't even like to think of, much less talk about. That ain't nothing to be ashamed of, ma. It is what it is, and anyone who tries to make you feel bad for learning a lesson—whether it's at fourteen or the big age of twenty-four—is a muthafucka who probably has their own shit they haven't dealt with. Lift that head up, baby girl. You ain't got nothing to be ashamed of."

She stares at me, her heavy-lidded eyes searching my face as if waiting for a punch line. The longer I remain silent, the deeper the stain across her rounded cheekbones. The faster her soft breath. Finally, she slicks her tongue across her lips, and of their own volition, my fingers tighten. Her eyes dilate as if I cupped her pussy instead of her shoulders, and shit, my body reacts the same way.

I should take my hands off her. Back up. She's my fucking employee. She isn't aware of how she's looking at me. What those eyes, those lips are begging for…

Those last two warnings should be enough to have me releasing her and falling far back, but damn. They got lust flashing into a gotdamn inferno. That innocence, bruh. Innocence tempered with curiosity, and her body pleading for something she probably doesn't acknowledge.

Let me find out lil' mama likes to be handled and to be fucked hard and nasty.

Her being my employee and me wanting nothing to do with breaking in virgins won't save her.

Caution alarms blare in my head, nearly deafening me, but they don't stop me from lowering my head, my gaze briefly flicking to Gia to make sure she's still occupied. I press my lips to the top of her ear. A hard shudder ripples through her, echoing in me, and *fuck*. Why didn't she hide that reaction from me?

Every restraint, every reason why I shouldn't be doing this, evaporates like smoke.

Sliding one hand across her shoulder blade and down the elegant length of her spine, I grip her hip, holding her. As small as she is, I'm almost folded over her, but these fucking curves… I squeeze the rounded flesh under my hand, my fingers grazing the top of that perfect, fat ass.

I pause, granting her time to object, to shove me off. But she doesn't move. Unless you count the shiver that rips through her again. Pressing closer, I growl at the softness of her small, plump breasts brushing my chest. The graze of her beaded nipples that the thin sweater she's wearing can't hide. The feel of those thick, perfect thighs against mine, granting me the perfect idea of how firm and welcoming they would be around my waist—my face. The give of her slightly rounded belly under my dick.

Shiiit. If it feels this good grinding against her stomach, pushing into that wet, soft pussy might take me the fuck up outta here.

Slowly, still silently offering her time to tell me no, I trace the outer rim of her ear with my teeth. Follow it up with the tip of my tongue.

A small whimper punctuates the air, and it's both a pump of my dick and a caress to my chest. Warring sensations, equally devastating to my body and senses.

Yeah, some of my original assumptions about Aaliyah might've been off, but one still stands.

She's dangerous.

Again, I should retreat, put the space of this house between us.

Instead, I suck her earlobe between my lips, tonguing it, sucking it like I would her clit if she gave me the word.

The dull prick of nails in my lower back has a rougher, deeper sound rumbling out of me. I want to rip my shirt up, grant her access to my bare skin and order her to do that shit again. But that would require releasing her, removing my own hands, and that I'm not ready to do.

Grinding my erection into her, I open my mouth over the line of her jaw and suck once more, rolling my tongue over skin that's both sweet and musky. Need, hot and urgent, floods my veins, converging in my dick so each rock of my hips shoots it higher and hotter.

The part of my brain that has retained some semblance

of sense rears its head, whispering that I don't have a lot of time. It's a minor miracle that Gia has been this quiet. But fatherhood has taught me I'm on borrowed time, and her barreling in here, declaring she's hungry, is only minutes away.

Yet, I don't hurry. I trail my lips up over Aaliyah's cheek, the bridge of her nose to the other cheek, following those cinnamon freckles like they're breadcrumbs. Her breath hitches, and she tilts her head back, offering me easier access. I press soft kisses to the place where a dimple dents her cheek when she smiles then finally, *fucking finally*, cover the pretty, carnal mouth that has been driving me to distraction for weeks.

There's no way I can contain my groan, even at the risk of Gia running in here at this moment. Aaliyah's too sweet, too delicious, too gotdamn *good*.

"Open," I harshly demand. "Let me get in, ma."

If I have my way, this won't be the last time I say this to her. Next time, it'll be me insisting she lets me in that tight, soaking wet pussy. That same *something* from earlier insists her cunt is perfect and will curve only to my dick.

That intuition—that promise—has me plunging my tongue between her lips, tangling, sucking, pulling. Where before my kisses across her cheeks and nose and jaw were gentle, tender, this isn't. It's a fucking, pure and simple. It's a command to give me everything she has, and when she believes she's done so, to fucking go further and unearth more to hand over.

It occurs to me I might be a little obsessed with having

her. Now that I know that fruity, sensual scent isn't a fluke, that it graces her skin, and I taste traces of it on her tongue and lips… Now that I've found out what that lil' sound of greed is like, I don't want to stop until I find out if her nipples will contain the same flavor, if those thick thighs will tremble around my head while I gorge myself on that pussy.

Yeah, obsessed could be an understatement.

Either she's a quick learner or I've misjudged her being a virgin—I don't really give a damn. I'm thankful for either one or both. Especially when she curls her tongue around mine and sucks so gotdamn hard my dick is jealous. My hand slides over her hip, and I cup that worship-worthy ass, squeezing hard.

"You don't kiss like a virgin, ma." I sink my teeth into her full bottom lip, draw on it with the tip of my tongue. "I don't know whether to thank or beat the shit out of the person who taught you that."

At my voice, my compliment—shit, both—she stiffens.

Fuck.

One moment, that beautiful ass is sitting on my hand, and in the next, my palm is tingling with the sensory memory of it.

Aaliyah stumbles back several steps, her wide, desire-hazed eyes on me, fingers lifted to her kiss-swollen lips. Her chest rises and falls, and I can't help dropping my gaze to those pretty breasts. Even with the distance she placed between us, I can clearly see the outline of her nipples against the sweater. I'm twisting between the protective urge to calm her, soothe her, and the more primal one to pull that sweater up and suck on the beaded tips. Could be she sees that in my face because she backs up even more.

"I—I think I should go," she softly stutters.

Minutes ago, I informed her she was staying, but now, I agree with her. I struggle to look unaffected by the…war our mouths just waged, but I'm fucking shook. How can she have my dick ready to bust with a kiss? I haven't been this close to nutting this fast when inside a woman, much less *not* inside her.

Now that the fog of lust is slowly clearing, and my common sense is coming back, all my mistakes, and why I shouldn't have touched her, flood in with a crash.

Nanny.

Gia needs her.

Young as fuck.

No relationships.

The hell was I thinking to say fuck all that—to risk all that—and kiss her? Gia is attached to her, and my daughter's emotional security is more important than getting my shit wet. Besides, even if Aaliyah's age, inexperience and where she is in life right now versus where I am weren't all relevant, there's still the fact that my marriage and divorce soured me on relationships of any kind. Having the mother of your child, the woman you thought would be by your side for the rest your life, end up betraying you—with one of your boys—strains the belief in love and commitment.

And the secrets, the agony of them, will have you saying fuck it altogether.

A kiss temporarily made me forget all that.

But now it's in front of my head like a billboard on the Loop.

"Daddy!" Gia barges into the kitchen and runs up to me. "I'm hungry."

Jesus, what if she'd run in here seconds earlier? I'd been so consumed by Aaliyah, I wouldn't have heard her. It was arrogance at its highest to think I had a handle on this. *Shit.*

"In a minute. Food's almost done. Go wash your hands, okay?"

"Okay." She spins around, but before she can leave the room, Aaliyah steps forward.

"Hey, sweetie, I'm about to leave. I'll see you on Monday, okay?"

Saturdays are my busiest days, but I don't make her work on the weekends. Aaliyah already stays late several nights of the week; she is young and needs a life. Gia stays almost every weekend with Sheree, and when she doesn't, my sister, Leslie, watches her for me.

Never have I been so grateful for a Saturday.

And even as I think it, I feel like a bitch. But after that kiss—a kiss branded on my mouth and dick—I need space. We both do.

"Why?" Gia whines, her shoulders slumping. My baby girl can be dramatic, but her disappointment is real. "You said you were staying for dinner."

"I know, and I'm sorry. I really am. But I have to get home. Something..." She pauses and my whole body stiffens. "Something came up, and I need to go, but I will be back bright and early Monday. And your dad has my number, so if you want to talk to me, you can always call, okay?"

I could stop her from leaving. Play off that kiss like it was no big deal and pretend nothing's happened. But I don't have it in me. Lust still runs through me like bad alcohol. Making me sweat. Got my body aching.

So I stay quiet.

"Okay," Gia says, voice low, soft. She bows her head.

That's when Aaliyah finally glances at me, and before she quickly shifts her attention back to Gia, I glimpse the confusion and…fear there.

Fear?

My head jerks back, and acid seeps into my stomach. What the fuck put that in her eyes? Did I do something? Was I too rough? Did she say no at some point and I…?

I shake my head. Hell no. *Fuck* no. If she'd, at any point, told me to stop, told me no, I would've backed up. My mama raised me to respect women, not hurt them. Not take advantage of them. Aaliyah had been as into that kiss as I'd been. Still feeling the sweet and sexy suck of her tongue on mine, I'm a hundred percent certain of it.

So what…?

I take a mental and physical step back. She's a complication, a puzzle and a distraction I didn't ask for and don't want. I should've never put my mouth on her.

And the thing about me? I don't need to burn my muthafucking hand on the stove twice to learn a lesson. Nah, it only takes once for me to back the fuck up.

Aaliyah kneels in front of Gia and cups her cheek.

"Hey, none of that. You've had a rough day, but your dad is right here with you, and I'm only a phone call away. And since you'll be home three days next week, you can come with *me* to school, how about that?"

Shit. I squeeze the back of my neck. I nearly forgot Aaliyah went to class while Gia was in school. We would have to figure out how to work around that because it isn't fair for Aaliyah to take Gia with her. I might have to take her with me to the shop until Aaliyah is finished.

We could figure that out later.

"Okay," Gia says, and this time, she sounds a little happier. "I'll call you tomorrow."

"Can't wait." Aaliyah stands but not before planting a kiss on top of Gia's head. "I gotta go, so give me a hug. You know I can't leave without one."

Gia throws her arms around Aaliyah's waist, and she bends down to return the hug. Moments later, she gathers her jacket and bag and heads toward the door.

"Be careful on the way home." I couldn't resist calling the warning out to her even though Aaliyah doesn't turn around to look at me.

She's still new to the city, and it's getting darker out earlier. And no matter how much I need her to get up out of here, there's something inside me that wants to make sure she's safe.

Aaliyah waves a hand but doesn't glance in my direction. Even after the front door closes behind her, I don't move.

Not until Gia comes running back into the kitchen, reminding me that she's still hungry. Turning my attention back to my daughter, I focus on her and getting food on the table.

But evicting my nanny from my head?

Yeah, that's going to take an act of God.

Seven

"Honor thy mother and father…except when in the strip club."

Aaliyah

"Do *not* answer that."

I glance up from my mother's name on the vibrating cell phone screen to meet my cousin's glare.

"I wasn't," I say, but it doesn't sound convincing even to my ears.

And from the arch of her perfect eyebrow, Tamara doesn't seem to believe me, either.

Sighing, I slide the still shaking phone under my thigh. She has a right to doubt the strength of my backbone. Ever since I answered Mom's call weeks ago and she issued that ultimatum, and I didn't show up at the Birmingham airport in two days' time, she's been calling nonstop. Her, my father, my uncle and, of course, Gregory. It's been relentless. And every time, I waver. One time I caved, and my mother's guilt trip had me curled up under the covers, crying for hours.

Even though I know this is a matter of survival, I bear their disapproval like wet sandbags around my neck, weighing me down. Except for the last few weeks, I've spent my whole life avoiding this feeling; it's not easy to *not* fall in line.

Tamara sees my struggle, but she's appointed herself my personal bodyguard and partner in rebellion. And she's on the job tonight. Literally and figuratively.

"Girl, stop lying. If you wasn't, you were damn sure thinking about it." She crosses her arms, and because they're *there*, my gaze drops to her breasts, which are lifted in a black bra covered in silver sequins.

Glitter dusts the dark brown mounds, and under the LED lights flashing across the strip club, she sparkles. Sequined bands crisscross her flat stomach and thick upper thighs, bracket the small black triangle covering her sex. Silver stilettoes adorn her feet, and the straps wrap around her calves, ending under her knees. My cousin is gorgeous and built like the proverbial brick house. And from the way all the men's eyes—a good amount of women's, too—keep traveling over to the section she insisted on getting for me tonight, I'm not the only one who thinks she's stunning.

Compared to her, I must look like a country bumpkin…

"Don't you do it," she snaps, and my hand pauses just before I reach the slit in my dress to tug the sides closer together. "Stop fidgeting and leave that dress alone. You look like the bad bitch you are, now let it go." She jabs a finger toward the leather couch. "Let it *all* go. I brought you out here tonight so you can finally have some fun. Life is more than work, school and worrying over helicopter parents. You didn't just move here for school. You came to experience the kind of life that's impossible in Parsons with Uncle Tim controlling every move you make. If you're going to hell, you might as well include partying in a strip club on your list of sins. Now—" she flicks her hair that's nearly hanging down to her ass in a beautiful, auburn weave "—I'm sending drinks over here, and I want you to get. Fucked. Up. No one deserves it more than you. When I leave here with you tonight, I wanna be pouring your lil' runaway bride ass into my car."

Giving her a small smile—which is a major feat, considering my phone is ringing *again*—I hold up a hand, palm out. "I solemnly swear to get drunk off my ass."

"That's my girl. And enjoy the show. These girls ain't me, but they're aight." She smirks. "Don't worry about anyone bothering you. I have one of the guys looking out for you while I'm up there."

"Got it," I assure her.

"Okay. Remember. Have fun."

I don't have a chance to reply before she steps out of the section, descending the short flight of stairs to the main floor. In seconds, and right before my eyes, she ceases being Tamara, my cousin, and morphs into Jade, the featured dancer at the sophisticated and sexy Inferno.

It should feel really wrong, looking at my relative's barely covered body as she works the room. Given all the denigrating things Daddy preached against places like this, and Tamara in particular, guilt should swarm me like a drone of angry bees. But…it doesn't. There's nothing sleazy about my cousin.

On the contrary.

Watching her strut among the people here to see her on that stage, I'm envious. She's comfortable with who she is—both Tamara *and* Jade. She's proud of her full breasts, small waist, thick thighs and behind, as evidenced in the confident stride that carries her past all the people reaching out to her. She's like a celebrity here, and from the videos of her on YouTube, I see why they're fawning over her. Tamara's a gifted dancer who defies gravity with her erotic acrobatics on that pole. And I'm not saying other strippers don't bring customers in, but it's Jade listed on the club doors.

People are crowded three deep at the bar that extends across one length of the wall and at all the circular high and low tables. Especially those close to the stage—like an LED-lit runway but with poles. Other private areas like mine—encased in glass with couches, tables and a private pole—dot the area. They sit above the rest of the club, offering unrestricted views of the stage and patrons below. I don't know how much Tamara had to pay to get me this space for tonight, but I'm guessing it wasn't cheap. Especially since I'm the only one up here.

God, I feel so conspicuous and out of place.

"Hey, boo. Jade said to take care of you and bring all the alcohol." A beautiful woman, her stacked body wrapped in a black bralette, boy shorts and boots, walks into my section, her long ponytail swinging over her shoulder. Her dark brown skin gleams under the low lighting. "She wasn't lying when she said you were gorgeous." She beams at me, her hazel gaze like a warm, physical caress over my face, breasts and thighs. "I'm Nikki. What can I get for you?"

Why does it feel like she's offering more than what's on those bar shelves? A little flustered—and shoot, flattered—I shake my head. "Nice to meet you, Nikki. I can't lie, I'm not much of a drinker. What do you suggest?"

Again, her gaze sweeps over my body, and nope, I'm not imagining the interest in her eyes. "Not much of a drinker, huh? Well, we don't want to overwhelm you, so how about I start you off with a cranberry and vodka and a bottle of champagne? If you don't like either of those, I'll bring you a different drink. But I think you'll love trying something new."

I'm pretty sure the "something new" isn't just the cocktail. And I can't help the smile that curves my mouth. I've never been sexually attracted to women—admired the hell out of them, yes, but not attracted. But Nikki's like the female version of Jason Momoa. Not Samoan. No, she's a beautiful Black woman. But I can't see anyone laying eyes on her and not having parts of themselves tingle.

I cringe a little at the queer-curiosity vibe I must be radiating. Like I said, I'm not really curious. I'm just not blind. And this woman is gorgeous.

"That sounds great," I say, praying the heat warming my throat and face isn't visible. "Thank you."

"You got it, boo. Be back." She winks and struts out of the section.

"Whew." Now that the server is no longer standing in front of me, I wave my hand in front of my flushed face.

If Daddy could see me now, he'd toss me into the baptismal pool and dunk me about six times. First leaving home, not answering his calls and now being attracted to another woman? I can just hear him preaching about being "of the world."

Don't get me wrong. I love God, and if it hadn't been for my faith in Him to take care of me and provide a way—which He has—I don't believe I would be here in Chicago.

It's just the judgmental, exclusionary God my dad preached about didn't match up with the loving, forgiving and compassionate one I worshipped. *My* God believed in free will, and that was something Bishop Montgomery didn't subscribe to. Especially not with his family.

Speaking of…

Even though I shouldn't, it's like an unseen force lowers my hand to my phone and slides it out from under my thigh. Tamara would curse me out if she caught me right now. Which is why I furtively glance around before going to voice mail to hear the most recent of the many messages left by my family and ex-fiancé. Closing my eyes, I hold the cell up to my ear, physically and emotionally bracing myself.

"Aaliyah Renee Montgomery," my father's beautiful, deep, intimidating voice resounds in my ear. And the whole government name *again*. That's never a good thing. "This is your father. Again. You are behaving immaturely by not answering your phone or returning messages, and I'm very disappointed. I raised you better than this. But with your recent actions, I'm not sure of who you are anymore or when you became a person who would purposefully break her promises, abandon her family and obligations, then worry her parents. You need to call me back as soon as you receive this. You've inconvenienced people long enough for this… rebellion. Send me your location immediately, young lady. I deserve more respect as your father and your bishop."

Click.

I flinch at the sound of the recording ending, as if Dad had slammed the phone down in my ear.

Shame and hurt battle it out for dominance inside me, and it's a draw. Both tear me apart, and *dammit.* I shouldn't have listened. I knew what awaited me. But like a masochist, I had to hear what my father thinks of me. How he's feeling toward me. And now…

I'm ungrateful.

Disrespectful.

Juvenile.

A coward.

Dropping the phone in my lap, I pinch the bridge of my nose, not caring about messing up the glitter or foundation Tamara applied to my face.

I don't belong here. I have no business here. What kind of person leaves their parents—parents who have provided and cared for them all their life—worried and upset? I'm so weak I can't even return a phone call—

"What's wrong with you, ma?"

That familiar voice of gravel and mistakes reaches me mere seconds before his earthy scent, which reminds me of the oil used to shine the wooden, leather-padded pews in my grandfather's old church out in the country. With my eyes closed, it's more potent, more sensual. Only I could equate church pews with sex.

In somebody's book, that has to be sacrilegious.

On a deep sigh, I lower my hand and open my eyes, meeting the sterling-gray ones belonging to Von. Immediately, my sex tingles, pulls tight. It's like his very presence—one look—triggers a thirst response. Which make sense since the man is a walking thirst trap. Like right now, for instance.

He makes a simple black T-shirt, black jeans and boots seem like fashion couture exclusives. His braids appear fresh as does the edge up, and his thick, dark beard is nicely groomed and seems to glisten. The tattoos covering his neck, arms and hands only add to the visual buffet he is, and God, I'm hungry.

As he sinks to the couch beside me, my gaze lifts from his powerful thighs that flex with the movement, up over his wide chest, and finally lands on his wide, dangerously carnal mouth.

Key word: *dangerously.*

Heat whooshes through me like someone opened a door to the simmering flames in my belly, and a backdraft incinerates me from the inside out. One look at that beautiful, sinful mouth, and I'm dragged back to yesterday in his kitchen when those same lips snatched my soul. Even now, I feel the demand of his tongue surrounding mine, the teasing edge of his teeth over my ear. The cool glide of his lip piercing against my tongue.

The faintly intimidating and wholly devastating pressure of his...dick against my stomach. I've seen a naked penis before, have had one inside me. But what Von's working with?

The logical, rational part of me wants no part of that thing. I like my insides arranged just the way they are, thank you very much. But the other part of me...okay, my vagina... literally weeps to be filled, stretched, pummeled. I've never been pummeled.

I so want it.

Swallowing past my suddenly tight, dry throat, I slide the tip of my tongue over my lips.

God, where's the waitress with that drink? Or bottle. I think I'll need the whole bottle.

"Aye, I know you heard me. What's wrong with you?" He nudges me in the side with his elbow before stretching his arm along the back of the couch.

I lean forward, trying not to be obvious about avoiding touching him. Shoot, I can still feel the print of his hand on my behind from when he grabbed and squeezed it.

Sweet Lamb, *alcohol*.

"What're you doing here?" I ask in return, evading his question like the high school gym dodgeball champion that I am. "I'm assuming Gia isn't with you."

He studies me for several long seconds, rubbing a hand down his mouth and beard. From personal experience, I know his facial hair is both soft and coarse. It added another sensory detail to obsess over when I lay in bed last night.

"I'ma let you make it, ma," he says, his gray eyes glinting like molten silver in the low lighting. I maintain a straight face as if I don't understand what he means by telling me he's very much aware I'm deflecting. He snorts. "I'm here with a few of my employees. I don't usually hang out, but Gia's with her mom so..."

He trails off as he slowly scans me from my half-up, half-down hairstyle over the strapless, black bodycon dress that hits me just below the knee and down to the black ankle boots with the highest heel I've ever walked on. His gaze retraces its path, lingering on the slit that has most of my thigh spilling out of it, before returning to my face.

"Gotta admit, ma. Wouldn't have ever expected to see you here at the strip club. I didn't think good lil' church girls did things like that." He cocks his head. "If that part of what you said to G's principal was true anyway, and you really are a PK."

Good lil' church girls.

Usually, that kind of condescension would've pissed me off. And, usually, I would've had a nice-nasty response that women of the South are famous for along with sweet tea and "bless your heart."

But it isn't irritation that stirs behind my breastbone.

Just as it isn't disdain that colors his words.

It's a heated insinuation, a raw suggestion. It's the same lust that drenched his voice when he told me I didn't kiss like a virgin.

And like last night, I'm caught between fleeing from the onslaught of need and staying right where I am, prepared to beg him to finish what he started.

Clearing my throat, I nod, and because I need something,

anything, to do with my fingers, I pick up my phone, clutch it in my hand.

"My father is a pastor back in Alabama. A bishop actually." Both his eyebrows arch high, and I huff out a small chuckle. "Yeah, he's a big deal at home."

"Damn, lil' mama."

I squint up at him, trying my very best not to let my gaze drift down to his lips. "What?"

"Some things make a little more sense now, but then others..." He shakes his head. "I'm more confused."

I wait for him to expound on that, but when he doesn't, I frown. "So are you going to leave me hanging? What are these 'some things'?"

"That innocence, for one."

My head rears back, almost bumping the couch behind me. "Innocent? Why would you call me that?" Before I can control it, my body recoils, an instinctive, physical reaction to that word. I *hate* that word. Hate more that only Von sees me that way. I inhale, breathing past the sudden tightness in my chest. "Contrary to how you speak to me at times, I'm not a child, but a full-grown adult."

Von studies me, and for a second, panic swirls inside me that his sharp gaze caught the flinch I'd tried to hide. Or that my face somehow betrayed my thoughts. But when he doesn't speak—doesn't poke in that blunt way of his—I deliberately release a breath.

The relief doesn't last long, though. As his unwavering gaze remains on me, the spacious VIP section seems to shrink, the loud music from beyond the glass dulls. Just like in his kitchen last night, I want to scramble backward. But I don't. Because there's a need in me that's desperate to be in his space, breathe in his earthy, intoxicating scent.

When I was younger, on Communion Sundays, Daddy used to let us kids eat and drink all the remaining crackers and grape juice after service. Right now, I want to gorge on Von—the sight of him, the sound of him, the scent of him… the flavor of him—just as I once did all the communion elements. Unlike those crackers and juice, Von's taste wouldn't be for my salvation. Only my destruction.

"So what you're saying is you don't kiss like a virgin because you're not one."

I snort, waving him off even as my heart throws itself against my rib cage at the reminder of how he'd rocked my world with just his mouth and a hand on my butt. "That's not a question an employer should be asking his employee."

"You're not on the clock. And if we're going to keep it real, we crossed the line of what we should and shouldn't be doing when I sucked on your tongue and your nails dug in my back because you loved it. At least, if that little sound you made as you pressed against my dick is any indication."

Shock ripples through me. I should be used to the things that fly out of his mouth by now. But not…this. Not words this bluntly sexual. No one has ever spoken to me like that. No one would dare. Not even my own fiancé. *Ex-fiancé.*

I try—and fail—not to squirm in my seat. Try—and fail—not to press my coochie hard against the cushion to alleviate the ache that throbs between my legs. Try—and fail—not to look into Von's gray eyes and glimpse the intimate knowledge that he knows *exactly* what I'm doing.

"I don't know about all that," I say, hating the breathless quality to my voice. "Who has or hasn't been inside of me isn't your business."

Those eerie, beautiful eyes flash, and moisture seeps out of me, wetting my flimsy panties.

"You're right." He nods. "And I don't care anyway. I don't give a damn if you've fucked twenty men in your past, or if the only thing that pussy knows is your fingers. What matters to me is *I* haven't been inside you. And keeping it one hundred, ma? It's probably a good idea I don't know how that pretty cunt would curve to fit my dick because I might body a muthafucka over something that good, wet and tight. So yeah, good look. Don't answer that question."

How in the *hell* am I supposed to talk, to *breathe*, after *that*? The drumming of my pulse fills my head, vibrates through my body. A flood opens between my thighs, and it's embarrassing how drenched I am. A part of me feels like I should demand he get up and leave for disrespecting me with his loose and reckless mouth. That part feels I should be cautious, even intimidated, by the blatant sexuality he doesn't try to hide.

But that half is a liar.

I'm not disrespected.

I'm not offended.

I'm not unsettled.

I'm turned on and hungry.

Nikki chooses this moment to return, and I forget my irritation that she didn't appear earlier. This is perfect timing. I could kiss her for saving me from myself and my vagina.

"Here you go, boo." She bends down, expertly balancing a bucket with a champagne bottle wedged in it and a drink. As she sets both of them down, she tosses a polite smile at Von, but her attention switches back to me. I might be sheltered, but I can read the invitation in her warm smile and the gleam in her pretty eyes. "Enjoy. And if you need anything, just send for me."

Giving me a wink that doesn't come across as douchey on her, she leaves, and desperate for something to do with my hands, I reach for the glass with the reddish alcohol in it. Sipping it, I taste the tartness of the cranberry with a hint of sweetness. Yuuum.

"You might want to slow down on that," Von cautions as I take another healthy sip. "Especially if it's gonna have you eye-fucking the waitresses."

I gasp, causing the alcohol to go down the wrong way. Like the lightweight I am, I bend over, coughing, eyes watering. Damn. Why can't I just drink like normal people?

"Why are you over here again?" I rasp once I get myself together. My eyes still water, but I can inhale. And since I can do that, I take another sip. Yes, it's a small rebellion, but I'm owning it. "Aren't your friends missing you?"

Subtle. Very subtle. And from the twitch of his mouth, he fully gets that I'm trying to get rid of him.

"Nah. I came over here for a reason. Don't think I'm letting go of what had you over here in the strip club looking like you lost your best damn friend. Start there and then finish with why you're here alone?"

"Listen, Daddy—"

"Find something safe to do, Liyah. Don't play with me like that."

There's a lot of eff-around-and-find-out in that low warning. My eyes widen, taking in his narrowed gaze, the downward curve of his mouth. I swallow hard and blow out a low, trembling breath.

That bright sensation skating over my nerves, spinning in my stomach? Why can't it be fear? I'd even settle for nervousness. But God, it's not. That's all excitement and shimmery want.

"Like I was saying," I whisper, then clear my throat. Speak louder. "Not that it's any of your concern because, again, full-grown woman here, I'm not alone. My cousin works here. She's the one who got me this section."

Surprise softens the hard line of his mouth, flares in his eyes, and he leans back a little. Thankfully, granting me the barest amount of room to breathe.

"You have a cousin who dances here?" He scans the room as if searching for someone who might resemble me. "Who?" Skepticism colors his voice.

"Tam—Jade." I catch myself before revealing her real name. But I don't even try to conceal the pride in my tone.

"No shit?"

"You know her?"

He snorts. "Who doesn't know her? Shawty's bad as fuck."

The spurt of jealousy catches me by surprise. Von isn't

mine. Nowhere near mine. So this…unnerving, twisty feeling doesn't make sense. I never experienced this with Gregory, and he was the man I'd been about to marry. As a pastor, he had women constantly coming up to him, hugging him, touching his arm, smiling up in his face. And I didn't care. Not once.

Jesus, if this is what being sexually attracted does to a person, I need to be raptured like yesterday.

"I can see it."

I jack my gaze from the depths of my cranberry and vodka and back to him. "See what?"

He nods his head, and I don't flinch from his close scrutiny. "See the resemblance to Jade. The same shape of the face and eyes. No dimples—" he brushes his fingers over my cheeks "—no freckles," he murmurs, tracing the constellation of marks scattered across my cheekbones and the bridge of my nose. "But the mouth and—" his scrutiny lowers and his teeth sink into his bottom lip "—and that body. Yeah, you and she are definitely family."

"Bull." The word explodes from me without my permission. When that silver stare returns to me, my face burns with embarrassment. But I don't mitigate what I've said with excuses. Maybe sitting here in a strip club with loud music, half-dressed women and people who won't be sitting with me in a church sanctuary tomorrow grants me courage. Or maybe it's the vodka. Either way, I meet his eyes and say, "You don't have to lie to me. I'm not so insecure that I need false compliments."

"One thing I thought you learned about me, Liyah," he

murmurs, using that nickname again. I really, *really* hate that I like it. Despite that it makes me feel special to him when I know I'm not. "I'm not a liar. Don't need to be. Now, if you don't see that those perfect titties, pretty hips, thick thighs and gorgeous ass would have every person in here throwing money if you got up on that stage, then you're the one with a truth problem, not me." He leans close to me, so close our noses almost bump. I taste the hint of alcohol on his breath, and my stomach caves in with the need to suck that flavor right off his tongue. "Let me clue you in, ma. Confidence is sexy as fuck on a woman. The only thing a man is going to do with a woman who doesn't know her worth is dog her out so he can keep her where she's at. Get that head up, lil' mama, and act like you know who the fuck you are."

I stare at him, blinking against the sudden sting of tears. He just praised my body and read me for being insecure at the same time. And that's why I'm fighting back, keeping the moisture from rolling down my face.

Get that head up, lil' mama, and act like you know who the fuck you are.

Tamara had said something similar not too long ago. Do I really come across so…weak? So timid and self-doubting? My stomach sours at the thought. And sadness coated in shame gels into a hard pebble in my chest.

"You still haven't answered my question. What was wrong with you?" he asks like he didn't just strip me uncomfortably bare with his brutally honest words.

"Did it occur to you that the reason I keep dodging the question is because I don't want to talk to you about it?" I snap.

He cocks his head. "If that's what it is, then stop playing word games and just come out your mouth and say that."

"Fine." I ball up my fists. "I don't want to talk to you about my personal business because it's just that—personal. Please and thank you."

He slowly nods. "There she is," he murmurs. "Been waiting on her to make an appearance." I frown. Who is this *she* and *her*? Before I can ask, he says, "Good. Glad you got that out. Now tell me what was wrong. Aye, church girl, roll those eyes again, and I'ma hand them to you. Go ahead and talk."

"You are irritating as hell," I snap.

A smile—slow and just a little bit sinister—spreads across his face. The sight of it has another flood drenching my panties. His lip piercing only adds to the picture. At this point, they're going to need to sanitize this couch when I leave.

"Is that the way you speak to your employer?"

"We're off the clock, remember."

He smirks and leans forward again. This time, his nose does bump mine. "Not much about you I forget, ma. Now do you start talking, or do I take that as an invitation to do something else with that mouth?"

We trade breaths, mine faster, softer than his. I know what my answer should be. Easily. But my trembling thighs and clenching sex are throwing in their votes.

"You're a bully," I whisper.

"Only when it comes to bullying that pussy." He straightens, his gray eyes refusing to let me go. Stealing my will, my choice. "Talk, Liyah."

That damn nickname. It's as bad as the *ma's* and *lil' mama's.* No, it's worse. I bet he's called other women the same. But Liyah? It's all mine.

Huffing out a sigh, I fall back against the couch. Mistake. His fingers graze my nape. Instead of moving his hand, though, he cuffs my neck, his fingertips pressing into the side of my throat.

Oh God. I *can't...*

How does he expect me to talk while he touches me? But his squeezing hand informs me he expects that very thing.

"I was just..." I close my eyes, lift my drink for a sip. "I'm not on good terms with my parents because I'm here. In Chicago. Not the strip club. But if they knew about me being *here*, they'd be angry about that, too."

A beat of silence, probably to wade through all that babbling.

"You miss them."

Do I? I lift my lashes, meet his piercing, unwavering stare. "Yes," I admit and wait for the sadness to slip in. But looking into his beautiful eyes, only calm wraps around me. It makes no sense. "Not enough to give them what they want, but yes."

"What do they want?"

"Me to return home." To fall in line. To go back to being the obedient, silent girl I was.

He's quiet but his fingers rub my neck, and *man...* They're speaking a language of their own. My vagina and nipples appear to be fluent.

"They don't agree with you leaving?" he asks.

I don't want to go into the details of the fractured relationship with my parents. A relationship that had been fractured long before I left for Chicago. Now, the splinters are just more obvious.

"God no." The confession bursts free, and I glance away from him.

Gentle yet firm fingers on my chin turn my head back in his direction. "No hiding, ma. Something tells me you're used to that. Baby girl, if you can't get naked in a strip club, then where else can you strip yourself bare?"

I snort. That's pretty funny.

The corner of his mouth twitches as if he's suppressing a smile. His hand drops away from my face, and I almost grab for it, bring it back to my chin. He steadies me, grounds me even as everything feminine inside me trembles.

"What's 'God no' mean? You run away from home?"

I choke out a laugh at how close to the truth he struck. "Something like that."

I'm not ready to talk to him about Gregory and why I ran out of that church. Because then I'd have to explain how I allowed myself to get to the altar before I found my courage to say no. And he's already called me out on my lack of confidence and strength once tonight. My feelings can't handle another hit. Particularly not from him.

I sigh, run my hand over my hair only to have my fingers bump against the bun at the top of my head.

"I wasn't that stereotypical PK who rebels, causes trouble and disobeys every rule. I tried to be the perfect daughter, obey every command, avoid causing my parents any kind of embarrassment or disappointment. I was willing to do anything to please them, especially my father. But when it really mattered—" when it came down to permanently tying myself to a man I didn't love in the eyes of God and the church "—I failed. And I left. Ran, just like you said. But not only because I wanted to get away. They didn't approve of me pursuing art. They saw it as a useless hobby. They didn't approve of me attending college so far from home. Graduating community college with an associate's in business administration was enough as far as my father was concerned. That way, I could use my degree to support the church." And my husband.

"Have you talked to them since you left?" he quietly asks, his fingers steadily stroking my skin.

If I didn't know better, I'd think he was trying to comfort me. I shake that self-serving thought out of my head. Von must take my shake as my answer to his question because he shifts closer to me.

"Why? It's been weeks." Something dark and intense passes through his gray eyes, momentarily shadowing them. His mouth hardens, taking on a cruel slant. "Did they do—"

"No, no, nothing like that." I adamantly shake my head again. "Neither one of them ever put their hands on me. And my father is a firm believer in spare the rod, spoil the child. I just never gave him cause to carry that out." I never defied him, and yet that still didn't make me good enough. Perfect enough. "I have spoken with my mother since I've been here. But that didn't go too well." My lips twist at the understatement. "I'm just not ready to talk to my father yet."

I shrug, and Von doesn't remove that penetrating stare from me. "And earlier..."

"My father called and left me a message. I told myself not to listen to it but—" Again, I shrug.

"Let me listen to it."

He holds out his hand, and before I even realize it, I pass the phone to him. He holds the cell up to my face to unlock it, scrolls to the voice mails and presses the phone to his ear.

Mentally, I cringe. Why am I involving him in my family drama? No matter what we've said to each other tonight, he's still my employer. This is crossing all kinds of boundaries. I can't explain why I let him listen. And as I study the lack of emotion on his face, my palms dot with sweat.

One rule we have in my family is what happens in this house stays in this house. And I'm violating that rule right now by inviting Von into the dysfunctionality between me and my parents.

Seconds later, he lowers the cell and passes it to me. The moments of silence have my nerves dancing beneath my skin.

"Don't let anyone have your peace, Liyah. They can try to take it, but only you can hand it over to them. Protect it at all costs."

I study him. It feels like he's not only advising me but himself as well. And it's on the tip of my tongue to comment, to demand he give a little quid pro quo, when he lowers his arm, signaling for a waitress. The woman who enters is tall, slimmer than Nikki but just as gorgeous. She strides into the VIP section, smiling widely, her dark gaze not even flicking toward me, fixed solely on Von.

"What can I do for you?" she purrs. The same bralette and boy shorts that barely covered Nikki's body wrap around hers, and she pushes out her substantial breasts, offering those right along with anything else he might order.

Another spike of jealousy strikes me dead center in the chest. I just manage not to rub the sore spot.

Not your man. Not your man, a voice inside reminds me.

Yeah, but she *doesn't know that*, my inner bitch snaps back.

I'm siding with the bitchy voice. It's just rude for ol' girl to be batting her lashes and flirting with him right in front of me. I know she sees me sitting here. I have a lot of issues, but invisibility isn't one of them.

Whoa, girl. I blink. Where did that attitude come from?

"You can bring a bottle of D'ussé and—" he glances at my nearly empty glass "—another cranberry vodka for her. And send some girls over for us."

She cocks her head, her gaze running over him in a slow, obvious scan. Subtlety? She don't know her. Anger simmers in my stomach, and I lift my glass, downing the rest of the alcohol.

I'm not the only one over here thirsty.

"I can do that. Anything else? If a lap dance is what you want, I would be more—"

"Aye, what's your name?" Von interrupts her with a hike of his chin.

The waitress's smile widens. "Draya," she says.

"Yeah, check it, Draya. You disrespectful as fuck." The smile drops from Draya's face, her expression going slack at his blunt words. But nope, he's not finished. "You see my girl sitting here and haven't even looked her way or asked her what she'd like to drink or eat. That's literally your job. Wait on people and serve. I don't like that. So no, you can't give me a lap dance. You can't even bring my drinks because I don't trust your thirsty ass not to spit in my shit. So hand over that order to another server and don't come back up in here."

He turns to me, lifting his hip off the couch and removing his wallet. Draya stands there, unmoving, mouth open for several seconds before whirling around and stomping out of the section.

Wow.

"What?" He removes a thick wad of bills then returns the wallet to his pocket all nonchalant like he didn't just tear that woman a new one. "What's wrong with you?"

"Did you…? Why did you…?"

I can't finish the sentence, but I don't need to because he pins me with a look that asks, *Really, though?*

"She got me fucked-up. I don't do that catty shit. What kind of man would I be if I let her disrespect you right in front of me? Why would she *want* a man who would do that?" He snorts. "Nah, no way I was letting her play in your face like that."

"But I'm not your…girl," I say, using the word he'd given Draya to describe me.

"And?" He arches an eyebrow. "Did she know that? Did she care?"

Since I'd just made that same point to myself, I don't reply. We stare at each other. I want to avoid that steady, beautiful gaze, afraid of what he will see in mine, but I can't. Lust swirls inside me—lust, need and a softer, warmer emotion I don't want to name.

I have a kindness kink. Be nice to me, say soft words, treat me like I matter, and I will spread 'em open for you.

It's humiliating. No one has ever defended me like that. No one. And now, I can't separate desire from gratitude. Longing from thankfulness.

"Someone wanted dancers?"

I jerk my head away from him and watch, my lips parted in confusion as three women enter the section. Is that what he'd meant by "send some girls over here"? Strippers? To do…what?

The "what" is answered right away.

One of the women—a dancer with beautiful pecan-colored skin, a long jet-black weave that reaches her behind and a red bra, thong and matching heels—stops in front of Von, standing between his spread thighs. But he waves toward me.

"This is for her."

Her? Does he mean *me*?

"What?" I gasp as the stripper moves toward me with a smile, turns, grabs her ankles and starts clapping her butt cheeks to the Latto hit the DJ's spinning. She's right there, inches from my face, and I gape at her, mesmerized by the rhythmic bounce and shake of her ass. "Umm, Von?"

"Relax, ma. You came out tonight to enjoy yourself rather than sitting home watching Tubi."

"Tubi's great!" So I might've become a bit of a Tubi addict since moving in with Tamara. The movies are so terrible and ratchet, and I love them.

He snorts. "Okay." He nods toward the dancer, who straightens, winding her hips as her fingers run through her hair. "Have some fun, Liyah. Get some lap dances, drink and let go. Here."

He shoves the handful of bills at me, and I gingerly accept it. He shakes his head, the corner of his mouth lifting. "Let that money fall on that ass, ma." Taking a few of the bills back, he rains the money down on the dancer, and the stripper bends over again, hands on knees. She glances over her shoulder at me, grinning. "Go 'head."

Slowly, I imitate him. The more dollars I sprinkle on her, the harder she twerks.

"Put some in her G-string," Von instructs, and I cautiously obey, slipping bills between her hip and the red string riding it.

"Thank you, babe." The dancer turns, her body twisting and grinding, and she's beautiful, the way her gorgeous body moves, hypnotic.

Another woman in a gold bra and G-string set with hair to match joins us, and she straddles me, her barely covered breasts almost touching my face as she grabs the couch behind my head and simulates grinding on my lap. The first stripper presses against her back, and they double team me.

In front of us, the third dancer twirls and swings around the pole on the small, raised platform in the middle of the section. I can't lie. Lust takes me by surprise, hardening my nipples and pooling low in my belly. I glance to my right and slam into Von's molten gaze. I'm unable to look away. The same heat that has moisture drenching my panties is reflected in his eyes.

God, I'm so turned on.

And yes, it's partly being surrounded by beautiful, undulating women. But more than that, it's his gray gaze on me.

Shame tries to spread like a virus through my blood. If my father saw me now, he would lose his mind. And then lay hands on me in intercessory prayer to save his prodigal daughter.

Yet, the shame, the guilt, don't get a foothold. They slip on the desire and longing filling me. The greed and hunger clawing at me.

Somehow, I whip my gaze away from Von's and focus on the dancers. When I run out of bills, more miraculously appear, shoved into my hand. And soon, just like Von encouraged, I let go. Push everything else out of my mind but the music, the alcohol, the strippers and Von.

A couple of hours and three cranberry and vodkas later, I find myself sandwiched between two dancers, arms raised, hips winding. Laughing, I peek over at Von, who hasn't moved from his spot on the couch. He's been like my guardian angel—or bodyguard—tonight, allowing me to let loose with no interference. A few times, some guys tried to enter the section, but one look from Von, and they all backed up, hands raised. Tamara came by, but after giving a head nod to Von, she shook her head and left, too.

Winded, I make my way back to the couch and plop down next to Von with a grin.

"I'm having *the best* time," I say.

He smirks, lifting his glass to his lips. When he lowers it, his full, sensual lips shine with the dampness from the amber alcohol. I slick my tongue over my own lips as if tasting the potent liquor off his mouth. His gaze lowers, tracking the movement of my tongue, sending liquid heat bursting through my belly.

"Do you want to kiss me?" I blurt out.

The vodka swimming inside me grants me eighty-proof courage. There's no other way those words would've escaped me. I let them sit out there, though, echoing louder than the music bumping in the club. The memory of exactly what magic he'd wielded with that mouth haunts me, and I sink my teeth into my bottom lip, imagining I can still taste him.

He leans back against the couch, watching me through hooded eyes that lower over my frame. He can't possibly miss the quick rise and fall of my chest or my thighs restlessly shifting, squeezing. When he lifts his gaze back to mine, his darkening eyes confirm he saw everything.

"C'mon, ma. I'm taking you home."

He stands and fire rushes to my face, setting my cheeks aflame. I duck my head, embarrassment over his rejection riding me hard and hanging me up wet. And not the good wet. The glowing buzz from the alcohol starts to thin until my mind is clear. Too clear.

As I scan the VIP room, I no longer feel free, but heavy and silly. A little girl playing at adult games.

"I should wait for my cousin," I say, avoiding his scrutiny on the pretense of scanning the club past the VIP entrance.

"I came with her, so that's how I should probably leave. You can go, though. We won't be here too much longer."

Tamara had danced over an hour ago, and my cousin had nearly brought the club down with the applause and cheers. The stage couldn't even be seen under all the money thrown up there.

"I'll send word that I got you." He walks toward the entrance. When he realizes I'm not behind him, he stops and turns. "Don't make me have to carry you out of here, ma."

His previous warning of me not liking it if he had to put me in a car echoes in my mind. For a brief moment, I consider making him come through on the threat. But I've humiliated myself enough for one evening, and I don't put it past him to do exactly what he said. Snatching up my phone, I rise and wave goodbye to the dancers, following Von out of the section and the club.

"Don't you need to let your friends know you're leaving? Won't they wonder where you're at?" I ask once we're seated in his truck.

I shiver in the early October air, having walked a block to reach his ride. He glances over at me then presses buttons on the dashboard. Soon, warm air streams from the vents and over my bare shoulders and arms. I lean forward, closing my eyes to bask in the heat.

"No, I don't need to check in with anyone. Here." Twisting his body, Von reaches in the back seat and hands me a black jacket. When I hesitate, he gives it a shake. "Take it. You're going to get sick wearing that little shit out here."

"I had a jacket earlier," I mutter, but still accept the piece of clothing. I'm no fool, and pride can't keep me warm. "I left it in the dancers' dressing room with my cousin. How was I to know I wouldn't be riding home with her..."

I sigh. There I go, rambling again. This man has that effect on me. As evidenced by my unwise invitation to kiss me. I swallow my groan. God, I just want to go home, crawl in my bed and stay there until I have no choice but to face him on Monday.

Slipping my arms into the sleeves of the jacket, I inhale his rich scent. It envelops me, just as the material of the jacket that's way too big for me.

"Thank you." I tug the lapels high, dipping my head and avoiding the stare that's like a heavy hand on my cheek.

"You going to look at me anytime soon, Aaliyah?"

Not if I can help it.

But I turn my head and meet his gaze, which seems darker in the shadows of the truck. Because *not* looking says so much more. And none of it positive.

"Did you need something?" I ask, injecting a nonchalance and calm into my voice that contradicts the chaotic swirl of humiliation and alcohol in my veins.

"Yeah." He leans back in the seat, for all the world appearing like someone settling in rather than a person about to pull into late-night Chicago traffic for a drive to the South Loop. "To know what's on your mind."

Before I can control my face, it balls up. Seriously? Like he has no idea what I could possibly be thinking? Okay, I have *just* enough vodka in my system to be honest and blame it on the booze.

"You want to know what's on my mind?" I ask, shifting toward him and tilting my head. "Yesterday you kissed me, and tonight you invite yourself to my night out. But when I ask you about kissing me again, you basically pat me on the head and treat me like I'm a pariah."

He arches an eyebrow. "Pariah?"

I make an impatient sound in my throat. "Go ahead. Joke. But I feel like you're playing some kind of game, and I don't know the rules. And this is where I excuse myself. You might get off on this, but it's not fun for me."

He stares at me, and I'm too in my feelings to be intimidated. All my life, I've been made to feel not enough—not male enough, not obedient enough, not perfect enough… not good enough. Jesus is the only perfect person, but in the gospel according to Bishop Montgomery, that was no excuse not to strive for perfection.

For one brief moment in Von's arms, I'd felt sexy, desired, needed. And even tonight, the way he'd listened to me, stood up for me… I'd allowed myself to forget who he was. Who we were to each other. Employer, employee. Gia's father and her nanny. But I wouldn't make that slip-up again. He couldn't have made it any clearer that he considers putting his mouth on me a mistake.

Anger simmers inside me like a boiling pot of water.

It's not like I asked him to kiss me the first time. *He* did that. Just like *he* walked over to my section tonight. I haven't inserted myself in places where I don't belong. That's all *him*. So it's not fair that I'm the one sitting here like I did something wrong.

"I'm too old for games, ma. What you saw as playing with your head or feelings, I see as trying to protect you."

"Did I ask you to?" The anger flares hotter, fueled by what I perceive as him trying to assume a role I don't need in my life. At least, not from him. "You see me as some wide-eyed, silly girl from some backwater town in Alabama, but newsflash—I can think for myself, care for myself and provide for myself. I've made it twenty-four years without your guidance and survived. I'm good."

Even in the dark, I can see his gray eyes narrow. "Survived. That's a strong choice of words."

I sigh, throwing up "Jesus, save me" hands. Of course, that's what he would jump on, out of everything else I've said.

And he can forget it; that was a slip of the tongue, and there's no way on God's green earth that I'm addressing it.

"Do you mind if we leave?" I ask through gritted teeth. "There's a bed with my name on it."

I probably shouldn't have mentioned beds. Not with arousal still trekking a path under my irritation.

"Nah, not until we clear this up."

I sigh.

But his only reaction is to peer down at me. "You're taking offense at what I said, but me wanting to protect you has nothing to do with how you believe I perceive you." I snort at that because the man *literally* told me day one that I didn't belong in the big city of Chicago. "Aye, ma. I'm letting you make it with your loose-ass mouth and you rolling your eyes, but keeping it real? I probably see you as more capable and stronger than you do, so check that shit."

I gape at him. He sees me as capable and strong? Since when? I want to ask him to explain so bad, but that would have him thinking I care about his opinion, and I don't.

Now who's the liar?

I mentally growl a warning at the know-it-all voice in my head.

"I'd do the same for my mother, sister or Chelle. Can they handle themselves? Yeah, damn right they can. But that doesn't mean I'm still not coming behind them. No one's taking advantage of them when I'm around. Not if I can stand in the gap for them."

"I doubt you kiss your mother or sister like that," I mutter before I can trap the words.

Damn liquid courage.

The atmosphere in the car changes. His big body stills, and a primal thing inside me reacts in the same manner. Tension crackles in the limited space like a live wire, and though I just slipped into his jacket, the heat rising between us, within me, has me almost whipping it off. Almost, because a purely feminine instinct cautions me not to move.

And though I've ignored other warnings when it comes to this man, this warning I heed.

"You want to repeat that?" he murmurs, voice cool and soft as silk.

I shake my head. My mama didn't raise no fool.

"Unhunh, lil' mama. You've had all that mouth, but now you don't know how to speak? Repeat that."

I swallow, then lick my suddenly dry lips. His tone demands I give in to him, and I really, really wish I didn't want to—but I do. Yet there's a glutton for punishment that resides within me who wants to push him. To see what he'll do.

And she wins out.

I shake my head again. Slower. More deliberate.

His eyes flash with heat—or maybe it's the headlights of a passing car. Either way, my vagina clenches so hard around emptiness that I worry for the state of my panties and his seat. My head swims at the hot girl level of my attraction to him. It's disconcerting, overwhelming and a little scary. But ask me if I move away. Ask me if I'm retreating, *knowing* it's all shades of wrong to indulge in this *thing* with him. The answer is a guttural, resounding and somewhat embarrassed "no."

God, my head hurts from all the flip-flopping I've engaged in.

"No?" He grants me one last chance to answer, and when I remain silent, he bites his lower lip, and I trap a groan at the sensual gesture. "No?" he repeats.

A big hand curves around the back of my neck, exerting enough pressure to make me lean forward with a whimper. Not of discomfort or pain but of pure desire. The feel of that hard, wide palm around my nape, and those long artist's fingers pressed to the sides of my throat, shoots sizzling arrows of lust straight to my womb.

He tugs me closer to him…closer still, until I'm straining across the middle console. I plant my hand on the lid of it, but there's no need. He supports me even as he controls me. Good thing I hadn't put on the seat belt yet, because it doesn't seem like he would've cared. Not as he leans forward, shoving his face within an inch of mine. I taste the woodsy, cinnamon scent of the alcohol he'd drunk in the club. Glimpse the black and light blue striations in his eyes.

My pulse thunders in my ears. So loud I almost miss his rumbled, "Repeat it."

I'm no match for him in this war of wills. The smart thing to do would be to surrender so I can retreat to my side of the car. Yes, the smart thing. But as my father has continually accused since I left home, I've abandoned reason and all common sense.

Through the rapid pounding of my heart, I whisper, "Make m—"

I brace myself for the carnal onslaught of his mouth. And the blitz does come. But not in the manner I expected. Instead of crushing his lips to mine, he advances with a tender kiss, a nibble to the corner of my mouth. It catches me by surprise. Out of the blue, I'm reminded of one of my favorite Scriptures, about God not being found in a wind or an earthquake or a fire. He was found in a quiet, small voice.

That's this kiss.

The one from last night was like one of those natural disasters—overwhelming, cataclysmic, world-shaking.

But this one… It's softer, gentler, but in its own way, no less earth-shattering. No less profound.

There's a part of me that yells, wanting the storm of his passion. It would be less dangerous. This slow glide of lips over lips, delicate peck to the corners of my mouth, this whispered caress over my jaw and cheek… I'm helpless to its onslaught. Susceptible to its deceptive meaning.

Nothing about Von Howard screams tender or gentle when it comes to sex. But he's showing me differently, and I don't know how to take it.

A whimper escapes me as he traces the seam of my lips with his tongue. I suck in a sharp breath, and he uses the opportunity to slowly penetrate me, slipping his tongue inside to tangle with mine. Cocking his head, he shoves deeper, his touch turning demanding as he sucks on me, licks the roof of my mouth, sinks his teeth into my bottom lip. Good God, if this man is this good with just his lips and tongue, how is he with his body, his…dick?

Desire pulls tight in my belly, and heat undulates through me, swirling in my aching, pulsing sex. I think my vagina just volunteered as tribute to find out the answer to that question.

Sex has always been a…complicated issue with me. I'm not afraid of it, just leery. And the experience I've had has never inspired a desperate need for it. I could take it or leave it, but mostly take it since I do want to have children one day.

But nothing about the lust urging me to moan and arch my neck so he can have deeper access pertains to reproduction. It's hunger, pure and not so simple. With Von, I want it all. Want to discover that hurried, messy urgency I've seen in characters in books and on TV. Want him to replace…

I shake my head as if the gesture can disrupt the path my brain wanted to take.

"What's wrong, ma?" Von lifts his head. "Where did you go just now?"

"Nothing. Nowhere," I answer each of his questions in

order and reach for him, to drag him back down and continue what he'd started.

But me fisting his shirt doesn't move him. Literally.

"What I say about lying to me?" He squeezes the back of my neck in warning, and my sex reciprocates with a spasm of its own. I close my eyes against the backlash of pleasure, and I could cry for the loss of his mouth. "Either tell me to mind my business or you don't feel like talking about it, but don't fix your mouth to lie to me."

I part my lips to tell him it's none of his business—hasn't that been preached to me for years?—but something halts the words. I stare at him, struck silent with the truth and the instinctive warning to be quiet both vying for dominance.

On one hand, I've been raised on the commandment that what happens in our house stays in our house. On the other hand, though… I'm tired of silence. I love my father with all my heart, but sometimes he contradicts what he preaches, and those occasions seem to always be to his benefit, not mine. God gave us voices not only to uplift Him but also to be truthful. Loving. And by not using mine, I've hurt myself. And only He knows how many others.

I lick my lips. "I—" My throat constricts as if it's aware of my intention and is intent on saving me from myself and my father's wrath. "I was…thinking about my uncle," I whisper although it feels like the admission is propelled out of me like a bullet.

Von doesn't speak, but his eyes narrow, roaming over my face, searching. I don't know what he sees, but one moment he's looking at me, and in the next, his hands are on my waist and he's yanking me off my seat, over the console and onto his lap. I straddle his powerful thighs, and the slight pull in my own has arousal beating inside of me like a separate heartbeat.

His big hand cups my chin, tilting my head up so I have no choice but to meet his gaze.

"Head up, Liyah." His low voice is a deep, resonant rumble in the silent car. "Tell me why you were thinking about your uncle while I was kissing you."

Jesus, when he puts it that way…

Shame tries to crawl through me, but I shut that down. I've fought hard and long not to take on that burden. I'll be damned if I allow it to place its crushing weight on me now.

I'm not that eleven-year-old girl anymore. I haven't been in a long time.

"When I was younger, my uncle David visited us. He lived in Norfolk, so I didn't see him often, but he was always fun and nice to me when he did come to Alabama. Where my father was strict, he was easygoing. Where my father was always busy with the church, he spent time with me, and I loved the attention. I loved him. One day, I came down with a bug, and that evening my parents left me with him to attend Bible study. We sat on the couch and watched all my favorite movies, and at some point, I fell asleep. I woke up to him…"

My heart shudders then pounds as if I'm right back there in my parents' living room. The metallic flavor of panic floods my mouth. I swallow it down, afraid to close my eyes. Afraid of the images my brain will supply in this moment.

Two hands cradle my face, and I latch onto Von's strong wrists as if he's my lifeline, the only thing preventing me from tumbling into a bottomless abyss.

"I got you, Liyah. Finish it," he roughly urges.

I nod, a breath shuddering out from between my lips.

"I woke to him trying to get under my pajama pants. My top was up over my—" I cut off the rest of the sentence, digging my fingers into his skin. "But I don't remember if he touched me there or not. When I realized what he was doing, I slapped at his hand, pulling free of him. I fell on the floor, kicking at him and screaming. He tried to grab me, shushing me, but I wasn't listening. I was so terrified, so hurt. This was my uncle, and I was old enough to understand what he'd tried to do. I ran to my bedroom, locked the door and didn't open it until my parents got home. I tried to call both of them, even knowing they probably wouldn't answer because they were in church, but I needed them. But the calls went directly to voice mail. The next two hours were the scariest of my life. I didn't know if David had left or was still in the house outside my door just waiting on me to open it. I pushed my dresser in front of it just in case and hid between my bed and bedside table. It seemed like forever, but when my parents finally came home, I couldn't move. All that time praying and hoping they would get there, and I couldn't go to them."

I'd been frozen, afraid of…everything. That Uncle David was still there, that he'd lied to them about why I'd locked myself in my room. Afraid they wouldn't believe me. Afraid they would.

I almost bend my head, but his hands, still clasped to my

cheeks, and his order to keep my head up prevent me from doing it.

Keep going. Get it all out once and for all.

"When my parents realized I was in my room, my mom convinced me to open the door. And as soon as I did, I fell on her, crying. When I got the story out, my mother lost it. I'd never seen her lose her temper or yell. And then, she screamed and ran to the kitchen. Before my father could stop her, she grabbed a bottle of wine off the counter and went upside David's head with it. I truly believe she would've cut him with the broken bottle if Daddy hadn't intervened. My father kicked him out, and I've never seen him again."

"Good," he snaps. His touch to my face remains soft, but there's nothing gentle about the brutal anger in his voice. "I wish your dad would've let your mother slice him up. If it'd been Gia, he wouldn't have walked out of that fucking house at all."

A coldness turns his gray eyes to chips of ice. I shiver, believing him. But anyone who would touch a child deserves all that and more. I have no sympathy for those monsters. Sometimes murder and theft can be justified, mitigated by certain circumstances. But not violating a child. There was no forgiveness in me for that.

"What happened after that? Did your parents press charges?"

"No," I murmur. "Mom wanted to. She was on her way to get me dressed so we could do just that, but my father stopped her." And this is the source of my shame, my hurt. "He told her going to the police would only be inflicting more harm on me since I would have to retell what happened to strangers at the station and then possibly in a trial. Also, how would it look that the pastor's brother tried to touch the pastor's daughter? And David had only *tried* to molest me. He didn't go through with it because I'd woken up."

"He didn't know that," Von growls, his hands dropping away from my face, falling to my hips. His fierce scowl doesn't intimidate me. Not when it's on my behalf. "He can't say for certain what happened before you woke up, just like you can't. Not that it fucking matters. He's *your father.* Fuck how it would look. Fuck everything but making that piece of shit suffer. It's his job to protect and support you through reporting it." He glances away from me, a muscle in his jaw jumping beneath his beard. "Man of God or not, your father's lucky he's in Alabama, because I swear to the God he supposedly stands for, I would stomp a hole in him right now for failing you."

For a moment, I'm lost for words. His anger nearly singes me, but it doesn't frighten me. It...warms me. Though nearly fifteen years have passed, his reaction soothes the jagged edges of something my father broke when he put his church and reputation before me. Because that's exactly what he did. Yes, he'd kicked his brother out and refused to have anything else to do with him, but he'd also silenced me, making his eleven-year-old daughter feel that if she confessed what happened to the authorities or anyone outside our immediate family, she would be responsible for the negative backlash.

I'd been turned from victim to potential perpetrator.

Von voiced what I'd been too scared to say before—my father had failed me.

As did my mother when she went along with it.

"So I take it they didn't bring you to the police. Have you ever told anyone what happened?"

"No, Daddy convinced my mother to leave it alone. He swore he'd never allow David back into our house. He made me promise to let our business stay our business. Outside of my therapist, I've only told one other person about it." I pause. "You."

"Not even your cousin?"

I shake my head and huff out a low breath. "I haven't because it's become a habit not to say anything about what happened, but my guilt also eats me alive. I don't believe I was the first child David tried that with. And because I kept quiet, how many more children has he—"

"No. Don't you fucking dare finish that thought." He lifts a hand, pinches my chin and tips it down so I'm staring directly into his eyes. "None of this is on you. You were a kid, a baby. You had no power then, which is why what the adults did and didn't do in this situation is all the more egregious. And your uncle's sins belong only to him. He's the criminal here, not you. If more kids were harmed, that's because he's a sick fuck. It has nothing to do with you. Let that shit go, ma."

I nod, absorbing his admonishment like a sponge run across a wet counter. I've told myself the same thing several times over the years. But hearing the words from another person—from him—it validates what my heart had a difficult time accepting.

"Thank you," I whisper.

His head jerks back. "Don't ever thank me for something like that, ma. That's what's wrong with muthafuckas now. Want credit for what they're supposed to do. Any person who's in your life—parent, friend, your man—should give you honesty and speak life into you."

My lips curl into a small smile as I tilt my head. "Speak life into me? Let me find out you go to church and listen."

He snorts, dropping his hand back to my waist. "I'm not a PK like you, but I do have a mother who didn't let me or my sister miss a Sunday school or morning service." He tilts his chin up. "Be honest with me, Liyah. This is important because I don't want to do anything to inadvertently cause you harm. Why were you thinking of your uncle while we were kissing? Is sex a trigger for you?"

"No. *No.*" I shake my head for added emphasis. "Maybe when I was younger, I had a problem with people touching me without telegraphing it. Or without my permission. But I'm better at that thanks to counseling when I was eighteen and old enough to get it without my parents' consent or knowledge. Still, sex hasn't ever been a necessity for me. That urgent need to have it? I've never experienced that. Until now." My palms dampen, and my belly churns at what I just admitted. Thank God for the shadows in the car. I don't think I could've had this conversation with him in a well-lit room. "You make me understand desire. And I—" my gaze dips to his chin, unable to look into his eyes as I whisper the rest of my confession "—want more of it. I want to replace my apathy with everything you make me feel when you kiss me, touch me."

The silence that throbs between us has its own heartbeat, its own texture. Because I can't *not* see what his thoughts are, I lift my eyes. The heated lust in his almost knocks me back against the steering wheel.

Without releasing me from his visual tug-of-war, he slowly slides a hand around to the front of my throat. He lightly cuffs me, and another whimper slips free, the light but possessive hold stirring the flames already licking at me. Who knew I would love this? Love the weight of his palm and fingers circling my throat, threatening to tighten and tighten… God, do I have a darker side that I never knew existed?

I squirm on his lap, and he glances down to my thighs, bared by the rise of my dress to accommodate me sitting on him. The material bunches around my hips, and only the very bottom of my dress hides my sex from him. If he lifts the material, he'll have a front-row seat to my scrap of black panties and how wet I am.

And I don't care.

Part of me—the part he's awakened with every look, touch, kiss—wants him to see.

Because though I know nothing good can come from this, I'm not moving. Not until he puts his mouth on me again. And anything else he has a mind to put on my body. Or in.

"I can't decide if you're really honest or just naïve enough to admit something like that to me while your pussy is sitting on top of my dick."

His blunt mouth is going to be the death of me, one way or another. And I can't lie. I'm feenin' for all of those ways.

"Are you looking for an answer?" I ask.

He cocks his head and studies me for a long, tension-filled moment then slowly shakes his head. "Not really. Not when whatever it is won't matter one way or the other. The only answer I need from you is yes or no about whether you're gonna let me pull this nut out of you."

Over the thunderous pounding of my heart, I nod.

"Unhunh, ma. Speak that shit."

"Yes," I say, surprising myself at how firm it sounds, when inside, I'm trembling like a storm-tossed leaf. I pause, holding my breath for a second, then blurt, "Pull this nut out of me."

The surprise that flares in his gray eyes mirrors my own shock at my boldness. And though a tiny voice screams, *Who are you right now?* I continue to meet his stare.

He chuckles, and the low, dark sound trips over my skin like both a caress and a warning. "Say less."

His mouth takes mine, and where it was gentle, tender earlier, now it's fierce and so erotic that a full-body shudder works through me. It's as if he's held back until now, and he's decided to fully unleash on me. My lips tingle under the onslaught, and I can barely keep up with the plunge and suck of his tongue. After a moment, I tilt my head back, surrendering, and the hand at my throat slips to my chin. I let him angle my head any way he pleases. Let him take whatever he wants. Give him whatever he demands.

When his other hand skims up the side of my ribs to cover my breast, I jolt against the lash of pleasure. The groan that slips out of my lips into his mouth is one that borders on pained. That groan transforms into a whimper as he massages my flesh over my dress, plucking at the nipple unashamedly making itself known. The material is no defense against his determined, brazen fingers, and neither am I.

Unable to control my body or manage the lust streaming through me, I inch my thighs wider, sitting fully on his dick. A wave of relief flickers through me as if contact with him telegraphs to my body that there's hope the fire raging inside me will be extinguished.

Like I said, I'm not a virgin, but I'm also not super experienced. Missionary was my one position, and it'd been… well, it'd been. Now, here I sit in a blacked-out truck, straddling my boss and grinding on him.

"Oh… God." Breaking away from his mouth, I drop my head back and breathily take the Lord's name in vain. But He'll forgive me. Because the pleasure striking my sex is divine.

I find my rhythm, not sure if I'm doing this right or wrong—not caring either way. Not when the slide of my feminine lips over the long, thick column under his jeans sends sparks skating over my skin, down my spine. As if they possess a mind of their own, my hips go to work. Experience be damned. My body—my vagina—seems to have a primal understanding of what will give me the most ecstasy. Thank God for the animal brain.

"Fuuuck." He releases my jaw and hip, lowering his hands to tear at his belt and zipper. In seconds, his jeans sag open and he thrusts them lower.

I greedily glance down, hungry for my first glimpse of his dick. Something tells me it's as beautiful as he is. I don't think there's anything unattractive about this man. Not the thick dark brows that arrow down over his silver gaze. Not the sensual, pierced mouth that's damp and swollen from our kisses.

And not the impossibly long, wide shaft he pulls free from his black boxer briefs.

Holy shit.

And hell yes, that curse is warranted. That one, too.

I feel my eyes pinch at the corners as they widen at the sight of him. *All* of him.

I'd be a liar if I didn't admit to the flutter of anxiety at the thought of *that* possibly getting inside *me.* No way in hell that's fitting into any hole my body possesses. I don't even think it's anatomically possible…or correct.

No, I don't have a ruler, but he *must* have more dick than I have vagina. Still… I hadn't been wrong. He's beautiful. Funny to think of a penis that way, but it is what it is. The dim interior of the truck can't hide the smooth, silken-looking skin stretched taut over every powerful inch of him. Can't conceal the broad tip that glistens with wetness at the very top. Or how heavy he must be if the tilt to the right is any indication of the weight he's packing.

Von's fist circles his flesh in a grip that appears punishing, and my core spasms in response. And when he pumps his hand up his length, making the head disappear for several precious seconds, my body lights up. My tongue dampens my lips as eagerness I've never equated with sex pulses through me.

"You looking at my shit like you want a taste." By sheer force of will, I drag my gaze up from his fist to his hooded eyes. I don't answer; I can't. Desire has stolen that capability. "Open," he says, staring at my mouth.

I obey. And not because I've been conditioned all my life to do so. No, I do it because I want—crave—whatever he has for me. I have a feeling Von's reward for deference will be vastly different from God's.

And I'm not wrong.

He slides all four of his fingers between my lips, over my tongue, stretching me to the limits. My mouth is full of him, of the musky yet fresh flavor I intuitively know is the precum that had dotted the tip of his flesh.

Should I be a little turned off by his assumption that I wanted the taste of him in my mouth? Should I recoil at his unapologetic filthiness?

Probably. I mean, I'm weeks out from almost marrying a perfectly respectable, different man.

Probably...but I'm not. If the moisture damn near coating my thighs is any indication, I'm not turned off in the least.

On a groan, I glide my tongue under his fingers, licking as best I can. Tickling the crevices between each digit, I soak in his grunt, hoarding each sound like manna from heaven.

God, I'm being so blasphemous right now.

Again, can't bring myself to care.

Especially when he withdraws his fingers until only the tips graze my lips...and then carefully but forcefully thrusts them back inside. I squirm, the simulation of sex not lost on me. He repeats the motion, this time reaching farther toward the back of my throat.

Heat sizzles inside me, burning me alive. My hips helplessly jerk, and his other hand returns to my hip, stilling me. Or tries to. At this point, my body has rebelled, seeking more of the acute need that has taken hold like claws sunk into giving flesh.

It's messy, beautiful and ugly. It's damn necessary.

"One more," Von goads, invading my mouth again, his hot, narrowed gaze focused solely on my parted lips. "If you're this pretty right now I can't even imagine how you gonna look stuffed full of my dick. You gon' take it like you are now? Or better, like the good little church girl you are?"

The taunt accompanies the deepest thrust yet, his fingertips tickling the entrance to my throat. My automatic reaction is to gag, my eyes tearing up. A thumb rubs up and down the front of my neck, the soothing touch in direct contrast to the demanding fingers.

"That's what I'm talking about, ma. You taking it so good," he croons. "Relax. Breathe slow and deep through your nose. There you go," he praises, holding himself still as I acclimate to him deeper inside me than anyone before. After several seconds, he slides free, and the fierce pride and lust branding his beautiful, harsh features are more than worth my stinging, wet eyes and aching jaws.

Mortification tries to attack me when he gently wipes spit from the corners of my mouth and chin. But Von tilts my head back so I have no choice but to meet his eyes.

"What're you looking embarrassed about?" He mugs me. Instead of giving me an opportunity to reply, he crushes his mouth to mine, making more of a mess of me. "Don't ever be ashamed of how much of yourself you give to someone for your pleasure or theirs. This—" he dips his thumb inside my mouth, and without instruction, I suck hard on it. "This," he growls, "is between us. It's natural and it's hot as fuck." He paints his assurance on my chin, over my cheek, with his damp thumb. "And sloppy head is the best head, ma. Don't nobody want neat when they're getting their dick sucked."

Declaring that as if it's the Gospel According to Von, he punctuates it with another hard kiss.

"Fuck, I ain't got no business doing this to you," he mutters. The admonishment might've hurt my feelings if he didn't tug down the top of my strapless dress, baring my breasts. The built-in shelf bra is sturdy enough—and my breasts are small and firm enough—that I didn't need to wear a bra tonight, and when that sexy mouth pulls into a snarl, I'm glad. "When I go to hell for dirtying you up, are you going to pray for my soul, Liyah?"

I would've answered—I swear I would've. If only he hadn't chosen that moment to vacuum damn near my whole breast into his mouth.

"Oh God," I wail, my hands flying to his head, clutching his braids.

He doesn't let my tight grip or my spasming body stop him from drawing hard or from pinching the other nipple.

I'm twisting closer, then bowing away. Hell, I don't know. I just don't know anymore. All I can claim for certain is I'm on the verge of breaking, and it scares me.

Von lifts his head, and despite my internal, erotic tug-of-war, I reach for him. But he evades me, leaning against the back of the driver's seat.

"Von," I whine, prepared to beg for that orgasm he promised me. The orgasm he can't deliver if he doesn't get back to what he was doing. Get back. Right. Now.

"Shh, ma. Let me get you right."

He doesn't explain that, and as his gaze and his hand lower to between my thighs, any question I might've had dries on my tongue. I'm speechless, but my body isn't. It screams with anticipation and greed as he grabs the hem of my dress and lifts it. Modesty should jump up and shout, *"Remember me!"* but no, it remains quiet, probably as breathless and eager as I am.

"Goddamn." His low, heated curse has my nipples beading tighter, has the coil of heat just below my navel pulling tauter. My hips roll all on their own, and his rough and *pleased* chuckle echoes in the confines of the truck's cab. "Why that pussy so wet, huh? Why she so pretty?"

On a hum, he traces my fevered skin just above the patch of thong that's barely covering me. A peek down reveals my puffy, drenched folds nearly swallowing the barely there lace. And in this moment, I'm relieved I let Tamara talk me into a spa day where I was waxed and plucked within an inch of my life. The pain was worth witnessing the lust stamping his features and watching him pull his bottom lip between his teeth. How did I go my whole life not knowing how sexy that one gesture could be?

Von cants my hips forward, pressing my back against the steering wheel. What if I hit the horn? Won't that telegraph to people—

A long, tortured groan eases out of my throat as he grips my hips and glides my sex up his dick.

Oh God. Who cares about a horn? Hell, what is *a horn?*

All thought flies from my head at the pleasure careening through me like a summer tornado. And when my clit nudges the rim of his tip, I can't even recall my name.

"Damn, ma." He grunts as he does some kind of twist/grind/roll combo that shoves his cock between my folds while circling my clit at the same time.

It's magic. Wicked sorcery. And I don't know whether to condemn him for this witchcraft or praise him for his skills. He slides me down his length then snatches me back up. I whimper.

Praise. Definitely praise.

"You got it, church girl," he urges, his pace quickening as he grinds me over and over his flesh. "Get it. Get me all wet and messy with it, too. Gimme my nut."

Desperate, I slap a hand over his mouth. If he keeps talking, I'm going to die. Expire right here and my ghost will be orgasming in his lap.

His lips graze my palm, and I don't need to see his smile to feel it against my skin. He lifts a hand, covering mine, pressing it against his mouth…and sinks his teeth into the heel of my palm. Electrical currents attack my sex, and like a marionette, my body twitches, pulled by the strings of pleasure.

And as powerful, as good as it all is, it's not enough.

I want more. I shouldn't. God knows, I've already gone a bridge too far. To do more, to tempt more, to dare ask for more…

Screw it.

Whether it's being drunk on the lust swirling in my veins or the reckless, desperate knowledge that this moment may never come again, I hurl caution and myself over that tenuous cliff called self-preservation and dive into the unknown. Into abandonment. Into danger.

Into him.

"Fuck me." The demand is a whisper but it's certain.

He stills but then his hand lifts, encircles my wrist and tugs mine away from his mouth. He remains silent but his gaze is busy, roaming my face.

Flames start to lick at my cheeks at his continued silence, and the "Forget it" sits heavy on my tongue when he reaches into the middle console and removes a condom.

"I can already feel the chokehold that pussy's gon' put on me and I want it. Make sure you do, too," he says while tearing the foil square open and rolling the protection down his dick.

In lieu of a verbal answer, I rise up, notch him at my opening…then slowly, so slowly lower myself down his dick.

Or try to.

What in the hell have I gotten myself into? Or gotten into me?

I whimper, caught between fiery pain and exquisite pleasure. Both vie for dominance, and honestly, I don't know which is winning.

"Gotdamn, Liyah." He sinks his teeth into that full bottom lip again, attention focused between us. "There's no excuse for this pussy to feel this fucking good. You should be ashamed of yo-damn-self."

If I wasn't currently trembling, stuck halfway on his dick, debating whether I want to climb off or sink farther down, I'd chuckle at his words. But here I am, trembling and stuck.

His big hands rub up and down my spine, his heavy, warm breath blasts the base of my throat.

On a low murmur, he lifts both arms and holds my bare breasts. His lips close around my nipple, sucking hard, his teeth grazing the hardened tip.

"Oh God." My head falls back on my shoulders as he switches breasts. Drinking from me and steadily fucking me from the bottom. "Von."

I can do nothing but hold on, and by the time I'm fully seated on his lap, I'm breathless, overflowing with dick and tipping over the edge into orgasm.

I cry out loud, shaking and creaming all over him, as the tip of that beautiful shaft nudges something within me that has remained untouched until this very moment.

Von holds me through it, dragging his mouth away from my chest to trail kisses up my throat to my ear and whisper things too low for me to catch given the roaring in my ears.

As soon as the first wave of the sensual storm passes, he presses hot, open-mouthed kisses to my jaw and then proceeds to fuck the little breath I gained right back out of me.

I fist his T-shirt with one hand and grip his head with the other, hanging on as he goes wild beneath me and I go just as hard, riding him with only instincts and pleasure as instructors. The smack of flesh, the suction of wet flesh releasing and welcoming each other fill the truck.

And when he reaches between us, rubbing my clit with unerring accuracy, I again rush headfirst into a full-on orgasm that gives me no warning. It slams into me, and my back arches so tight I dimly hear the blast of a horn. It's drowned out by the roar of ecstasy filling my head, tumbling through my body, pulsating in my sex. My...pussy.

Like he demanded, I'm a hot, sticky mess, and I'm making it all over him.

"Fuck." Von's voice penetrates the swarm buzzing in my ears. "Fuck, fuck, fuck." He punctuates each curse with a thrust against me, and seconds later, he stiffens and he throbs hard and deep within me.

The harsh blasts of our labored breathing echo in the truck's hot interior that smells of sex. As the red haze clears, cold reality seeps in like a biting winter wind slipping through the cracks.

The modesty and embarrassment I wouldn't let myself feel earlier creep through me now. *What have I done?* I cross my arms over my breasts, then quickly yank up my dress, covering myself.

"Hold up." Von stretches across the console for the glove compartment and removes a handful of napkins and a bag of wipes. Wipes he probably keeps in his car for his daughter. The daughter I nanny.

Oh *God*. What have *I done*?

While I spiral into self-recrimination, he gently lifts me off his dick and efficiently cleans me up, and I'm so deep in my thoughts I don't even flinch as he swipes between my legs. It's only when he's removing the condom and dragging the disposable cloth over his dick that I scramble back over to the passenger side, tugging down the hem of my dress. It's either put distance between us or offer to replace his hand with my own.

This is bad. So bad. I shouldn't have ever kissed him, touched him. Because even as I mentally tear myself a new one for being so reckless to have gotten physical with my employer, the greedy need for a repeat simmers low in my belly.

I turn my head, staring out the window still foggy from our…activities. No sooner does the word pass through my head than I'm palming my forehead, silently groaning.

What does this mean for my job? God, no wonder my father didn't want me out here, out of his sight. Just weeks and I'm forgetting who I am, what my morals are…

But who are *you? Shoot, you don't even know what your morals and opinions* are *since the only ones you've known have been dictated by your father.*

I flinch away from the voice in my head that sounds a lot like Tamara.

Pinching the bridge of my nose, I bow my head. My father's stern rebukes fill my mind, and I shrink from them.

I didn't raise you to be a woman of loose morals. Only a prostitute advertises her wares.

Cleanliness isn't just of the body but of the spirit.

To be in the flesh is to be separate from God.

Each sermonized statement strikes me like pebbles. Since what happened with my uncle, I've tried so hard to be virtuous, as if I somehow drew his attention even though I was a child. And Dad didn't do anything to discourage that line of thought. He became stricter afterward, more watchful, more…controlling. As if he had to make sure my soul remained pure since the flesh had already been sullied.

Maybe he had a point to be so concerned, so wary. Maybe he'd seen something I hadn't. The something that would lead me to—

"Aye, I don't know what the fuck you're over there thinking, but stop it."

I only had seconds to process that rumbled order before firm fingers bit into my chin, lifting my head and turning it toward Von.

A fierce scowl darkened his face more than the shadows surrounding us. "Was this shit the wisest thing to do? Probably not. And since you still work for me—don't even get it into your head about quitting, ma—we shouldn't repeat it. But do I regret it? Hell nah. Life's too short for that shit. And since I've been wondering about how you taste from the moment you walked into my office at the shop, I'd be fake as fuck to say I have regrets. Baby girl, we grow from mistakes, not use them as memorials to our fuckups. And if you're not given the opportunity to grow, you don't learn a muthafuckin' thing in this world."

He drops his hand away from my chin, and I stare at him, a little stunned, a lot mesmerized. Sometimes I forget that Von has me by ten years. But then there are moments like these, when he drops profanity-laden nuggets of wisdom, that I'm reminded.

"You good?" he asks, arching a dark eyebrow.

Since I've been wondering about how you taste from the moment you walked into my office at the shop…

I would be good as soon as I exorcised that bit of truth-telling from my mind. As for the rest…

"Yes." At least, I would be.

Maybe.

"Good." He nods. Without removing his narrowed gaze from me, he turns on the car, the engine rumbling to life. "And I meant what I said, Liyah. Don't make me have to come hunt your little ass down on Monday. You went to the wall for my baby, you stuck with her now. And she's stuck with you."

Not us. Not stuck with us.

Oh God. Here I go. Prime reason why I shouldn't have kissed this man or fucked him. Say what he wants, I have regrets.

I have real world, intimate knowledge of what Von Howard looks and feels like when he comes.

My regret is that I'll never do it again.

I can't.

Not if I know what's best for me.

Eight

"Can't no pussy whip me. It might give me some love taps, though."

Von

I wipe a paper towel down my client's shoulder, cleaning off the excess blue ink and blood. Leaning back, I study the dress I just finished coloring in. I toss a glance at the picture taped to the drawer of my Craftsman, comparing the image on her skin to the one in the photograph. I love what I do, creating art, immortalizing it on a person's body. It's more than leaving my mark in this world, like Picasso left behind his *The Old Guitarist* or Jean-Michel Basquiat his *Untitled*. Yeah, it definitely is that. But it's also this right here.

A client like Ms. Iman Johnson, a middle-aged math teacher at one of the local high schools, who lost her mother to cancer and wants to always carry her mother with her, no matter how many years have passed. It's giving people living art—art that breathes in their hearts, their souls, their memories.

That's what Sheree will never understand.

King Tattoos is more than brick and mortar and glass. It's more than money she can spend to flex for her so-called friends. It's more than a pawn to hurt me.

It's my dreams, my salvation, my refuge, my legacy. It's me.

And I'd be a liar not to say the thought of giving up any part of it scares the fuck out of me.

Pressing the pedal and turning the tattoo machine back on, I bend over and add a little more shading to the folds in the dress. Minutes later, I finish cleaning off the tattoo with green soap, admiring my work. It's gorgeous. Ain't no point in being modest about the shit. I'm damn good—hell, one of the best. After over twenty years of doing this, shit, I better be.

"Aight, Ms. Iman. I'm finished. You can have a look before I wrap it up."

She stands, stretching and rolling her shoulders after sitting for three hours. Turning around to me, she smiles, and it lights up her pretty face. "I can't thank you enough, Von. I'm so excited to see what that tattoo looks like."

Returning her smile, I motion toward the full-length mirror in the corner of my room. "Over here." I pick up a handheld mirror from my shelf and follow her across the room. When she turns, I hand it to her.

"Oh my God," she breathes, staring into the reflection, studying the tatted image of her mother. As Iman lifts her bright, misty eyes to me, a sense of satisfaction and accomplishment crowds into my chest.

"Thank you," she whispers, her fingers covering her mouth. "Thank you so much, Von. It's simply beautiful and *her.* God, it looks just like her." Her lashes flutter, and a soft sob slips out. But when she meets my gaze again, that smile curves her lips, and her eyes, though wet with tears, are gleaming. "I can't express how much this means to me. Thank you again."

"Of course. It was my pleasure. I'm honored to do it for you." Taking the mirror from her, I cross the room and grab the ointment and plastic wrap. "Let me wrap it up for you."

Minutes later, Iman stands at the front desk with instructions on aftercare and a tube of ointment, waiting for Malcolm to take her payment. Giving her one last wave, I return to my room and thoroughly sanitize it. My next appointment doesn't arrive for another couple of hours, and it's an original piece.

Picking up my Surface Pro, I sink down on my stool and turn the tablet on, navigating to the design I've been working on for a week. I frown down at it. My client requested a back piece that I'm doing the outline for today. We'll set up another appointment for the color. That's not the issue. The design is.

Usually, this part of the creative process is my favorite. After all, my love of art is what brought me to tattooing in the first place. My client wants an elephant. That's her only stipulation, leaving the other elements, such as the tattoo style, all up to me. I continue studying the design, trying to pinpoint what's bothering me. What about it I *don't* love. Because if I can't stand behind it, there's no way the piece is going on someone.

A knock sounds on my closed door, and without removing my gaze from the screen, I call out, "Yeah?"

"Hey, Von, your nanny's here," Malcolm says.

That snatches my attention from the art piece.

"What's that silly-ass smile for?" I snap, and his mouth only widens into a big grin. No fucking respect. "Y'know what? Never mind. I don't want to know. Send Liyah back. She's only here waiting on G."

And why did I feel the need to explain anything to him?

"So it's *Liyah* now, huh?" He arches an eyebrow. "You know I've been meaning to ask if you had a good time at Inferno. I mean, after you disappeared on us to go chill with *Liyah*."

"Malc, don't get thrown around this room, aight?" I glare at him.

"Fine, fine." He holds up both hands, but that grin remains. "I'll just go get your nanny. Just let baby girl know if she ever wants to join us at the strip club again, I don't mind making it rain—"

"I swear fo' God, Malcom…"

"Aight, aight! I'm going!" He laughs, backing out of the tattoo room, leaving the door cracked.

Moments later, Aaliyah appears in the doorway, hovering there as if she's torn between coming in or running in the other direction. I'm a little glad she's hesitating. It gives me a minute to get myself together, seeing her for the first time since Saturday night.

And gotdamn, do I need that minute.

It'd been two days since I'd had my fingers in her mouth, sliding over her tongue and tapping the back of her throat. Two days since feeling that juicy clit jump under my fingers. Two days since fucking in my truck like horny-ass teens and she'd come all over my dick and I'd painted her pussy with my seed.

And in not one of those days, minutes or seconds had I forgotten anything that happened between us. Not her delicate, intoxicating scent and taste. Not each whimper, groan or catch of her breath. Not the slick, soft glide of her pussy. Everything clung to me like a cranky kid, not leaving me in peace. I've been both dreading and looking forward to today.

Dreading because I would have to stand ten toes down on what I told her in my truck after my heart decided to crawl up out of my ass from that nut. What we'd done was a mistake and shouldn't be repeated. Regardless of my dick wanting to find itself back inside her slick, tight walls, I can't go there again. Have to somehow flip this back to the status quo.

And yet I'd looked forward to seeing her again. Something about that pretty face, those gorgeous eyes that I now know can gleam with lust and still somehow retain their air of innocence. Something about that peaceful yet ferocious spirit that could be a lamb one second and a lioness in the next.

Maybe the smartest thing to do would've been to let the nanny agency find her another job. It for damn sure would've been the safest. But just like Saturday night, just the thought of someone else caring for Gia…just thinking about walking into my house and not seeing Aaliyah's shyly smiling face… Yeah, no. Call me selfish, but I meant what I said. I would've ridden to Aaliyah's cousin's place, tossed her ass over my shoulder and hauled her back to my house.

Just 'cause I can't have her doesn't mean me and Gia can't *have* her.

She shouldn't have taken up for my little girl. That sealed her fate.

"Why're you standing in the doorway like you stole something?" I cock my head. "Come on in, ma. Gia isn't here yet. She should be on her way. Her mom's bringing her."

"Sorry." She moves fully into the room, and as she closes the door, I scan her petite frame, taking in that beautiful ass sitting up pretty in black leggings. A short jean jacket covers a green hoodie, and black-and-white Chuck Taylors adorn her feet. This woman—at least on the outside—is a far cry from the buttoned-up evangelist who walked into King Tattoos for an interview weeks ago. Both are pretty as fuck, though. She could be in a muumuu and a bonnet, and my dick would still brick up.

"I sent you a text that my last class was letting out a little late. Usually, if that happened, I still would've left to make sure I picked up Gia on time. But since she's not in school, I figured it would be okay…"

I don't say anything, just stare at her as she rambles on and then eventually trails off.

"You finished, ma?" I calmly ask.

She nods, releasing a heavy-sounding sigh. "Yes, sorry about that."

I shake my head. "You can cut out the apologizing. I texted you back that you were all good, and I meant that. Sheree decided to take G out for breakfast and some shopping anyway, so you're still on time."

My grip on my stylus tightens. Now, I'm not mad at Gia for how she handled herself down at the school, but I'm not rewarding her behavior, either. Not so with her mother. Instead of sitting her daughter down and reinforcing what I've already told her, Sheree decides to take Gia on a spending spree. I'on know if she's trying to win some popularity contest between us, but she fo' damn sure should be putting being a responsible parent above making me look like the Grinch. God… Sometimes she's one hell of a mother, and then other times she leaves me questioning her life choices. Shit, mine too for ever marrying her ass.

"Good…and thank you."

Waving a hand toward my tattoo chair, I return my attention to my tablet. Better than obsessively studying every detail of Aaliyah's face and trying not to stare at her curvy little body.

"What class were you in? And how's school going for you so far?"

Out of my peripheral vision, I catch her moving to the chair and settling onto it. She frowns down at the Saran Wrapped arms for a moment then says, "It's going amazing." For the first time since she entered my office, her voice loses that hesitancy and brightens, filling with enthusiasm.

"I love all my classes and professors. And everyone I've met has been so nice."

It's on the tip of my tongue to demand if any dusty-ass muthafuckas been pushing up on her, but I manage to bite it back. It's none of my business. What she does outside of taking care of Gia is none of my business.

And yeah, I'm lying and trying to convince myself of that shit.

"The school is huge, and I'm only in my general courses, but still, it's like I've found my own little community in my classes, with like-minded people who have the same interests and passions that I do," she continues to gush on. "Take the class I just finished for the day. It's called Film and the Moving Image. We're studying perception, comprehension and interpretation regarding film and other moving-image media. We're studying texts and documentaries, doing screenings. It's hard work, definitely, but it's so interesting. I'm analyzing films, videos, broadcasts and other media and seeing things like dialogue, text and expression in ways I've never looked at them or even noticed." A small, self-deprecating smile flirts across her mouth, tugging at the corner. "I'm sorry for going on and on. I must sound like a nerd, getting excited over classes and school."

"Nah, you good. I like it. And what I tell you about apologizing? You're excited over school. What's there to be sorry for?"

She shrugs. "I'm so—understood," she modifies when I arch an eyebrow. Huffing out a chuckle, she says, "I guess

I'm so used to hiding my love of art or making excuses for it that it's difficult changing my mentality."

Yeah, that right there.

My jaw clenches as I breathe deep, attempting not to reveal the anger that flares to life inside me. I haven't forgotten a damn thing she confided in me Saturday night. Not what that fucker uncle of hers did or her bitch-ass daddy's reaction. Even her mother ain't getting a pass from me. One tried to violate Aaliyah—nah, ain't no "tried to," he did because he violated her trust—and the other two completely failed her. There ain't no way if Gia came to me with something like that I would have told her to keep it to herself so we wouldn't be embarrassed. Shit. I'd disappear a muthafucka and give condolences to his mama right over his casket. Even though her father's a "man of God," he should've fucked his brother up first and prayed for forgiveness later.

I don't understand that shit to save my life. Don't want to, either.

"On your résumé, I remember seeing some college. You didn't major in art or at least take some classes before now?" I return my attention to the design on my tablet so she won't spot my disgust for her parents. For some reason, she obviously loves and respects them.

Fuck 'em.

She releases a small laugh that carries zero hint of humor. "God no. First, my father paid for community college, and if I'd majored in anything other than business administration, he would've pulled all financial support. And since he was able to access my academic records and see my schedule, I couldn't even sneak art classes."

I tap the screen, erasing the safari landscape that I'd drawn in the background. Too expected. Too boring.

"What did he have against art? It's not like these days people can't make money from it. Between graphic design, animation and even education, there're plenty of jobs for a person to get into and earn decent money."

She sighs, and I flick a glance in her direction in time to catch a pained expression waver across her face. It's there and gone in a moment, but I saw it. I file it away.

"That might be true for a lot of people but not Bishop Montgomery's daughter. My great-grandfather pastored his own church as did my grandfather and now my father. Because he didn't have a son to continue the legacy—"

"I don't know if he's heard of this thing called women pastors." My sarcasm game is strong.

She gives me a rueful smile. "Not in our family. My father didn't even consider that, not that I would've wanted to anyway. But the option that was pounded into my head from the time I can remember was *marrying* a pastor, becoming a first lady and helping him run the church in whatever capacity he needed—or allowed. That's the reason Daddy okayed business administration. It could come in handy with church business."

"If he planned your life out to that degree, I'm surprised he didn't have a man lined up for you to marry," I mutter.

"Right," she murmurs, then practically leaps out of the chair and approaches me. "What are you working on?" She steps to the side of my stool as I lean back, so she can see the design. "That's beautiful." She glances at me then back to the tablet. "You're so good."

I snort even as warmth barrels through me at her compliment, at the admiration in her voice. "Why do you sound so surprised?"

"Silly, isn't it?" She smiles, and I drag my fascinated gaze from her mouth and return it to the screen. "Of course, you can draw. The first time I came in here, I saw your work on the walls in the lobby. But seeing it here…" She shakes her head. "Have you decided what to do with the background? Or is the elephant the whole design?"

"Nah, that's what I'm having trouble with now." I frown, and before I can question why I'm sharing this with her, I admit, "My client didn't specify what all she wanted in the tattoo, just an elephant and a back piece. She's leaving everything else up to me. And she'll be here in—" I peer down at the face of my Patek Philippe "—a little over an hour, and I'm still not finished with the sketch."

"Hmm." She inches closer, and her citrusy scent infiltrates my space and senses.

Damn, she smells good. And as of two nights ago, I can attest to the fact that her skin tastes like that beautiful fragrance. Yeah, I shouldn't be thinking about that, not in this moment, with her leaning over me, and my black joggers no defense against my dick print.

"Who is your client? Do you know anything about her?"

"Just the little I learned in her consultation. Single mom

of a little girl, works as a manager in a steakhouse, loves elephants because her grandmother collected figurines of them."

"They also symbolize strength and determination." When I look at her, she smiles with a small shrug. "My mom is a Delta," she says in explanation. I didn't attend college, but I get the reference to the Black sorority, one of the Divine Nine. "I, too, grew up with elephant sculptures and figurines around the house. Do you mind?"

She extends her hand toward my tablet, and after a brief hesitation, I hand it to her, curiosity curling inside me. More than a few times, I'd come home and found her curled up on my couch, a sketch pad balanced on her knees, her head bent over it. But I never got a chance to check out anything she was working on because no sooner did she hear me than she flipped the cover down and stuffed the pad in her bag. I'd be lying if I said stealing it while she was out of the room hadn't crossed my mind.

Most of the time, I don't let anyone have a hand in my designs. They are mine, and I am territorial. Shit, it annoys me when I scroll through social media and see someone with my exact shit that didn't credit me for it. But with the internet, people see something they like, take it to a tattoo artist and say they want it, and sometimes the artist doesn't care about who the design came from, just getting that money. Still…annoys the hell out of me.

But, as I hand over the Surface Pro to Aaliyah, none of that irritation makes itself known. Nah, I just stand up, waving toward the stool, indicating for her to take my place. She settles down, her head already lowered and her hand hovering over the tablet. I stand back, giving her room, but I can't take my eyes off her.

This side of Aaliyah is new. And since she's started working for me, I've been introduced to a few of those sides. The unassuming, pious church girl. The fierce, protective nanny. The sensual, greedy siren.

Now the talented, passionate artist.

I can't choose which one captivates me more.

It's like she tunes out me and the world as she works. Sometimes her hand moves slowly, deliberately, and a moment later, it'll fly as if caught in a sudden burst of inspiration.

She's…magnificent.

Twenty minutes later, she lifts her head, the hand holding the stylus lowering to her side. I push off the wall from where I posted up, hungrily taking in everything about her.

For a long moment, she stares down at whatever she drew then, finally, shifts her gaze to me, and, for a second, I'm snared in that beautiful brown gaze like a starving animal caught in a trap. Only by sheer will do I snatch my scrutiny away from her face and drop it to the design she worked on for nearly a half hour.

Shit.

As if of their own accord, my feet carry me closer—so close my chest bumps her shoulder. But the first physical contact with her since Saturday night barely registers as I stare down at what she created.

"Damn, Aaliyah." Baby girl has left me fucking speechless.

She left the elephant I'd drawn as it was, but even with

that as the centerpiece, it appears to be a different design. A smaller, somehow daintier elephant—if an elephant can be called dainty—is protected in the shadow of the larger one. In the background hangs a moon with twinkling stars and tall grass that seems to sway against the animals' feet. Lush lilies peek out from behind the elephants' large ears, under their tusks, near the arch of their trunks. The flowers shouldn't have worked—they shouldn't go with the large animals and the glimpses of a savanna. But they do. They add this ethereal beauty that makes the art seem photographic yet almost otherworldly.

In a word, it's stunning.

Perhaps taking my shocked silence for disapproval, she waves a hand over the drawing.

"I know I took liberties with the design," she rambles, nerves clear in her voice. "But I thought with her being a single mother, incorporating the juvenile elephant could reflect her protectiveness and love for her own child as well as reflect the girl she once was with her grandmother. The African landscape symbolizes home, while the lilies signify innocence, purity, both her child's and the love they share..." She chuckles nervously. "Well, say something."

"It's beautiful." That's so inadequate. And for someone whose dream has been ridiculed and discounted time and again by people she admired and respected, "beautiful" isn't enough. "Nah, Liyah. It's fucking gorgeous. I had no idea you could..." Still staring at it, I'm *awed* by her talent. By *her.* "You took what I said about my client and created a piece that's not just stunning but thoughtful and intimate to her alone. I don't say this lightly, ma. But you're gifted and meant to be on the path you're on. Art is what you were born to do, and anyone seeing this—" I dip my chin toward the tablet "—would clearly see that. If they don't, then they're willingly blind." Though touching her is unwise, I pinch her chin between my finger and thumb. "Thank you."

Lowering my head, I press a gentle kiss to her full lips. It's not sexual but admiring, grateful. At least, I didn't intend it to be sexual. But as soon as her lips part on a soft gasp, I can't stop myself from slipping my tongue inside, lazily tasting her. I half expect her to pull away, to push me away. But she doesn't. Instead, she tilts her head, silently offering me deeper access. And I take full advantage, reacquainting myself with every bit of her.

She moans, nearly drowning out the knock at my door.

"Hey, Von—oh, shit. My bad." Malcolm slams the door shut after his timely—or untimely, I can't decide—interruption.

Releasing Aaliyah, I take one last, hard look at her—at the flush staining her cheekbones, at the damp, kiss-swollen mouth. Irritation and regret sweep through me, but at the same time, I can't be too mad at Malcolm. He saved me from myself. So much for my determination to not touch her again. Took me less than an hour of being in her company, and I failed that challenge.

Swiping a hand over my braids, I shift back a step and call out, "Come in."

As if he never moved from the other side of the door, Malcolm opens it again, a sheepish grin on his face. Curiosity brightens the gaze he switches from me to Aaliyah then back to me.

"Sorry about that," he says.

"Yeah, what I tell you about waiting for me to actually answer before coming in?"

He winces, but the smile still decorating his face ruins his remorse. "My bad, Von," he repeats. "Believe me, I won't forget that again." He snickers.

Gritting my teeth, I glare at him. "What, Malcom? You came in here for a reason."

"Right, right. The Wicked Bitch of the West Side is out in the lobby with G. You lucky I didn't let her run back here like she tried to. That could've been…awkward."

Fuck.

I got so wrapped up in Aaliyah, I'd momentarily forgotten Sheree was on her way here with Gia.

"Thanks, Malc. We'll be right out." With a nod, he leaves, closing the door behind him, and I turn to Aaliyah. "Aye—"

"Let's go." She jumps off the stool, setting the tablet down and damn near flying for the door. "I've missed Gia, and we don't want to keep her waiting."

Sighing, I swipe a hand down my face and over my beard. I shake my head. It's a good thing I let her go because I apparently don't know my head from my ass when it comes to her. I follow Aaliyah and catch up with her just as she reaches the doorway leading to the lobby. Grasping her upper arm, I slow her down. I'm not so in my head that I'll allow her to walk out there to deal with my ex-wife unprotected. On a good day, Sheree is on some bullshit. Seeing as how I don't know what the hell she's going to be on today, I'm not taking any chances. And nothing in me believes she'll keep it together just because Gia is with her.

I rub a hand over the back of my neck, feeling the dull throbbing of a headache coming on. Not an unusual reaction when having to deal with Sheree.

As soon as I step out, I spot Gia, and even the fact that her mother stands behind her doesn't dim my joy at seeing her. It's been three days since she's been home, and I miss her every time she's at Sheree's house.

"Liyaaah!" Gia shrieks, sprinting toward Aaliyah. I reach out and put a hand on Aaliyah's back to steady her as Gia crashes into her, hooking her arms around Aaliyah's thighs. "I missed you!"

"Well, damn." I snort. "I'm standing right here, and I'm just your daddy."

"I missed you, too, Daddy." She grins up at me, her pretty hazel eyes wide. "I just missed Liyah more."

"Shawty, you don't know nothing about loyalty." I mug her and she laughs, and the sound reaches right into my chest and snatches up my heart like it stole something.

"Ahem." Sheree clears her throat, and I glance over at my ex. Her narrowed gaze is fixed on my hand that's still pressed to Aaliyah's back. When she shifts her attention to me, I silently sigh at the anger simmering in the same hazel eyes she gave Gia.

"I take it you're the nanny I've heard so much about *from Gia*," she says to Aaliyah, although her glare doesn't leave me.

"Yes, I'm Aaliyah Montgomery. It's nice to finally meet

you." Smiling, Aaliyah steps forward despite Gia not letting her go.

She extends her hand toward Sheree, and after a hesitation that borders on rude and awkward, Sheree accepts Aaliyah's hand, briefly shaking it then dropping it like her palm's sticky with shit. She scrunches up her nose as if she smells it, too.

Irritation scratches at me. How is it that every day Sheree wakes up and chooses to be a bitch? And for no gotdamn reason. The shit's gotta be exhausting, I know it is for me since I have to deal with it.

"Yes, *finally.*" Sheree's lip curls up at the corner. "It's only been weeks that you've been caring for my daughter. This should've happened before now. No offense, but it would've been nice to have been consulted about hiring you. She's my daughter, so I should've had an opinion about who's taking care of her."

That irritation flares to a deep, burning anger. Sheree's words were deliberately chosen, I have no doubt about that. And though I know she's being petty as fuck, it doesn't stop the pain from stabbing me in the chest.

It's some shit. When she wants something from me, she's our daughter. But when she's pissed, Gia becomes her daughter.

The "get the fuck outta here with that" sits on my tongue like a live coal. A glance down at Gia keeps me from cursing her mother out, no matter how much her trifling, deceitful ass deserves it. Sheree doesn't give a damn that our daughter has a front-row seat to the shit show she's stirring, but I do.

Holding out my hand to Gia, I wait until she takes it

then I walk her over to the front desk. "Baby girl, go with Malcolm for a few minutes, aight? I bought your favorite Pop-Tarts for you. Go have one, okay?" She could eat the sugary breakfast food any time of the day, she was that obsessed with them.

"Okay, Daddy." Some of the joy has dimmed from her voice, and that has my hands itching to shake some sense into her mother.

I wait until Malcolm disappears into the back with Gia before turning and stalking back to Sheree. Thank God the lobby is free of clients because I don't do drama, and that's all my ex-wife is about.

"Look, Sheree, I'm not doing this with you. Now you know how I get down, so don't think just 'cause our daughter is back there that I'm gonna let you come up in here and show your ass. Not in my shop."

"Your shop, your shop. That's all you care about as usual." She waves a hand, resentment dripping from every word. "All I'm saying is, you could've included me in hiring a nanny for Gia. How do I know she's even capable or experienced enough for the job? I'm sorry—what's your name again?—Amira? How old are you anyway? Nothing personal, but you look young enough to need a nanny yourself." She chuckles at the tail end of the insult.

I part my lips to tell her to get the hell on, but Aaliyah tilts her head, the same sweet smile on her face.

"It's Aaliyah, but you know that. And usually when someone starts off any sentence with 'no offense' or 'nothing personal,' they mean just the opposite. But since you seem to be upset and in a bad mood, I'm not going to charge it to you because I totally understand that we all have difficult days when we wake up on the wrong side of the bed. And bless your heart, you *should* be concerned about who's in your daughter's life, as you're her mother. That's your right, another reason I will gladly excuse your bad behavior. I'm twenty-four and quite capable of caring for Gia, as I'm sure she's expressed to you. And from the time I've spent around her father, I am very assured he wouldn't hire anyone if he didn't have the confidence they could protect and care for his daughter. So please don't worry, okay? I hope that makes you feel better."

Well…shit.

I glance at Sheree, and her stunned expression reflects the same surprise reverberating inside me. I don't know why I'm shocked, though, after how Aaliyah took down the principal up at Gia's school. Still… This must be that nice-nasty I hear about with Southerners. She even threw a "bless your heart" up in that muthafucka. And I didn't have to be from there to know exactly what that meant.

Apparently, so does Sheree because the surprise washes away from her face, anger pinching her mouth and darkening her eyes. Yeah, I'd be embarrassed, too, if someone who looked like they were woken up by chirping birds and dress-making mice gave me the business.

"Excuse me," Sheree hisses, leaning forward.

I shift forward, too. Now if she thinks she's gonna put hands on lil' mama, she got the wrong one.

From the fury tightening her face, Sheree catches my

movement, and she barks, "Who *the fuck* do you think you are talking to me like that?"

Aaliyah shrugs, lifting her palms. "The nanny."

I try to swallow down my laughter. I really do. But the bark of laughter from the back tells me two things: one, Chelle and the other artists are listening to everything that's going on out here, and two, they're enjoying their selves at Sheree's expense.

"Bitch," Sheree snarls, stepping closer, but I'm faster and step in front of her, blocking Aaliyah.

"Nah, yo. Watch that *bitch* word," I say, even though minutes earlier Malcolm had used it toward Sheree. Funny how hearing it applied to Aaliyah has me feeling some kind of way, but when it was directed toward Sheree? Yeah, she earned that. You had to give respect to earn it. And Sheree had lost all of mine a long time ago. "Now I told you I'm not gonna let you bring this bullshit up in here. You've dropped Gia off, so you can go."

"Oh, it's like that?" She crosses her arms, loosing a cackle. "You must be giving ol' girl the dick for you to be standing here defending her 'n' shit, and for her to think she can talk to me any ol' way." With another bitter burst of laughter, she leans around me, smirking at Aaliyah. "You think just 'cause you bussin' it open and giving him that young girl pussy that you can keep him, sweetie? Got news for you. Men like him don't stay, and they for damn sure aren't loyal or faithful—"

The fuck? "You for real, Sheree?" I growl. "This what you want to do? Right here?" The hurt seethes, and only

Gia being in the building keeps me from airing *all* her shit for everyone to hear.

"Since that was directed to me, please let me clear up any misconception," Aaliyah says, her tone still sweet as sugar. "You are the only one who seems preoccupied with who Von is giving 'dick' to, as you put it." And goddamn. Even though I'm mad as fuck, hearing that prim, soft voice wrap around the word *dick* has my own hardening as if it came accompanied by a hand job. "Von is my employer, and whatever is between y'all isn't my business or concern, so please leave me out of it."

It's like every time Aaliyah opens her mouth or makes her presence known, it stirs an anger in Sheree that should be directed at me.

"Whatever," Sheree snaps. "Just know your place. You're the *nanny*. Not Gia's mother. So next time you want to take yourself up to *my baby's* school and show your ass, remember that. Yeah—" she smiles, looking like a shark showing all her teeth as she switches her attention to me "—I called up to the school to find out why Gia wasn't in school today since you didn't see fit to give me the full story. The principal told me how this one—" she jabs a thumb in Aaliyah's direction "—came up there. I think my lawyer would be interested to know the nanny had to go up there 'cause you couldn't be bothered until *she* didn't know how to act. Got my daughter up there fighting. I wonder what the court will think about that?"

"You threatening me?" I quietly ask, studying her.

I love my baby girl; God knows that I do. But her mother?

I'm questioning my life decisions right now, staring at her smug expression. There are times like this one when I really do believe she hates me more than she cares for Gia.

"They'll probably wonder why the school didn't call you in the first place," I say. "Then they'll probably ask when was the last time you were up at the school for a parent-teacher conference, a parents' day, hell, to bring Gia lunch? And just in case they do ask, best believe I'll have the answer. Then they'll most likely wonder why a mother who spends her days taking selfies for the 'Gram is even in their court on some bullshit. Then they'll revisit why they didn't give her physical custody of her daughter in the first place. And we both know the extraordinary circumstances of them giving that to me instead of you, don't we? Want me to remind you since you insist on standing in my fucking shop when I've given you chance after chance to leave?"

Several beats of silence pass between us where we stare at each other, until she balls her face up and whispers, "I hate you."

Not giving me a chance to return the sentiment, she storms out. My heart pounds in my chest, the fury, the fucking pain, coasting through me. Fists clenched at my sides, I inhale a deep breath, bowing my head, trying to fight past the emotion assaulting me.

When a small hand covers one of my mine, I almost snatch my fist away, not wanting or needing her sympathy or pity. But at the last moment, I stifle that urge. I don't pull away. And though it sends splinters of fear through me, I call out my lie, admitting the truth.

I do want her touch.

Her softness grounds me in the here and now, reminds me that I can't allow my resentment and hurt about Sheree and our past to harden the part of me that Gia needs.

Flipping my hand over, I thread my fingers through Aaliyah's and ignore the words whispering through my head like an indictment.

You need her, too.

Nah. Been there, got the ex-wife to prove it.

I'm good.

Nine

"If God watches over drunks and fools, then no worries, I'm sufficiently covered."

Aaliyah

"Liyah, can I ask you something?"

I pause in the middle of grabbing a book for Gia's nightly bedtime story to look over at her. With her freshly braided hair under her silk bonnet and her pink unicorn pajamas on, she's so cute tucked under the covers. After meeting her mother today, I can see where Gia inherited her pretty face. And though I don't see much of Von in his daughter, that confidence and boldness is all her father. Even though her mother is a…piece of work, Gia is a perfect combination of her parents and, still, all her own person. I've quickly come to love this little girl in the weeks I've been taking care of her.

"Sure, sweetie, you can ask me anything," I say, slipping *Broken Crayons Still Color* by Toni Collier from her shelf for our nightly read. Gia has an impressive library, and we are working through all the books. "What's on your mind?" I settle on the edge of her bed.

She scrunches her face up, then a moment later, she softly asks, "Why do Mommy and Daddy hate each other?"

The question knocks the wind out of me, and for a moment, I struggle for air. I easily see the sadness in her pretty hazel eyes, and I just want to hug her close, shield her from all the hurt no seven-year-old should feel.

This isn't my place. Truthfully, I should tell her to wait and talk to her father when he comes home from work. But I can't. I won't be an adult in her life who ignores her feelings or lies to her.

Carefully, choosing my words, I say, "Baby, your parents don't hate each other—"

"Un-huh," she interrupts me, nodding her head so hard her bonnet slips forward. "I heard Mommy tell Daddy she hates him today. And she tells Aunt Jasmine all the time on the phone when she thinks I don't hear her."

Jesus.

I briefly close my eyes. After having encountered her mother this morning, I don't know why I'm surprised. She'd been ready to throw down in front of Gia at the shop if Von hadn't convinced her to leave. So it shouldn't shock me that she's careless enough to badmouth her ex-husband—*Gia's father*—within her earshot. Even if it's accidental. How 'bout not do it when she's in the house and there's even a chance of that happening?

"She might say that sometimes, and those words are hurtful. We shouldn't *hate* anyone. But I don't think she means it, and I don't believe your father feels that way, either." When Gia frowns again, I try another tactic. "Don't you sometimes say things you don't mean? Didn't you just tell me last week that your friend Khamari gets on your nerves? You didn't mean that—"

"Un-huh!" Gia interrupts again with another adamant head nod. "I meant it. She wouldn't stop singing whenever Halle sung 'Part of Your World' in *The Little Mermaid*, so I told her she got on my nerves."

Lord ha' mercy. I can't argue that logic.

"Okay, you might have meant it in that moment, but does she always get on your nerves? You still like her, and she's still your friend, right?"

"Yes," Gia says. Her frown deepens for a moment then it clears. "So Mommy and Daddy only hate each other sometimes?"

"They don't hate one another, sweetie. Is your mommy mad at your daddy sometimes, and he gets mad at her right back? Yes. But we all get upset at people, and our feelings get hurt. When they do, we can say things we don't really mean at the time—not like with you and Khamari," I add, cutting her off when she parts her lips to correct me. In spite of the serious topic, a laugh bubbles inside me. I wait a second to tamp it down then continue. "We can say mean, hurtful things, but it doesn't mean we have hate in our hearts for the other person. The most important thing, Gia, is they love *you* so much. And their love for you will always be so big that nothing else matters, okay?"

She stares at me, and finally, she says, "Okay. But, Liyah?"

she asks before I can breathe a sigh of relief that I waded through that minefield.

"Yes?"

"When they fight, my stomach hurts. And I get sad."

"I know, sweetie, and I'm sorry. Have you ever told them that it makes you sad?"

She shakes her head, dropping her eyes from mine. "I don't want them to be mad at me," she whispers.

"Oh, Gia, they would never be mad at you for telling the truth." I can say that for a certainty with Von. Just from what I've witnessed, and the kind of father he is with her, I think it would hurt his heart to know she's feeling this way. "Why don't you do this? Tomorrow, tell your father how you're feeling and see what he says, okay? Start with him. I bet you'll feel so much better after you do."

Another beat of silence where she studies me, as if judging if I'm being honest with her. Then she nods and a smile spreads across her little face. "Okay. Now can you read me a story?"

Children. Their attention can switch like lightning. Especially when they feel secure.

"*We* can read the story. You're such a good reader, we can do it together."

She beams, sitting up. "Okay!"

About a half hour later, I pull her bedroom door closed, leaving it open a small crack. Sighing, the heaviness from my conversation with Gia settles back on my shoulders.

It's not your place, I remind myself. Especially after that scene with Sheree and Von at the shop. She'd made it abundantly clear she didn't want me included in anything that didn't have to do with nannying. Honestly, I understand where she was coming from. It must be hard watching another woman with her child when she doesn't have her on an everyday basis. I can only sympathize with her. And with a daughter like Gia, who's such a joy? Yes, it must be difficult. But her nasty attitude and mouth had me popping off.

Yes, I'm quiet and some people mistake that for weakness and not having a backbone. As Tamara would say, they eff around and find out. Well, Tamara would say the f-bomb…

You're only spineless when it comes to your father.

Bitchy inner voice, one. Me, zero.

I head for the living room and drop down to the couch. Like I do most nights while waiting for Von to come home, I pull out my sketch pad and flip to my current drawing. It's one I started a couple days ago of Gia running across the park playground. Smiling, I start working on the background, capturing the jungle gym, seesaw and swings. In class, I'm learning how to perfect depth and perspective, and I can already see the results in my work.

Without my permission, my mind drifts to earlier today when I drew the tattoo design for Von. Other than my professors and students in my classes, he was the first person to see any of my art in years. After being told time and again that drawing and my interest in art was a waste, I stopped sharing. I stopped talking about it at all. What does it say that I trusted Von with that part of me? Or that my stomach had been in knots as I awaited his opinion? Or that his opinion had mattered?

Oh, I don't need to think too hard.

It means I'm getting in too deep, and I should save myself before there's no coming back. Tamara had warned me about catching feelings for Von, and I'd assured her that wouldn't—couldn't—happen. God, I'm a fool.

The alarm announcing the opening of the front door beeps, and my belly bungee jumps. I don't turn around to watch him enter, instead keeping my gaze trained on my drawing pad. After the way we parted—not to mention that kiss in his tattoo room—I'm all over the place on how to deal with him, talk to him. He has me so confused, off-kilter and…well, hot, that my instinct is to withdraw.

Anything I want as bad as I want Von can't be good for me. It can't be *for me*, period.

I know who I am—or, at least, I'm getting there. And I'm not built for the reckless, overwhelming passion Von introduced me to days ago and got me reacquainted with today. I, who has been starved of affection and love, would too easily mistake tenderness for affection and lust for love.

For so many years, my father smothered me with his overprotection and chains of religion. Now, it's up to me to protect myself. Choose myself. And I choose not to leave Chicago wrecked and in pieces.

"Aaliyah."

His low, rough-silk voice sends pleasure tripping over my skin. I work not to betray my reaction. "Hi, Von."

"Gia in bed?"

"Yes, she's been asleep for about thirty minutes now."

"Okay." The rasp of his beard beneath his hand tickles my ears. "Thanks again for staying late."

"It's no problem. It never is."

"You not going to look at me, ma? And you call me rude."

My head jerks up from my pad, and I scowl at him. "Seriously?"

"There you are," he murmurs. "Now what's up, ma? What's going on that you're up in here hiding from me?"

"I'm not..." He arches an eyebrow, and I trail off. "Whatever," I mutter.

He stares at me for another few long moments then turns, heading out of the living room in the direction of the kitchen.

"We saved you some dinner just in case you're hungry," I call after him, stuffing my pad in my bag. "Your plate is in the microwave."

I grab my book bag and purse then stand, setting them both on the couch while I go to the closet to grab my coat. It's almost November, and the nights have gotten colder. Most native Chicagoans aren't fazed by it, but my thin Alabama blood has me shivering against the cool air.

"Let me ask you something." He appears in the entryway to the kitchen, plate of chicken and mashed potatoes in his hand. "You can't cook, can you?"

I stare at him, the answer stuck in my throat. Is this a trick question? I mean, this far into my employment, I don't *think* he'll fire me but...

"Um...why do you ask?"

"Because I know Church's chicken when I eat it." He smirks, biting into a leg. Why seeing his strong, white teeth sinking into the meat is so sexy, I can't even begin to explain. There's something wrong with me. "And every time you stay late, there's some kind of takeout container or bag in the garbage. Either you can't cook, ma, or you lazy as fuck. And ain't shit lazy about you. So…"

"In my defense, I didn't include cooking skills on my résumé," I mutter.

He snorts. "Since you taking care of my daughter includes her not starving, being able to fix a meal was implied. I believe it's called a lie of omission."

He doesn't *look* angry. Still, I purse my lips, studying him.

"Am I fired?" I ask.

He huffs out a laugh. "No, Liyah, you're not fired. Even if I wanted to, Gia would probably leave to go live with you rather than stay with me. But let me know how much you spend on food so I can include that in your check. You shouldn't be coming out the pocket to feed my daughter."

I nod even though I don't mind. Especially since I have to eat, too. But as a student paying for the part of tuition the scholarship doesn't cover, I'm not turning down extra money. I might have my pride, but I'm no fool.

"Thank you." I turn around, intending to head back to the living room, grab my stuff and leave. But I only go a couple of steps before I stop and face him again. And I'm speaking before fully acknowledging my intent to do so. "Can I… talk to you? If you're not too tired."

He bites into the chicken again, swallowing before replying, "Yeah. Sit while I finish eating." Dipping his chin toward the breakfast bar and the stools lined up in front of it, he sets his plate on top and retrieves a bottle of water from the refrigerator while I follow his command. Water in hand, he sits across from me and resumes eating. "What's up?"

Inhaling a breath, I hold it, formulating in my head exactly how to explain this now that I've broached the subject. Smoothing a hand over my ponytail, I meet his steady, bright gaze.

"I don't feel like I'm betraying Gia's confidence since she promised me she would talk to you tomorrow..."

The fork in Von's hand pauses halfway to his mouth, and after a second, he slowly lowers it back to his plate. "What do you mean? What about Gia?"

"Tonight, she confided in me." I relay to him my conversation with his daughter. He sits quietly as I talk, not interrupting me. When I finish, he remains silent, seemingly no longer interested in his dinner as he hasn't touched it since we sat down. "I encouraged her to talk to you about how she's feeling, and she agreed to, but I didn't want you to be blindsided. I also wanted you to be prepared so you wouldn't inadvertently...well..."

"Hurt her. Reject her," he finishes, staring down at his plate, hands flattened on either side of it. "The last thing I wanted was for Gia to be traumatized by this. Of course, I knew she would be affected by her parents divorcing, but I tried to minimize the hurt and confusion as much as possible. But they don't make DIY shows on how to break up a marriage without fucking up your kids."

"Von," I whisper. "You're doing your best."

"Am I?" He looses a hard chuckle. "When my daughter walks around here scared and worried about how she's going to make me and her mother feel by being honest with us,

I'm not so sure. Her one job is to be a kid. To go to school, clean her room, play with her friends and enjoy herself. Not deal with mine and Sheree's shit. Definitely not be emotionally responsible for us. Nah, Liyah, even if we are doing our best, it's not fucking good enough."

I don't know what to say to that. There's nothing I can say that will change his mind or stop him from beating himself up. So I just lean across the breakfast bar and cover one of his hands with mine. After a long moment, he flips his hand over and grasps mine.

"You're an amazing father," I say, breaking the long, heavy silence.

I'd hoped my words would comfort him, but instead they seem to have the opposite effect when his grip on me tightens. His big body stiffens, and it's almost like he's rejecting my assurance with his mind and body.

"Von, are you o—"

"Did you believe my ex-wife today? What she said about me not being loyal? Or faithful?" he asks, interrupting my inquiry into his well-being.

I blink, straightening and slowly sliding my palm back across the bar top until it rests in my lap. "I didn't think about it one way or the other. I just took it as her being petty and trying to throw shade."

He gives another of those sharp chuckles and scrubs a hand down his face, his tell that he's in his emotions.

"Is it—" I pause, my pulse echoing in my head "—true?"

Why does the thought of him being a cheat cause my stomach to churn?

He stares at me, his gaze unwavering. "Would it matter if it was?"

I want to say no, that it wouldn't matter, that their marriage and divorce was their business, just as I'd said in the tattoo shop earlier. But I can't lie. How I was raised and my own standard of right and wrong won't allow me to lie. Fidelity, faithfulness, they are character traits, and if he could lie and betray his wife—the woman he'd promised his heart, loyalty and future to—what else would he lie about, who else would he be disloyal to?

"Yes," I admit. "It would."

"Good." The fierceness in his voice and the hardening of his eyes take me aback. "It should change how you see me. People get it fucked-up. When you cheat, it isn't just betraying your partner. It's saying fuck you to your relationship, your family. It's stealing time from not just the person you married but from your kids, your extended relatives. It's jeopardizing your world, not just your marriage. It's saying getting a nut is more important than other people's hearts, other people's emotional pain, their security. It's selfish, and I couldn't do it. I wouldn't do it." He pauses. "But Sheree did."

I rock back on the stool. Shock slaps through me in ice-cold waves. I don't know what I expected, but it wasn't *that*. From the animosity and…bitterness that seeped from his ex, I wouldn't have guessed she was the one who'd violated their vows. If I'm honest, she seemed more like a woman scorned than an ex-wife with no emotional ties to her ex-husband.

"Yeah." He nods. "I was faithful. And shit, keeping it a buck, I had plenty of opportunities to cheat. Do you know how much pussy is thrown at me in my shop alone? I'm not gon' lie and say I've never been tempted. But crossing that line? Hell no. Not even when the communication between me and Sheree dissolved to arguments and silences. Apparently, her definition of faithfulness was a little looser than mine. By the time I found out, the affair had been going on for years. Four to be exact, off and on. Whenever she got pissed with me, she'd run back to him."

Wow. I shake my head, stunned. Four years? That's not an affair; that's a full-fledged relationship.

"How did you…?"

"Find out?" His lips curl into a smile that hurts to look at. "Her cell, of course. She guarded that muthafucka like there was a ransom on it. The phone went with her everywhere, including the bathroom when she went to take a shower. As suspect as that was, it still didn't occur to me she was on some snake shit until Gia ended up with her phone one day, just playing with it, and Sheree lost her fucking mind. It's one thing to be protective of the damn thing but to go off on your daughter because she handled it? Nah, that's when I knew she was doing something. Then she slipped up one night and forgot to take it into the bathroom with her. And when her phone rang, I answered it. It was a friend of mine on the other end. And since he ain't ever called me 'baby,' I figured out real quick he wasn't looking for me."

"That's… Wow. I'm so sorry that happened to you. And with your friend. That's a double betrayal."

He crosses his arms, leaning them on the counter. "No cap, I felt like a lil' bitch answering that phone. What's the saying? What you go looking for you'll find? I ain't really give a fuck about him. We weren't that close, but I didn't ever expect it of her."

Pain for him radiates through me. I didn't even love Gregory, but discovering he'd betrayed me like that? It still would've hurt me. So I can't even imagine…

"I'm sorry, Von," I whisper again. "I'm so sorry."

He flicks a hand as if waving off my words. "I could've gotten past the cheating. Or the stealing. I didn't mention that, did I? Yeah, she stole money from me, too. We wouldn't have stayed together because I couldn't ever trust her again. But neither devastated me. Nah, that came when I hung up with ol' boy and scrolled through her phone, looking for a text thread between them. That's when I found a text from a couple of years earlier when he asked her if Gia was his."

Oh my. *God.*

"What?" I rasp, grasping the edge of the bar top to keep myself from swaying right off the stool. I had to have misheard him. He didn't…he couldn't… "Are you saying there's a possibility Gia's not your biological daughter?"

A sadness so deep, so profound flashes across his face, it's like a spasm of agony. He turns his head, glancing away from me. When he returns his gaze to me, a mask claims his features, but his eyes… His eyes tell the true story. I didn't misread that expression.

"It's not a possibility," he flatly says. But before relief can make a full sweep through me, he adds, "It's a fact. When I confronted Sheree, she confirmed it. Gia isn't mine."

I can't *not* touch him. Even as astonishment continues to clash inside my head, pounding against my temples, I grasp his hand again. Like when I reached out before, he stiffens, and then his behavior takes on new meaning.

You're an amazing father.

That's what I'd said to him, and though he hadn't said anything in response, I can tell now that he'd physically recoiled from the praise. From "father."

"Don't you ever say that again," I snap. Anger pours through me, burning away the shock.

Von's head snaps back, and he studies me through narrowed eyes. "The hell?"

"Don't," I repeat, emphasizing it with a hard squeeze. "I don't care if God Himself donated His DNA to Gia, *you* are her father. You provide for her, care for her, support her. But more than that, you're her hero. You show up for her. You make her feel safe. You make her feel like the most beautiful, smartest and most loved little girl on this earth. And this isn't something I'm guessing at—I see it every day I'm with her. You are her world. And from a person who grew up with a father in the house who wasn't necessarily present… A father who I knew loved me but didn't affirm me… A father whose love felt conditional on my behavior and obedience… You are a gift. You're a gift to her and to me. I look at you and know fatherhood isn't something to fear but to revere."

My breath heaves out of me, and embarrassed at my outburst, I snatch my hand back. What am I doing? Well, besides crossing boundaries that shouldn't be crossed. Again. I'm making this about me, not him. Not Gia.

I'm revealing too much.

Handing him ammo to use against me later.

He's not your father.

The fact that my inner bitch's voice is soft and comforting when she imparts that particular nugget only deepens my shame.

"Thank you."

The quiet, almost solemn gratefulness in his voice stops my emotional spiral. I inhale a breath and slowly exhale it.

"You're a wonderful dad. And I don't know the ins and outs of your divorce. But I'm assuming the court most likely had full knowledge that you're not Gia's biological father yet still determined you were the more appropriate choice to be the custodial parent. You have to know that's unusual. Doesn't matter that she was born into the marriage, the court chose you. And I bet if Gia had any idea, she would choose you over and over again."

Slowly, he rises, rounds the breakfast bar and stops in front of me. He spins my stool until I'm facing him, and he moves in between my thighs. My voice and breath are stuck in my throat as he lifts his hands to my cheeks, cradling them.

Tipping my head back, he sweeps his thumbs over my cheekbones and brushes a gentle kiss over my forehead. "Thank you." He presses another kiss to the bridge of my nose, directly over the freckles he often mentions. "Thank you." Another to my cheek, right over where my dimple would be. "Thank you."

He covers my mouth with his. And I'm helpless. I open for him, allow him inside.

No.

Nonono.

I'm not helpless. I'm not powerless. I'm choosing this, choosing to surrender to the heat that's never far away with Von. Choosing him once more.

There's power in that, and it sends a new wave of arousal coursing through me. On a whimper, I curl my hand behind his neck and use him as leverage to rise up a little and press my lips harder to his. Demand a deeper, more carnal, more…dirty kiss. I want him to corrupt me, and in turn, I can set myself free.

Free from my chains of religious propriety.

Free from my own insecurities of not being enough.

Free from…me.

And yet, finding me.

Joy mingles with hunger, and it surges within me, incinerating the last of my inhibitions and doubts. As if sensing what I need, he threads his fingers through my hair, fisting the strands, and the tiny pricks across my scalp have me gasping into his mouth. It's like when he puts his hand to my throat—I didn't know until being with him that edges of pain could get me so…wet. Because God, I'm so wet.

It should be embarrassing how just a touch from him can send me into flash-flooding territory. And maybe later, it will be. But right now, with him sucking on my tongue then my bottom lip like I'm the sweetest lollipop he's ever tasted, I really don't give a damn.

"You've been teasing me with this pussy, walking around here pretending she's not mine. Like she isn't fucking crying for me. This is my shit." He reaches between us, cups me through my leggings, and part of me wants to contradict what he's just said. Tell him he doesn't own anything over here.

But I'd be a liar.

I only want him. My body has only ever reacted like it's one touch away from internal combustion with him. At this point, it's so his, he should have the signed deed to it.

"You gon' let me have you again, Liyah?" With the hand not filled with my sex, he squeezes my jaw.

Where do we go from here? What's going to happen after this?

The questions fly through my head at lightning speed, but I have no answers. Don't need answers. No, my only concern in this moment is how he can have me and where.

"Yes."

It's all I can manage. But it's more than enough.

As if that one word snatched all the brakes off, he hikes me up in his arms and sets me on top of the bar. Within dizzying moments, he has my leggings and panties stripped off and his face buried between my thighs.

Holy…

I clench my jaw, locking down the feral and shocked scream rising up from my chest as Von swirls his tongue in a figure eight around my clit and through my folds.

Of course, I've read about this before and seen it on videos but experiencing it? No, experiencing it *with this man*? I bite my bottom lip and fist my hair. No comparison.

"Von," I rasp as he rolls my hips up, pushing my thighs toward my chest.

"I knew this pussy was gon' be good." His voice vibrates through my flesh, adding to the pleasure, and I arch toward him…well, as much as I can with his arm banded across the backs of my legs. He hums, sucking on each lower lip then releasing them with a wet pop. "You know you fucked up letting me get a taste, right? This the kind of pussy you kill a muthafucka over, ma. That murder pussy."

I don't answer—not that I can. Not when he thrusts his tongue inside of me, setting off a fireworks display in my core.

"Oh shit," I gasp.

His dark chuckle rumbles against my flesh, and he pulls back, replacing his tongue with his large, long fingers, and I choke on a cry as moisture burns my eyes. This shouldn't feel this good.

My mind tries to intrude, tries to warn me that this is sinful, that I'll regret this, pay for it.

Maybe.

Maybe all of that is true.

But I don't care.

And right now, I'm willing to pay the cost.

Von finger fucks me, and it's not gentle. And I love it. No, I *crave* it. As I do the wet sound that echoes in the kitchen every time he pulls free of my pussy. He latches his mouth onto my clit and with one hard suck, I explode.

I'm a shuddering, whimpering mess, and I try to squirm away from Von as he cleans me up with his tongue, chasing every drop that leaks out of me.

"Unh-unh." Straightening, he lightly slaps my thigh and hauls me off the bar. "Don't tap out on me, ma. I'm not finished with you yet."

He spins me around then yanks my shirt over my head and removes my bra. I shiver, not really cold but at the prickling sensation of standing in the kitchen fully naked and… exposed.

But Von burns that feeling away with the settling of a hard palm to the center of my back.

"Bend over, Liyah," he says, exerting slight pressure and guiding me until my breasts and cheek meet the chilled bar top. "Arch that back and get that pretty ass up in the air for me."

Raising on my toes, I do what he wants—what I want, too.

The rustle of clothing and crinkle of foil telegraph that Von's donning a condom before he moves between my legs and, without any hesitation, buries himself deep inside me.

I groan, rolling my forehead over the tile of the bar. Maybe it's our position but there seems to be more of him than last time. I swear, I can damn near feel him in my chest.

"You can take this dick, ma. Fuck a church girl. You taking it like the boss bitch you are. Now put that hand back up there and give me this good pussy."

Something swells within me, and I close my eyes, inhale deep and surrender in a way I haven't in…ever.

A low rumble echoes behind me, followed by "gotdamn" and another rustle of clothing. In the next moment, his bare chest covers my back, and his hot mouth opens over my shoulder. My own lips part on a soundless gasp at the skin-to-skin contact and his dick digging deeper and deeper inside me.

He grips my chin, turning my head toward him, and we

kiss in a nasty, wild mating of lips and tongues, all while he fucks me with a grind and punch of his hips. My walls grab at him, milk him. And already I'm on the verge of orgasm, feeling it sizzle its way up my spine.

"Shit." He grunts. "Go on and give it to me, Liyah. Rain down on my dick."

And I do. With a sharp cry, I let go, and he laughs, but there's pride in that soft, strained chuckle. Pushing off me, he grips the back of my neck with one hand and my hip with other, and slams into me. Over and over. Before my release starts to ebb, he's shoving me into the next one, the tip of his dick knocking against that spot high inside my pussy. He slides his fingers over my hip and down between my thighs, unerringly finding my clit. As he brushes the bundle of nerves, I flinch from the almost too-sharp pleasure.

"Oh God. Oh God," I chant.

"That's it, baby. That's it." Von's hold on me tightens as he buries that beautiful dick in me again and again. "One more. Give me one more."

This one is going to kill me. I can feel it as the electrical current crackles in the soles of my feet, the base of my spine, my brain. With a breathless cry, I break apart, and with several more thrusts and an almost tortured groan, so does he.

Ten

"I need you. Fuck, I want to hate you for that."

Von

I stare down at my desk, not seeing the open folder of invoices. They're a jumbled mess of numbers, lines and signatures. One that I can't begin to make sense of—not with Ronald on the other end of my phone, flipping my world on its ass.

"Von, as hard as this is, I need you to try not to worry," Ronald says, speaking to me in a voice I'm sure he's used often when convincing his clients not to do anything stupid. "Let me handle this—that's what you pay me for. And for God's sake, please don't go anywhere near Sheree." When I don't say anything, he says, "Von, do you understand?"

"Yeah, man, yeah, I hear you."

But I don't. Not for real. Not when Ronald's news is still

ringing in my head. Fury and fear fight it out in my chest like boxers in a championship fight.

"Listen, I don't want you to do something you might regret. And by that, I mean something Sheree and her attorney could possibly use in court against you. Which is why I'm serious about you not going to see her. Don't call her. As a matter of fact, you might want to think about having your mother handle visitation exchanges. Just until this is either thrown out or settled. Tell me you understand what I'm saying, Von."

"Yeah, I got you."

I can hear the skepticism in his voice when he says, "All right. If you have any questions or need me, don't hesitate to reach out. I'm about to immediately jump on this, so let me do my job."

I tell him goodbye and end the call. Carefully setting my cell on the desk when I want to hurl the thing across the room, I close my eyes. Sounds from the shop filter through my closed office door, and a part of me wonders how everything is still going on as usual as if my life didn't just get fucked.

"Hey, Von, your three o'clock just called up here to cancel their—what the fuck's wrong with you?" Chelle shuts the door behind her and approaches my desk with a frown.

I don't even have the energy to curse her out for busting up in here without knocking. Who cares about that now?

"Aye, what's going on?"

I stare at her, silent, unable to form the words because

saying them aloud seems to make the shit real. Not that it matters. This is happening.

"Von, I swear to God—" Chelle growls.

"Sheree is suing me for full custody."

Her expression blanks, and she falls into the chair in front of my desk. Her gaze roams over my face, probably searching to see if I'm joking, but nah. It's true. It's fucking true.

"What? No way in hell."

"My divorce attorney just called me. She's taking me back to court to get full custody of Gia and to give me only limited, supervised visitation."

"That bitch," Chelle snarls, fury glittering in her eyes. "On what grounds? You were awarded primary physical custody for a reason. What possible cause is there to limit your interaction with Gia when you've been nothing but a good father?"

I can't stop my flinch at the word *father.*

I don't care if God Himself donated His DNA to Gia, you are her father.

Just days ago, Aaliyah uttered those words to me, and then, I grabbed on and held them close. I'd believed that wound had started to heal that night, but here I am. The scab ripped back off it while it bleeds all over my chest.

The rage that had swirled inside me during Ronald's call fades under a sheet of ice, leaving me numb. No, that's not completely true. Fear still lurks, scratching at the ice with long, skeletal fingers.

"On the grounds that I'm not Gia's biological father."

Silence booms in the room, damn near blowing out my

ear drums. I'd kept this secret for so long. Out of love and the desire to protect Gia. Out of humiliation that my wife at the time had gotten pregnant by another man and made a fool of me, lying to me. Out of terror of losing my little girl. And now look at me. In a matter of days, I'd confided the truth to two people.

And soon, if Ronald couldn't squash this new filing, everyone would know. And yeah, I don't want people in my business. But the most important person in my world would discover the truth and be devastated by it.

Gia.

"Von," Chelle whispers, leaning forward in her chair, her gaze fixed on me. Shock widens her eyes. Clearing her throat, she says, "Von, what're you talking about you're not Gia's biological father? How…? That's not…" She shakes her head, continuing to gape at me.

Sighing, I fall back in my chair and look away from her. I can't stand to see the shock and…pity that will undoubtedly claim her face.

"I didn't tell you Sheree was cheating on me for four years. It wasn't something recent and short like I let you believe. Nah, she let Malik raw dog her for years, and when she got pregnant, she let me believe Gia was mine. I didn't find out until much later. That's why I got a divorce."

"Does Gia…" She trails off, and I shake my head.

"No, she doesn't know anything about it, and that's what Sheree and I agreed on. I've been Daddy since she was born—before she was born. I'm all she knows, and though I think Sheree had several reasons for not wanting me to find out the truth, being Gia's father is one thing I've never regretted. Paternity didn't even come up in our divorce. But now..." I loose a disbelieving, sharp laugh. "This is going to crush Gia and tear her world apart. Sheree's sole goal is to hurt me."

I've never truly hated my ex-wife. Not after discovering the cheating, the theft and Gia's true paternity. Did I curse her out? Hell yeah, but I couldn't hate her because of the years we spent together and because Gia loved her.

But now?

Yeah, I hate her. More so because she doesn't give a fuck about anyone but herself, her own agenda and pain. It's fuck Gia and fuck me, so it's fuck her.

"Hold up." Chelle puts up a hand. "Is this because of Aaliyah? We all overheard it when she came up in here earlier this week. Is that why Sheree's doing all of this?"

"She doesn't mention Aaliyah by name, but she does refer to undue influences and worry for Gia's safety and emotional state. She's also requesting a paternity test to prove I'm not Gia's biological father to bolster why I shouldn't be the custodial parent. It's some bullshit, Chelle. And when she threatened this, I thought she'd cool off and wouldn't ever go through with it. But I underestimated her."

"Listen, I can't stand the woman and wouldn't put much past her, but this? Nah, she got me fucked-up on this." We fall silent then Chelle murmurs, "What're you going to do, V?"

"Fight it. Ronald's going to try to get this and the modification for half my shop dismissed. But in the meantime, I have this fear hanging over my head. Every moment I spend with my baby I'll be hoarding because the future where she'll think of me as her father won't be promised to me. *Fuck!*"

I slam my hands down on the desktop, making the keyboard, invoice folder and desk phone jump. My palms sting from the impact, but I barely feel it. Not when the icy numbness is wearing off and every emotion—the pain, fear, anger and panic—is seeping back in.

"Since your three o'clock canceled, go home. I'll get Malcolm to contact the rest of your clients and get them rescheduled. We'll tell them you had a family emergency," Chelle says. I shake my head, but Chelle pops her hand up to stop my objection. "I'm pulling my nonexistent rank. You shouldn't be working on anyone in your frame of mind anyway. Go home. We're good, and I'll stay and close up."

For a moment, I consider arguing, but at the last minute, I don't. She's right. Inking someone when my head is fucked-up would be damn near criminal. What I want to do is leave, drive over to Sheree's and ask her what the hell she's thinking. The only thing stopping me isn't Ronald's warning; it's Gia. She's with her mom for the weekend, and soon enough, she's going to be dumped in the middle of our shit. I'll give her every second of peace I can until it's no longer an option.

"Yeah, I'ma go." I shove back my chair and stand, grabbing my keys and wallet from my top drawer. "Call if you need me?"

"Okay, but we won't." I round the desk, and she pulls me into a tight hug. "We gotchu, Von. Everything's gonna work out for the best. And by that, I mean Gia isn't going anywhere."

I squeeze her then step back. "Thanks for that, Chelle."

"No doubt. But, bruh, next time you shoot up the club, can you make sure she's like a saint or something? I'll even settle for a nun. Someone who isn't going to transform into the devil if things don't work out."

I shoot her a "what the hell?" glance, and she shrugs.

"I'm just sayin'..."

For some reason, Aaliyah flickers across my mind, and it leaves me shook. The fuck was that?

"I'm out, Chelle." Deliberately shoving any thoughts of future baby mamas out of my mind, I exit the office and leave out the rear entrance to the parking lot. Soon, I'm hitting the interstate, but the thought of being up in my house in all that fucking silence with reminders of Gia everywhere seems like a cruel punishment.

Before my mind acknowledges what my hands and feet are doing, I'm heading in the direction of the South Loop instead of Edison Park. Though I've only been by Aaliyah's cousin's apartment a couple of times, I drive like I can do it in the dark. I speed to the condo, praying that Aaliyah's there.

Instead of obsessing over Gia and losing custody, I've found a new fixation.

Get to Aaliyah.

I don't know when I began to think of her as my safe harbor but here I am, running to her.

The urgency drums in my veins like a primal beat, and thirty minutes later, I'm stepping off the elevator and stalking down the hallway to her door. I pound on it, sounding like damn SWAT, but I can't stop myself.

After several seconds, the door swings open and Aaliyah stands there, sweatpants and a tank top on. And at the sight of her, the panic shoving me here dissipates and a relief sweeps in, so sweet, so sharp it physically hurts.

"Von?" She crosses her arms, and it's too late for all that shit. I already noticed she isn't wearing a bra. "What're you doing here?"

I open my mouth to apologize for just popping up, to explain, to…beg. But I can't.

All I can say is one truth.

"I need you."

And I take that step forward, crossing the space separating us. I trade words for the low moan that crawls out of my throat as I take her mouth in a hard, almost brutal kiss that carries all the chaotic emotion assaulting me. I take it out on her lips, her tongue, her neck.

"Von." She gasps, but she doesn't push me away. No, she slams the door shut and wraps her arms around me.

Another groan escapes me, this one originating from gratefulness. For her selflessness. Her trust. Her surrender. She doesn't ask me questions. She just gives me all of her.

Thank. God.

I roll over, my brain dragging me to consciousness from a good-ass sleep. The fresh scent of citrus and the earthy musk of sex tickle my nose, reminding me I'm not home in my own bed. A peace blankets me as memories of where I am and how I got here creep into my head.

Aaliyah.

I'm in her bed.

My body calls for a stretch, but I resist and indulge in the inane need to just be still and savor this...peace. A peace that I've been hesitant to name or recognize but can't avoid anymore.

It's Aaliyah.

I fought my attraction to her, my need for her, the joy she brought my daughter, the light she brought me. I fought and lost. But I don't feel like a loser. As soon as she opened her door to me and took me in her arms, accepting me, protecting me with no questions asked, I became the victor.

I'm so used to scrapping for everything in my life—my shop, my daughter, my fucking dignity—that when a gift strolled right through the front door, I did my damnedest to force it right back out.

But not anymore.

Not anymore.

I reach for Aaliyah but only touch an empty sheet. Frowning, I open my eyes, turning my head to search the room. The door is cracked, so maybe she just went to the bathroom. I'll give her a few more minutes before I hunt her down. I'm ready to dive back in the sweetest pussy I've ever had. Pussy that's as much of a goddamn miracle as the woman.

My frown deepens as a sound penetrates the quiet in the bedroom.

Muffled voices.

Is that what woke me up?

It's probably her cousin; a glance down at my watch shows it's only a little after six. Too early for Jade—or Tamara, as Aaliyah told me her real name—to have left for work.

An unmistakable deep, male voice echoes down the hall. I can't tell what he's saying, but it's definitely raised.

The fuck is that and who're they yelling at?

Hurriedly, I swing my legs over the side of the bed and locate my jeans and T-shirt. I drag them on, and seconds later, I'm out the room and striding barefoot down the hall.

I thought I would be squaring off with an asshole who didn't know when to leave, but instead I come face-to-face with a tall, distinguished-looking older man, a woman who is the image of Aaliyah with a couple of decades added to her, and another man, younger, slim and wearing a scowl directed toward Aaliyah.

Oh, he got me fucked-up.

"Aye, bruh, I don't know who you are, but you might want to fix your face before I do it for you," I warn, stopping behind Aaliyah and Tamara, who stands shoulder to shoulder with her cousin.

Tamara glances at me, and though she doesn't lose the mug on her face, I catch the relief that flashes in her light brown eyes.

"Who are you?" the younger man asks, his mouth twisted up as he somehow manages to look down on me even though I got him by no less than five inches in height. "Aaliyah, who is this…person?"

"Gregory—" She pinches her nose, and I don't miss the quiver in her voice. "I—"

Instantly, I want to lay hands on this muthafucka for causing that tremble.

"Ma, you don't have to explain shit to him. Especially when he's being disrespectful as fuck with how he's looking at you."

"Von," Aaliyah whispers. "It's okay."

I scowl. The fuck she mean it's okay? Ain't shit "okay" about what's going on here.

"Young man, if you'll excuse us," the woman who must be Aaliyah's mother—which would make the older man her father—says. Her tone is more polite, so I don't snap on her. Though front and center is what Aaliyah told me about her and her husband. Only being her mother and a woman is saving her right now. "This is a family matter."

"If you'll excuse me, ma'am, this isn't your place, and unless Tamara wants to put me out, then I'm not going anywhere."

Aaliyah's mother raises an eyebrow. "Tamara? This discussion should be among family."

Yeah, that seems to be their motto. I don't even try to contain the disgusted curl of my lips.

Tamara shrugs, crossing her arms. "I don't have a problem with him staying."

"Why am I not surprised?" Aaliyah's father, *the bishop*, sniffs. "Given your *occupation*, the words *discretion* and *private* aren't in your vocabulary. I pray with your father for you, but—"

"Daddy, that's enough," Aaliyah quietly interrupts what was undoubtedly about to be some self-righteous bullshit. I'm glad she got to him before I did. The same tremble still occupies Aaliyah's voice, but it's firm when she adds, "This is Tamara's home, and she shouldn't be disrespected in it."

He stares at Aaliyah, a deep frown slowly settling on his face. "Excuse me, Aaliyah Montgomery." His shoulders draw back, and he glances at his wife then at Aaliyah again. "Is this what you've been learning while you've been hiding up here? To talk to me like you've lost your mind? I shouldn't have let your mother convince me to give you time to come to your senses. Considering what I'm seeing and hearing, I should've come to fetch you as soon as I found out where you were." He tosses a derisive look at Tamara then at me. "The influences you've been under have you forgetting who you are and where you come from."

"Bishop." I huff out a laugh and pinch the bridge of my nose. Aaliyah tucks her hand behind her and gropes for my hand. Finding it, she squeezes. I don't know if she's holding on to me for support or if she's trying to tell me to shut it down. I'm going to take it as the former because I want to. "For my mama's sake, I'm going to try to keep it civil with you. But your daughter isn't a dog or a possession for you to come fetch. She's a grown woman fully capable of making her own decisions. And has been doing a damn good job of it. If you took half a second to climb down off that pulpit and actually listen, you'd see that."

"Damn," Tamara breathes. Then snickers.

Aaliyah's father's face grows so dark, I want to ask if he's got blood pressure issues. If he passes out, I'm not catching his big ass.

"Young man—"

"Von, Bishop. Von Howard." I curl a hand around the nape of Aaliyah's neck, and though she stiffens under my touch, I chalk it up to her being nervous with this confrontation that's way overdue.

I don't know why he had to bring an armor bearer or whatever purpose this other asshole has for being here.

"Are you serious, Aaliyah?" her father hisses. His gaze drops to the hand I have on her, and when his eyes lift, settling on his daughter's face, Aaliyah flinches at the fury and disapproval there. The movement is small, but I feel it. So does Tamara, if her shifting closer to her cousin is any indication. "Who have you become since you left home? I thought you'd just had a lapse in judgment, running away from home like a child, but allowing a strange man to put his hands on you in front of your parents and fiancé? What're you think—"

"Fiancé?" I cut off the bishop's tirade, zeroing in on that one word, dropping my hand.

In my head, the word echoes. It drowns out all sound, then like a great vacuum has sucked me back into this fucked-up reality, everything becomes painfully clear. The hardwood underneath my feet feels too slick, too cold. My pulse blooms to a loud drone in my ears. And Aaliyah's scent—so delicate and fruity and carrying the faintest trace of sex—crowds into my nose, choking me while only minutes ago, I wanted to roll in that same fragrance.

"Von." Aaliyah turns, reaching for my hand. She tips her

head back, and the alarm and sadness there has my stomach bottoming out, my chest caving in. "Let me explain."

"Aaliyah, you and this man seem…familiar. And you didn't tell him you were engaged?" her mother chides.

"Mom, please," she replies without taking her gaze off me.

And my stupid ass can't look away. Hoping against hope that somebody will say something to clear the shit up. To make me feel like I haven't been fucked over by another woman. Haven't been lied to by another woman I…cared for.

"This is perfect." Her father barks out an incredulous laugh. "Yes, young man, Gregory here is my daughter's fiancé. Though after he's seen her behavior here tonight, I wouldn't blame him if he decided otherwise."

"I can't believe this shit," Tamara snaps. "Are you fucking kidding me?"

"Watch your mouth, young lady," the bishop thunders.

"This is *my* house, *Uncle Tim.*" Tamara pops her hands on her hips. "We're not in Parsons, and you don't run me."

"Von, I can explain." Aaliyah's grip tightens, maybe becomes a little desperate. But it doesn't move me. Not when I read the guilt on her face. "Please…"

"Aaliyah, I think you and I should talk in private," Gregory interjects, moving closer to her. And even though anger and a knee-buckling pain punches at me, I mug him, daring him to get in her space.

Fuck.

She's not mine.

Never was, apparently.

What the fuck is wrong with me? Am I defective, fundamentally broken? Because how did I attract two women who are cheaters? And I confided in her how Sheree did me, how her betrayal hurt me. And with that innocence that I'm beginning to see is a fucking lie like the rest of her she agreed with me that infidelity was a dealbreaker. Sheree might've been a cheater, but Aaliyah made me one right along with her. Like the side fuckboy.

Backpedaling away from her, I drag a hand over my braids. I scan the room, taking in her father's and fiancé's smug expressions, her mother's confused one. And Aaliyah. Still fucking playing me, looking hurt.

To think she'd had me almost believing in… Yeah, I'm not finishing that thought.

I'm just…finished.

Snatching free of her grasp, I stalk back down the hall to her room, put my boots on and slide into my coat. When I return to the main part of the apartment, I don't spare any of them a glance. Humiliation burns my skin, and the only thing that will relieve the pain is getting the hell up out of here.

"Von, please!" Aaliyah calls after me.

But I ignore her, already pulling the front door open and shutting it behind me.

Shutting her behind me.

Eleven

"Y'all up in here just testing all of my Christianity."

Aaliyah

I squeeze my eyes closed, listening to Tamara's front door closing behind Von, ringing with finality.

With loss.

Pain wraps around my ribs and tightens until I'm gasping for breath.

"Aaliyah, I didn't think it was possible to be this disappointed in you." Daddy's sonorous voice penetrates the agonized haze cloaking me. "What happened to my daughter?"

"Oh my God, could you stop with the guilt trip?" Tamara snaps. "She's not a child."

"Tamara, your uncle deserves your respect," Mom admonishes her.

Tamara tilts her head. "And I don't? The three of you popped up in my place uninvited. Who does that? And to do what? Lie? Embarrass your daughter? This right here—" she wags a finger back and forth, encompassing my parents and Gregory "—is exactly why people avoid church. They see who the so-called Christians are, rolling up in there every Sunday, and want no part of your religion. Now call me a heathen all you want, but I bet God is no more pleased with y'all."

My mother gasps, splaying her fingers across her chest, while Daddy looks damn near apoplectic. And Gregory. Jesus, Gregory. How in the world did I ever agree to marry him? His disgusted scan of Tamara's body tells me everything about how he treats others.

I would've been miserable as his wife.

"Aaliyah, pack your stuff. You're coming back to the hotel with us, and we're leaving out of here first thing in the morning," Daddy orders, his voice cold and brooking no disobedience.

My first reaction is to obey. Since Tamara opened her door to the three of them standing on the other side, I've felt myself shrink smaller, my voice grow fainter. A part of me is still entombed in shock going from the warm bliss of being wrapped in Von's arms, up under his big body and thrust into this cold, judgmental space. Even with Von and Tamara having my back, I couldn't… I couldn't…

A sob crawls up from my belly at the thought of Von. At his disbelief, his hurt. But the worst was his terrible indifference as he walked out of the apartment.

Walked away from me.

He took joy with him. Took the peace and contentment I'd found with him and Gia. Took my safe space I'd only started to appreciate.

I close my eyes again and try to capture the ephemeral sensation of his hand in mine.

Anger boils up inside me.

Anger at myself for reverting to that voiceless, powerless woman who arrived in Chicago months ago.

Anger at failing the woman I'd become.

Anger at my parents for their grasping control and refusal to really see me.

Anger at Von for not believing in me, trusting me. For walking out.

Was this karma? I'd run away from Gregory all those weeks ago, and now the man who'd become so important to me—so vital—had done the same to me.

You reap what you sow.

Screw that.

Then I'm due to reap kindness, acceptance. Joy.

Love.

"Aaliyah, don't make me repeat myself," Daddy says.

"Sweetheart, do what your father says, please."

And on top of her order, Gregory says, "We can talk when we all get back to the hotel."

"Shut. Up."

The room falls quiet, the clicking on of the central heating is like one of those loud cannon firecrackers the neighborhood kids set off every Fourth of July.

My parents and Gregory gape at me, and my chest heaves, nerves attacking me. But satisfaction and…power sings in my veins, and I don't think I've ever heard a prettier song.

I turn to Tamara, who's wearing a smirk though her gaze shines with something like…pride?

"Not you, Tamara."

"I wouldn't even care if that was directed toward me, babe. You got it."

"I know you're not talking to us like that."

"Aaliyah Renee Montgomery, I raised you better than this!"

"This is unacceptable."

When Daddy's, Mom's and Gregory's shocked and highly offended voices trip over one another, I hold up both hands, and miraculously, they all go quiet.

Didn't expect that.

I might need to check Tamara's bottles of water to see if they've changed into wine since it seems to be a night for miracles.

"Thank you." I lower my arms. Though there's still a tiny part of me that wants to cower under those heated glares, I refuse. That part is going to have to grow up like the rest of me. "Now, Daddy, Mommy, I love you, and let me apologize for running away. I should've had enough courage and integrity to sit you both down and tell you how I was feeling and what was going on with me."

"Yes, you should've," my father agrees with a soft grunt. "Then we could've talked past normal wedding-day jitters."

"Or me," Gregory interjects. "After all, we are to be husband and wife—"

"Gregory, I'll get to you. And, Daddy, I'm not finished. While I'm sorry for *how* I did it, I don't regret *doing* it. This may be hard for you to hear, but I'm not going back to Parsons. Not now, and not anytime in the near future. For now, my life is here in Chicago."

"Sweetheart, you can't mean that." Mom steps forward, her hand outstretched toward me. "Parsons is home. You've been here just a few weeks. I get it may seem shiny and new, but home is what you know, where you have family."

"I have family here, too. Family and a best friend." I glance at Tamara, and she smiles at me, nodding. "Just because Alabama is home for you doesn't mean it's enough for me. Or even what I wanted for my future. Have you even stopped to ask yourselves why I chose Chicago?"

Daddy humphs. "Your cousin. No doubt she convinced you to do this foolishness."

I give a small, disbelieving chuckle. "You still refuse to listen, to see me as a grown woman instead of the girl you've tried to keep me. Leaving was *my* decision. I went to Tamara and begged her to take me with her. You think you corner the market on family, but my cousin offered me a place to live, refusing any money. My cousin put clothes on my back and supports me without expecting anything in return. That's family. That's love. But you're so judgmental, so critical, that you can't see past your own plans, expectations and standards for *my* life. You can't even thank her."

I inhale a deep breath, and for once, none of them say anything to interject. Knowing that won't last long, I continue. "Like I asked, have you stopped to consider why I chose here? It's because I was accepted into the University of Chicago art program and received a partial scholarship."

"College? Art?" My father balks, and nope, that precious

judgment-free zone didn't last long at all. "Aaliyah, you went to college and got a practical degree that will serve you in life. Why are you wasting those people's money on a degree you can do nothing with?"

"And why is this the first we're hearing about it?" my mother adds. "You never said anything about wanting to further your education."

"I told you weeks ago, Mom. I told you when I ran out of that church," I say, voice low, solemn. "It's not my fault you didn't listen. That you're still not listening. Daddy, I got that associate's because it's what you wanted, not me. I said yes to Gregory's proposal because it's what you intended for me, not what I desired for myself. This one time, I made my own choices. I *am* making those choices. I don't care if the only job opportunity I have is drawing on a paper menu at Denny's, it's my dream. My decisions. My life. And I'm through living it for everyone else."

Turning to Gregory while my parents digest that, I smile. "I'm sorry for embarrassing you by running out on the wedding." I refuse to call it *our* wedding because it was never mine. "I should've come to you long before then and told you that I didn't love you the way you deserve, and I have no desire to be anyone's first lady. Honestly, I shouldn't have accepted your proposal in the first place. That said..." I narrow my eyes on him. "Let me make this abundantly clear right now. I am not and will never be marrying you. I'm not your fiancé, and to think that I still am is bordering on delusional. Move on and do better than pursuing a woman who ran out on you. I sincerely hope you find a woman you love who will be proud to stand by your side."

His lips part then snap closed, his face contorting into an insulted mask.

"Aht aht." Tamara holds up her hand, stopping anything about to come out of his mouth. "She said what she said, and we don't need an epilogue. Move around." She shoos him with a flick of her fingers.

Smothering an inappropriate snort, I return my attention to my parents. Would I love for us to part on terms where we understood and accepted each other? God, yes. But one glance at my father's sternly set expression, and I know that's not happening. And that's okay. The little girl inside me who still seeks her father's approval is hurt, but the grown, capable and independent woman who's standing in front of him will be fine.

"When you find the mind you've apparently lost between Alabama and here, you know where to find us," he says. "Let's go, Georgia." He immediately turns and strides for the front door, Gregory on his heels.

But Mom doesn't follow.

My heart pounds in my chest as she remains standing in front of me. Even when Daddy whirls around and snaps her name.

"In a minute, Tim." She doesn't glance over her shoulder to see his shock, but I do. And I'm as stunned as he is. Mom moves forward and pulls me into her arms. After a brief, astonished hesitation, I hug her back, and her embrace tightens. A sob wells up inside me at her familiar sent and the unfamiliar joy that she chose me. Put me first. Even if only for a couple of moments, my mother chose me.

"I love you, sweetheart," she whispers in my ear. "Anytime you need me, I'm just a phone call away. And, Aaliyah… I'm so proud of you."

The words are just between us, but they still have tears stinging my eyes. She briefly cups my shoulders before releasing me with a smile. Then she walks toward my father, who leaves the apartment without a backward glance. Mom waves to me then steps out, pulling the door closed behind her.

"Did that shit just happen, or did I smoke too much weed earlier?" Tamara asks into the silence.

I snicker. "Yes, that just happened. Even though I'm still not sure what 'that' is."

I glance over at her, and we stare at one another for a long moment then crack up, our laughter loud, obnoxious and cleansing.

I stood up to my parents, and I'm good. Most importantly, though?

I'm free.

"I'm so proud of you, Aaliyah," Tamara says. "For a minute there, I was a little worried, but you telling them 'I think the fuck not' without one curse was something worth buying tickets to see." She laughs, but then sobers. "Are you okay, though? Not just with your parents and fuckboy but…Von?"

That quick, the peace and happiness bubbling inside of me goes flat.

"You warned me not to fall for him," I murmur.

"I did," she agrees, sliding an arm around my shoulders. "But what the fuck do I know? The way that man had your back—"

"The way he walked out of here without a word or even a look at me, you mean."

She sighs. "He was hurt and didn't have the full story. And shit, your parents and a man claiming to be your fiancé would overwhelm anybody."

"He hurt me, too," I softly admit. "He encouraged me to find my voice, to use it. He's come to know me, the real me, over these past couple of months. And at the first sign of trouble, he ran. He left me alone. No." I shake my head. "I don't know what this means about my job, but if I don't stand up for myself, who will? For the first time, I'm having my own back. And that'll have to be enough. It *is* enough."

Besides, I can't erase his hard, implacable expression as he walked out that door from my mind. For a man who's been betrayed like he has, the wounds go deep. And those aren't wounds I can heal; he can only heal those himself.

The love and acceptance I crave—from my parents, from him—has to start with me.

"Damn, girl. Who the hell are you and what have you done with my cousin? I'm asking so you can tell her ass to stay over where she at. I want this woman right here."

Though the pain in my heart hasn't abated, I laugh at this fool woman. "You're crazy, you know that?"

"You love it."

"I do," I say. "And I love you, too."

"Oh fuuuuck." Tamara tips her head back, scrunching her face up. "Did you really just go there? Don't make me *feel*. That's not fair."

Cracking up, I hug her tight. And she hugs me back.

This right here?

This is enough.

Twelve

"See, what you not gon' do..."

Von

I open the front door as Gia climbs the steps. Her usual cheery and loud demeanor is missing, replaced by a subdued frown. Well, the cheery and loud stopped when Aaliyah stopped being her nanny two weeks ago. And though she's talked on the phone with Aaliyah several times, the frown has become customary on my baby girl's face. And for that I feel like I've more than disappointed her; I've failed her. Because if I'd used my brain instead of my dick, Aaliyah would be here. That's on me.

Falling for Aaliyah...that's on me, too.

"Hey, baby girl." I step out onto the porch. Guilt swarms in my chest but so do love and joy at having her back home. "Did you have a good day at school?"

"Yes." She hugs me then asks, "Is Aaliyah back yet, Daddy?"

I swallow down a tired sigh. “No, baby. Remember we’ve talked about this. She’s not working for us anymore.”

Her shoulders droop like the weight of the world is pressing on them. And maybe for a seven-year-old it is. And that weight is the bullshit that belongs to the adults in that world.

“I remember, I was just hoping she came back. I’ve been praying that she will, but God’s moving so slow.”

In spite of the heaviness we both seem to bear, I softly laugh. “Well you know what Grammy’s always saying. He doesn’t come when you want Him but…”

“He’s right on time,” Gia finishes. “I just wish I knew what time He was coming,” she adds with a pout.

I hold back my bark of laughter, remove my phone from my pocket and pass it to her. “How ’bout you give her a call and see what she’s doing?”

That suggestion gets me a little smile, and she takes the phone. “Okay.”

I hold the door open for her, and she slides past me, her head already bent over the cell. I catch movement in my peripheral, and instead of following her inside the house, I glance over my shoulder. And frown.

Deliberately schooling my face so it doesn’t betray my anger and disgust, I call out to Gia. “Hey, G, I’ll be right in. I’ma talk to your mom real quick. Go ahead and get started on any homework you have after you get off the phone.”

“Okay, Daddy,” she replies, her voice coming from deep inside the house.

Still, not wanting her to accidently overhear anything

that's said between me and Sheree, I close the storm door and descend the short flight of steps to meet a smiling Sheree.

"Hey, Von. I'm surprised to see you here this time of day."

Her voice is pleasant enough, but I'm not buying it. And I'm not having this fucking conversation, either. I haven't hired anyone to replace Aaliyah yet, though I could've easily called the nanny agency again. I just can't bring myself to do it. And with Sheree's custody hearing still in the works, I've been home more. Not just to strengthen the case, but because these last few weeks have felt like I'm in a mental countdown. If her custody hearing goes left for me, I need to have as many stored-up memories with Gia as I can get.

But I'm not telling her none of this shit.

"What're you doing here?" I cross my arms. "The agreement was your mother is supposed to be dropping Gia off from now on."

I'd taken Ronald's advice and arranged for an intermediary who would handle the custody exchanges. It didn't used to be like this. Sheree and I could at least deal with each other for this part of the divorce. But now, that shit is dead.

Sheree shrugs, that smile still curving her mouth. "I told Mom I'd handle it today since I wanted to talk to you. This is silly, Von. We can handle pick-ups and drop-offs like adults."

"Nah, we can't. I'on trust you like that if we keeping it a buck."

Oddly, she winces as if my honesty hurt her. Then again, I've come to learn Sheree is a fantastic actress. I give her a slow clap in my head.

"You make it sound like I'm standing here recording our conversation," she mutters.

I just arch my eyebrow because hell no, I don't put it past her. "What do you want, Sheree? And make it fast so I can get back in the house."

"I just want us to be civil. For Gia's sake."

That's got me seeing red. Gritting my teeth, I pinch the bridge of my nose, willing the rage to recede. At least enough so I can form words.

"Did you really just say 'for Gia's sake'?" I laugh, shaking my head at this silly bitch. "Sheree, get outta here with that. Sweetheart, ain't none of the moves you've been making lately been for Gia's sake. You don't put her first when you run me down on the phone with your thot-ass sister so G can overhear. You don't put her first when you come up to my shop starting shit. You for damn sure didn't put her first when you filed this custody modification. Everything's been about you. Don't stand here thinking you gon' play in my face."

She glances away from me, but I see the ticking of a muscle at her jaw and wait for the hate that's about to come out of her mouth. If Sheree knows how to do anything, it's defend her indefensible actions.

"Gia told me that woman isn't her nanny anymore," she calmly says, returning her gaze to me.

"Not your business."

"It is," she insists, shifting forward. It takes everything in me not to warn her to put one hundred feet between us at all times. "That's the point. You didn't consult me on who was watching over my daughter. Why do I have to hear about everything from her? You are responsible for telling me."

I cock my head, scrutinizing her, and chuckle when I see she really means that shit.

"Let me ask you this. Do you call and inform me of who you leave Gia with when you go clubbing? No, you don't," I answer for her. "And I don't trip because though you're a trash-ass wife, I considered you a good mother and trusted your judgment, confident you wouldn't leave G with anyone who would harm or neglect her. After being married to me and knowing me for all these years, you should know the same thing about me. I hired a person who cared for G and loved her like her own. If you'd get out your bag for two seconds, you'd admit that, especially since your daughter can't stop talking about her. But you don't give a fuck about none of that. You went on some control trip knowing you ain't got any. You don't run what goes over here in my house."

Doesn't she, though?

Aaliyah isn't here anymore.

And while Sheree no longer has any say in what goes on at my house, she's still for damn sure running my feelings, getting in my head. Dictating my actions and reactions. For the last couple of years, everything that happened with Sheree has colored my interactions with people, not just women.

Everything that had gone down with Aaliyah, hearing her father call another man her fiancé… I'd reacted based off my past with Sheree. How she'd lied to me. Betrayed me. Fucking used me. Had Aaliyah should've told me about her engagement? Hell yeah. But I also could've allowed her to explain, off the strength of our relationship. Off the strength of who we'd become to one another.

After being married to me and knowing me for all these years, you should know the same thing about me.

My accusation against Sheree bites me in the ass, and shame fills me. What I expected, I hadn't offered Aaliyah the same grace. And now it'd been two weeks—two miserable-ass weeks—without her.

Once, I'd accused her of being a runner.

I had it wrong.

I'm the runner.

Running away from my feelings for her despite my resolve to not get emotionally involved.

Running away from the hurt and the risk of future betrayal.

Running away from myself.

Scrubbing a hand down my face, I blindly stare at a point over Sheree's head. You'd think I'd eaten enough crow since Aaliyah had come into my life. Apparently, I had one more serving to shove down my throat.

"Von, I'll drop the custody modification," Sheree softly says, drawing my attention back to her.

I study her then bark out a laugh. "What you want me to say, Sheree? Thank you? Nah, shawty. I'm not thanking you for that when you should've never filed in the first place. You don't get credit for doing something you should've *been* done. Especially when we both know the reason you did it."

Aaliyah.

Her jealousy over her assumption that we were fucking.

She hadn't been wrong, but again, not her business.

"You used Gia as a pawn to press your fucked-up agenda, not sitting your ass down to even think about how it would affect her. How it would devastate her. You've had weeks to reconsider and do what was right. But because of a woman who was never a threat to you—*because you're not my wife anymore*—you decided getting back at me was more important than your daughter's well-being and security. You were ready to rock her world to the fucking foundation for that bullshit."

"Von, I—" She thrusts her fingers through her hair, pulling the straightened strands back and away from her face. Blowing out a breath, she says, "You're right. About everything. I guess since our separation and divorce I haven't seen you with anyone, so I tripped and acted out of emotion. Hearing Gia go on and on about that woman and then seeing how you looked at her and acted all protective even though she was just supposed to be the nanny had me feeling some kinda way. I'm sorry. I..." She exhales again, and her hazel eyes soften, a plea in them. "I just want my family back. I fucked up. Fucked up bad. I wish you would forgive me, that we could get past it and make our family work again. I didn't treat it or your love like they were everything to me, but they are. I can't begin to list all of my regrets, but the top of the list is losing you."

Part of me wants to laugh in her face. But I can't. One, I'm tired of fucking fighting with her. And two, for the first time in years, I glimpse a peek of the woman I once loved.

And I can't throw her vulnerability back into her face. I can be a muthafucka, but I'm not intentionally cruel.

"Sheree, for one, I been forgiven you. But there ain't no going back. Our divorce isn't one hundred percent on you. Though how you decided to handle it, with a four-year-long affair, was fucked up, your reasons were valid. I did work a lot. Everything I did to get you, I stopped doing to keep you. I get that you were lonely, and yeah, some of that's on me. But lying to me, giving another man that part of you that you promised only to me? Being irresponsible and letting him run up in you raw, saying fuck me and the consequences? Yeah, I got G out of that, but nah, shawty. We can't go back. I could never trust you again. We both got to live with the consequences of our actions, but we don't have to be miserable as hell doing it. This back-and-forth shit—" I wave a hand between us "—is only hurting G. We can't give her a mother and father living together under one roof, but we can give her co-parents who at least don't hate each other."

Sheree lowers her head, and she doesn't say anything for several long seconds. "I don't have any choice but to accept it."

When she lifts her head again, tears swim in her eyes, and I'd like to say they move me. But they don't. Maybe one day I can get to the point where I don't feel anything but a polite fondness when it comes to her. But today ain't that day. All the shit she's put me through is too close.

"I meant what I said about dropping the modification. Both of them."

I nod. Still not going to thank her.

"You should know I'm going after Aaliyah. If I have my way, she'll be a fixture in my and Gia's life. You probably need to know that before you talk about dropping the filings."

Sheree's threats, the stranglehold she had on me, ended today. Even if after hearing my intentions, she decides to let the modifications ride, I'm not changing my mind. She's not going to dictate my moves any longer.

I am through letting my past control me.

Pain spasms across her face as does anger. But finally, she dips her head. "I hear you. And I'm still withdrawing them. For Gia."

This time, I don't contradict her or remind her how fucked up her actions have been. Maybe even a small part of me is proud of her for finally owning her grown-woman shit.

"Aight. I gotta get back in the house. I'll have Gia call you later before bedtime."

"Okay. And, Von?" I stop mid-turn and glance over my shoulder at her. "I'm sorry."

"Yeah, me, too, shawty. I'm sorry for anything I did in the past to hurt you. All that's in the rearview now. See you."

Heading back for the house, I don't wait around for her to drive off. I meant it when I said it was behind me. And except for her being Gia's mother, so was she.

My main focus now is Aaliyah.

Seeing her. Talking to her.

Getting her back here. Because at some point during my conversation with Sheree, I had to be honest with myself.

I...I've fallen in love with Aaliyah. Even if she's engaged and ol' boy is really her fiancé, there has to be some reason she didn't tell me. Now I'm willing to listen, like I should've that night. I *know* Aaliyah. And she isn't Sheree. If she kept it from me, it wasn't on no snake shit. I trust her. I love her. And the house, my life—my and Gia's lives—aren't the same without her here.

Ironic as hell it took talking to my ex-wife to get that revelation. Or to allow it in. Because deep down, I knew it all along. Fear kept me from accepting it.

But like I just told Sheree, all that's behind me.

Ahead of me is Aaliyah.

Besides, if I don't do something, Gia might take drastic measures. I'm not saying she'd run away to go find Aaliyah. But I *am* saying baby girl's book bag been a little heavier these past couple of weeks.

I better go get our Aaliyah and bring her back where she belongs.

With us.

Thirteen

"Well, if you're going to play the love card…"

Aaliyah

Another class down, and one more to go before I'm done for the day. Can't say I'm happy about that. For the past few months, I had Gia to look forward to after I finished. But now, without her, I just go back home—yep, I now call Tamara's apartment "home"—and clean, do homework, try out new recipes (that's been an epic fail), binge Amazon Prime… everything but think on how much I'm missing her.

And her father.

Nope. Nopenopenope.

Not going there.

"Hey, Aaliyah, hold up."

At the sound of my name, I draw to a halt and look over my shoulder. Amari, a guy from my Readings in World Literature class jogs up to me, smiling. I return it, waiting on him to reach me. He's a nice guy, and we've shared notes once or twice.

"You headed to the caf?" he asks, shifting his book bag higher on his shoulder.

I shake my head. "No, I don't have a meal plan. I'll probably grab something from McDonald's."

"Gotchu. Want some company? My next class isn't for another couple of hours."

I glance at him, searching his face to see if this is a platonic offer or…

"Nah." He chuckles, holding up his hands. "It's not like that. A *friendly* lunch, that's all."

My laughter joins his, and why not? Shoot, I don't want to be alone anyway. And he's smart and funny and will be good company. It'll keep my mind off… *Stop it, Aaliyah. God, can't you go twenty minutes without thinking of him?*

"That's sounds good. You okay with McDonald's or do you want to go somewhere else?"

"Mickey D's is good."

We hike over to one of the student parking lots, talking about our class and what'll probably be on the final after Thanksgiving break.

Thanksgiving.

At one time, I imagined spending it with Tamara, Von and Gia. That dream looks a lot different now. Sadness spears me in the chest, and I rub my knuckles over the aching spot. Gia has called me more than a few times, and those conversations have been the bright spot in my days. But it's not the same as seeing her and spending time with her.

God, I miss her.

"Uh, Aaliyah. Please tell me you know that Ryan Henry looking dude mugging the shit out of me. I mean, I'll cape for you if I have to, but damn, that muthafucka huge."

"Huh?" I toss him a startled look, but he dips his head in the direction of my parked car.

"Over there."

I follow the line of his sight, and my heart stalls behind my ribs before speeding up so much I'm light-headed. "Von?"

I'm not even aware I said his name aloud until he pushes off the side of my car and walks forward, pausing at the rear of his truck. The truck I'm just now noticing is next to my car.

"Aaliyah." He switches his attention to Amari. "Who're you?"

"Her friend and classmate who has zero interest in her other than her class notes, bruh." He glances at me. "Tell him, Aaliyah, before he knocks my ass to sleep."

"Seriously, Amari?"

"Dead ass." He laughs. "Look, I'll get up with you later. Looks like you have different plans for lunch. See you."

With that, he walks off, leaving me alone with Von.

My heart still pounds, throwing itself against my chest as if trying to get back to its owner. The traitorous thing obviously hasn't learned its lesson.

"What're you doing here?" I ask, proud of myself when my voice emerges cool, unbothered.

"Came to see you." His gaze shifts in the direction where Amari disappeared. "Who's he?"

"A friend. Not that it's your business. What did you want?" An alarming thought suddenly pops in my head. "Is it Gia? Is everything okay with her?"

"She's good. Well," he grunts, "she's fine anyway."

"What does that mean, she's fine? Did something happen?"

"Yeah, you left. She hasn't been good since then."

Guilt seeps inside me, but so does anger. As if he didn't have anything to do with my resigning. I bear the responsibility, too. I knew better than to get intimately involved with him.

"I miss her, too."

"She's not the only one who hasn't been good."

My mouth and throat go dry.

Then that anger flares bright, incinerating the guilt. It covers the sadness, the hurt, the love that still simmers beneath.

Anger is better.

"Is this fun for you? What kind of game are you playing? You walked away from me. You left me. And now, two weeks later, you show up here, and I'm supposed to do what? Forget there's been radio silence? That I'm not important to you?" *Not as important as you are to me.* I flick my fingers at him. "There are other nannies out there, Von. I'm not irreplaceable."

"Yeah, there are other nannies, but there ain't another *you*."

"That's what you're going with?" I don't try to conceal my skepticism. Or disbelief. Even though my heart swoons a little at the corny words. "No thanks. Now if there's anything else?"

"Liyah," Von murmurs, and I want to melt, sink into him at the sound of his low, graveled voice wrapped around my name.

Reminding me of when he growled it into my ear as he plastered his chest to my back, sliding deep inside me.

Reminding me of when he held me close and whispered it just before he brushed a kiss across my forehead.

Damn him! I was doing so good before he showed up here.

Well, not good, but I was managing. I was keeping it together and moving forward. Now his presence here has knocked me yards backward.

"Von, I don't—"

"I'm sorry, ma. I violated that night at Tamara's place. I left you to the fucking wolves when I should've stayed there, continuing to have your back and giving you a chance to explain instead of walking out and leaving you behind." He takes a step closer to me, and I stumble back one. Stopping, he sinks his teeth into his bottom lip, and I snatch my gaze from his mouth, returning it to his eyes. But God, that's not any better.

"I'm sorry," he repeats, gentler.

I want to cave. I want to erase the distance between us—both physical and mental—and forget about how he hurt me. How I hurt him. But it's not that easy. Love…is not that easy. Especially when I'm the only one suffering from it.

"Oh, now you're willing to hear me out?" I cross my

arms, not caring how defensive I might appear to him. "I asked you to let me explain that night, and I was willing to explain for days afterward. But now, on your time, you're giving me the grace to listen?" *Shut up. Shut up*, I order myself. I'm letting my hurt feelings splatter all over this student parking lot. But I'm on a roll, and I can't stop. "I never lied to you, never betrayed you. You, more than anyone else, know me—even more than Tamara, if I'm being real. And yet you were so quick, so willing to paint me with the same brush as Sheree."

"I know, baby."

But I barely register his agreement or the endearment that makes tears sting my eyes.

"Yes, I was engaged. But on the day of the wedding, I ran. So you were right about me being a runner, but I ended up running to something. Toward me. And finding me. That 'me' didn't have a fiancé anymore. I stopped having one as soon as I jumped in that Uber and rode to Tamara's hotel. As you saw firsthand, my parents are stubborn and only believe and accept what they want. Gregory, my ex, is cut from the same cloth. Although, I suspect his being here had less to do with him loving me and more to do with pleasing my father. Either way, I never mentioned it because Gregory was—is—a nonfactor in my life. I never loved him, and I only agreed to marry him out of obligation, the same reason he proposed to me. I never once deliberately lied or hid him from you. I just didn't *think* about him."

Silence beats between us, and I look away. It's getting too

hard, and my feelings are too close to the surface. "Von, look..."

"Thank you for the explanation, but I didn't need it. I've already accepted that you weren't on no bullshit. You're right. I did take out my past with Sheree on you when you're nothing alike. You'd never lie to me. Never deliberately hurt me. And even that night, in the back of my mind, I knew that. But I was too scared to accept it. You'd become too important to me, too necessary, and I panicked. I was the runner that day, Liyah. Running and looking for any excuse to avoid experiencing the pain I'd suffered in my marriage. I'm sorry. I can't say it enough."

I don't reply. God, I *can't*. I'd need breath to accomplish that.

"I love you, Liyah. I think I started falling when I walked into that school and saw you sitting at the table with my little girl, looking like you'd move all the furniture in that office for her. And everything you've done and been since then has only dragged me deeper until I can't see, think, smell, fucking *be* without you. I get I hurt you. Give me a chance to make that up to you. Come back to me and Gia. Please."

I could've held out against the declaration of love.

I could've even held out against him tossing Gia in there.

But that "please"? I have no defense against it.

Oh hell. Who am I kidding? I couldn't have held out against none of that. He had me before he opened his mouth.

Letting my book bag slide to the pavement, I take four strides and throw myself at him. His strong arms catch me and close around me. His embrace is tight, nearing painful, but I'm not complaining. I wish he'd hold me tighter, closer. I'd crawl inside him if I could. Because here, in his arms, against his body, I'm at my safest. At my happiest.

At my most content.

"Kiss me," he rasps, and I have no problem obeying him.

Tipping back my head, I cup the nape of his neck with one hand and the back of his head with the other. I rise on my toes and meet his mouth halfway. At my first taste of him in weeks, I whimper. I needed this. I *missed* this. So much. Yes, the passion. I mean, *yeah*. But more, I missed the closeness, the connection. Him.

"I gotta correct myself. I said there ain't another you. That's true, but there ain't another pussy like yours, either. And fuck, ma. I've missed you both."

"Whose pussy?" I mock frown.

He grins, probably at my question as much as me saying the word. For the first time since I've known him, his smile is carefree, bright and so wide I'm staring at all thirty-two of his teeth.

"You're right. *My* pussy."

I chuckle, and when he kisses me again, he takes my mouth and my laughter.

"Yaay!" I jerk my head up to see the back door of his truck fly open, narrowly missing a side swipe of the car next to it. Gia climbs down and dashes over to us, throwing her arms around both our waists and grinning up at me. "You're back, Liyah! You're back!"

I crack up, bending down and returning her hug. "Aren't you supposed to be in school, ma'am?"

"Daddy said I could come with him in case he needed a secret weapon."

"Oh really?" I straighten, arching an eyebrow. "That's just sneaky, using her."

He shrugs. "I ain't never said I would play fair when it has to do with you. I'm coming behind you hard, ma. And I always will. That's a promise."

"Me, too, Liyah!" Gia chimes in, and when Von bends down and lifts her, she circles her arms around my neck, smacking a kiss on my cheek.

I blink back my tears. This is what I was running to when I left home, even if I didn't know it at the time. Not that it matters.

The only thing that does matter is I made it.

I made it home.

★★★★★

Look for Tamara's story,
coming in 2026!